DRAWING DOWN THE MOON

JAMES ISLAND TRILOGY • BOOK I

SHAWN KELLER COOPER

shawnkellercooper.com

Cover photograph: wideskystudio.com

To Jim,
…you're still the one…

ACKNOWLEDGMENTS

Writing is a solitary pursuit, but producing a book is not. Organizations, friends, and family have contributed to help me reach this point in my career.

I have benefitted greatly from my professional memberships in the North Carolina Writers Network and the Women's Fiction Writers Association. I have learned from the seminars and conferences and shared the writing life with these talented people. Thank you to Michelle Ganeles of Wide Sky Studio for the incredible cover and interior design.

This is a work of fiction, but I drew inspiration from my time with my sisters of Kappa Alpha Theta at the University of North Carolina at Chapel Hill. For four wonderful years, they were my family and home away from home. Over the last three decades, our bond has remained strong, and those women are still my family.

At one point in my life, none of this would have been possible. For their expertise and intellect, I want to thank Julie Fleck, Dr. Dijiana Christianson, Dr. T. Michael Sherrill, and Dr. Bryan Edwards.

For their editorial assistance and encouragement, I want to thank Bobbie and Karen, and my Red Barn women, Kimbo, Jo-Elle, and especially Jules, who yelled at me one night in Washington, D.C., reminding me that it was time to stop dreaming about writing and just do it. It made a difference.

I want to thank my family, Dean Black, Bob Keller, and my grandmother, Wylene Keller for their love and support, and my mother, Bobbie Black, a living example of perseverance. I must thank my cat muses who sit on my feet while I write and my sweet dog who always gives me a smile.

My children, Cannon and Sydney, encourage me, always, and endure my stories and the many voices talking in my head. With time and dedication, you can reach your goals.

My husband of twenty-six years, my friend, my man, Jim Cooper, is the one who always believes in me, sacrifices for me, and loves me unconditionally. I promised I would do this.

Boundaries
Like pieces of a puzzle,
I rearrange and replace
Parts
Of my identity.

Tattered and misused,
I force them into
Places
They never fit.

So bound and obligated
By the straight edges,
The inside
Is forced to conform.

Creating an image
I do not recognize,
Pretending
It is still me.

PROLOGUE

1944
James Island, North Carolina

MOONLIT RIBBONS OF LIQUID SILVER swirled around my feet, unraveling and pulling sand back into the gray waters of the Atlantic Ocean. I walked deeper into the frothy waves, salty spray showering my naked skin. Two more steps and I was beyond the breakers where swells of cool water swayed like butterflies, their soft wings fluttering, massaging my sore muscles. The fear and anxiety that tightened my body into knots began to loosen. Lifting my arms and stretching into the night air, I felt calmness flow into me.

So many nights I had walked into the ocean searching for answers, seeking solace, needing to feel the water wash over me. Tonight, I needed the ocean to cleanse me, forgive me, and restore me. It wouldn't be long now. My fingers touched my firm breasts and traveled down to the swell of my abdomen. I hardly recognized myself anymore. So many changes had occurred in the last nine months. My body was strong, my muscles tight from beach living, running with the wind, swimming in the waves, and wading through the marshland. Now I felt softness around my edges as the child inside me grew.

Ripe and ready, the time was close. Young, unwed, and pregnant was completely unacceptable to my family yet I had never felt so alive and connected to the world. This was the circle of life, creation in its purest form. Energy flowed through me, bringing harmony and purpose. Water, fire, earth, and air all united within me. I had spent my entire life surrounding myself with nature, and now inside me was the greatest offering I could make to mother earth. No longer was I alive in nature. I was creating nature.

I drew strength from the elements; never had I needed their energy more. This child, my child, needed protection. These times were ominous and emotional. The world was at war with itself, and although the devastation and tragedy were on another continent, my homeland was still at the center. I felt the land weaken, drowning in the blood of boys too young for violence. The air was suffocating from a lack of tolerance and compassion. Nothing would ever be the same. Even here on my tiny barrier island, people hung blackout curtains over the windows at night. German subs were just offshore, according to the newspapers. I was sickened to think of my pristine waters being infected with hatred, but I knew it was true. Learning long ago to trust my instincts, I felt darkness seeping like used oil around me, permeating and sticky, deliberately clogging the balance of nature. I was falling into something that would change me forever.

The water dripped from my skin as I walked from the ocean into the dunes. Sea oats brushed my bare legs and I left a trail of water spots as I climbed over the mountain of sand. Among the reeds and beach grass, I stooped to retrieve a hidden bag. The opaque moon lit my path, but nearing the maritime forest it was considerably darker. The dense undergrowth was a crouching beast waiting to grab my ankles. I could smell its musk, earthy and pungent, raw and acrid, it burned the lining of my nose. Prickly scrub bushes and spiny leaves nettled my skin as I picked my way through the path, one hand cradling my smooth, round stomach. The stunted wind-blown oaks formed a canopy overhead blocking out most of the moonlight. But I was not afraid, never had been, this was my world. I had made this trip many times to the small clearing where the cool sand caressed my feet, and the crooked arms of the live oaks protected my solitude. This place was my refuge from a world that would never understand me, and a sanctuary into a world that would never forsake me. It was here that I gathered my strength, channeled my energy, and sought guidance for my actions. This was my church.

Still naked, rivulets of sea water dripped from my hair and ran down the straight column of my spine. I turned, facing north, and kneeled before an altar of eggshell smooth stones. Opening my bag, I placed its contents in the sand, sprinkled a handful of sea salt around the clearing, and drew a circle with a slender birch rod. I had cleansed my body in the ocean, cast my circle, and invoked the elements. It was time. I must protect my daughter.

I had felt the dark, evil stalking my happiness. It had been rising for days, soon it would attack. Its oppressive weight pressed on my body. The hope I had for this miracle was crumbling like a sandcastle in the rising tide. It would never be as I wanted. My connection to Jackson would vanish forever. Weighing the danger and tempting the spirits, I had postponed this moment, almost waiting too long. But it had to be this night, the longest day of the year, the midsummer solstice. I felt the Old Ones surround me with love and the white light of the Spirit. This night was for acknowledging dark and light, finding inner power, and protection. I celebrated Lithia tonight as a night of fulfillment and expectation. Tonight, I would give my child to the Old Ones, for she would be in their care now. The moon was full, shining with the brightness of my love, a mother's love. This was the night to channel the most powerful energy in existence. This would be my ultimate sacrifice.

Exhaling slowly, fighting my body for control, I focused on my heartbeat, asking the Goddess to hold me with gentle hands. I picked up the diminutive dagger, its pearl handle cold to the touch in my unsteady fingers. Lifting it straight above my heart, I looked to the heavens and closed my eyes. It was time to draw down the moon.

PART I

CHAPTER ONE

Present
James Island

THE WAVERING WATER DISTORTED my feet as I stepped into the moonlit tide pool. Blurry and indistinct, I saw flashes of my chipped toenail polish, sexless pale pink, nondescript and anonymous. I thought this would be harder, but my body moved mechanically, recognizing sweet release. The ocean beckoned, swaying and swelling, offering eternal peace. My path was lit by the opalescent moon just beyond my fingertips. Euphoric, weightless, mesmerized by the rhythm of the water, my pain washed away as my beloved Atlantic cradled me in acceptance.

Surrender Jade.

I couldn't spend another day knowing my dreams were dead, like my babies. Another miscarriage, motherhood elusive, I was a failure.

Let go. I'll take you as you are.

No pain, no judgment, drifting forever in her watery embrace.

Drown your despair.

Never to feel again, never feel, never again… never feel. Never feel warmth… or Ian's touch… chocolate melting on my tongue. I was so tired. There was nothing left. My life had drained from my body long ago with my tears and lost babies.

My lungs burned. My chest was going to rupture, leaving fragments of me churning in the surf. The manic voice in my head screamed, *Coward! Fight goddammit!*

"It's too late," I cried to the dark, raging core tearing inside. "Empty…no strength." My words were saturated with saltwater.

What about us?

Their voices were whispers on the wind, barely audible in the rolling fields of black.

What about us?

Stronger, clearer, pleading with me. Then I saw the three young women. Exuberant. Hopeful. Kicking foamy surf with tanned legs, posed fearless on the edge of a continent and adulthood. The echo of their voices bounced snapshots of college through my mind.

"Can't. I can't. I can't hold on anymore."

We'll hold on to you.

Frustration, anger, insanity, the hard lumps of failure rose from the depths of me and spewed out my mouth to bubble overhead. Fluid fingers of a watery hand crushed my throat. Desperate and urgent, I strained against its grip, kicking to break from the hold, my soul pleading for my body to respond. I wanted to laugh with them again, eat popcorn and drink beer, debate through the night. I wanted to feel my husband touch me, flickers of desire tingled in my cells.

Desire left me long ago, but now I wanted. Astonished, I really wanted. To live. I wanted to live. Panicked and dying, I inhaled the salty air, thrashing my leaded muscles, shocked and gasping. Scanning for the shore, I was lost, heels over head, I tumbled in the undercurrent. There were no dunes, no hope. The irony of my life, now when I wanted to live, I was going to die.

There was only me and my instinct to survive. I released the torment of the last years, kicked hard, breaking the surface. Refusing to die, I roared, "I will not die! I will not give up! I will not!"

I saw the beach illuminated in the moonlight. Images of newly hatched sea turtles flashed through my mind. As a child, I had watched them burst through their sandy nest to scramble furiously toward the moon for the sanctuary of the sea. Predators be damned, they wanted to live. Now I wanted to live. I longed for the sanctuary of the sand. Crawling into the dunes, I collapsed among the sea oats.

Just after dawn, I awoke to the fiddler crabs scuttling about my feet and gulls shrieking overhead. Confused, I tried to stand but my legs buckled and I fell into the damp sand knocking over a bucket of clams.

"It took me the better part of the morning to get all those." Startled, I turned toward the voice, shading my eyes from the sun.

"My name's Agnes. I wondered when you were going to stir." I didn't have any words for her. Still disoriented, I tried again to stand, my head throbbing at both temples. "You might as well stay down," she said. "You look like hell." Sitting beside me, Agnes took a brown paper bag from a pouch slung around her shoulder. She handed me an apple and what looked like a piece of dried leather then took out the same for her. Rubbing it between my fingertips, it was rough to the touch and smelled like smoke.

"Go ahead child. It's beef jerky. Protein," she said. "Then maybe you can stay on your feet."

"Jade," I mumbled, nodding in her direction, but eating was more than I could do. Just the pungent smell of the jerky was sending bile rising in my throat. Everything about these moments, surreal, I didn't even remember yesterday. Was this woman even real? Snippets were just beyond my mental grasp, of sadness, hopelessness, and water overtaking me. Had I deliberately tried to drown? A vision of myself and college friends from two decades ago floated to mind

9

and I heard voices telling me to save myself. Now, I sat on the beach, hung-over and sun-bleached, watching a small woman gnaw on a piece of meaty shoe leather. She was at least eighty, wearing a baby blue windbreaker and cut-off fatigues ragged at the knees. She handed me a mason jar of water she took from her bag.

"I come out here every morning to see what the sea gods wash in."

The lilt of her voice interrupted my flashes. She didn't seem to be bothered by my silence or state of mind. "I come out here at night too, when the moon is full, like last night." The last three words sunk slowly into me, cold and slimy, I felt them slide all the way to the center of my soul. Trance-like, I turned slightly to study her. The woman's wispy white hair framed her pinched pixie face. Her skin was tan and tough like old canvas, and crinkled from decades of sun and wind. Gnarled hands and feet, calloused with old age and hard work, they reminded me of the maritime undergrowth behind me. But there was nothing elderly or clouded about the crystalline blue eyes that studied me. Such eyes could see everything, I realized, including my desperate descent into madness last night.

"I go swimming sometimes at night," I said finally.

"Yeah, I took a swim like that once," she replied. Neither of us needed to say anymore. We both understood. The sun was journeying west, now right above us, heating the sand like smoldering coals. Thanking Agnes, I stood and brushed sand from my clothes.

"I think I'm fine now," I said. "Just got a little too close to the edge."

Agnes picked up her bag and bucket of clams then started walking north up the beach. Departing, she called over her shoulder, "It's a long way down," she warned. "And even further back up."

CHAPTER TWO

Present
James Island

THE PAPERY STRIPS OF paint peeled from the rails of the porch, like thin, scorched skin of a sunburned swimmer, and drifted on the breeze. I sat at my family's beach house contemplating my near suicide. That word, suicide, sounded so strange in my head. I felt defeated and relieved. This had been my happy place, and why I came to James Island. It was my favorite place as a child, full of memories of joy and peace. I had wanted those memories with me as I drifted away.

My parents bought the beach house the summer I turned ten. Although it was a real estate rental investment, we used it frequently when it was vacant. Mom packed the car while dad woke me. We left before dawn, and I would nestle in the back seat with my pillow and blanket, falling back asleep to the quiet conversation between my parents. We stopped for breakfast after several hours, always at the same café, where they put real whipped cream on my chocolate chip pancakes. After that, I knew it was slightly over an hour until I could see the ocean. The bridge across the canal was a swinging bridge. Periodically, the caution gates lowered, and the mechanical beast heaved and stretched to life extending its arms wide to let the waiting boats pass through. Dad would sigh at the delay, but I loved watching the slick sailboats with tall masts, sails folded, gliding through. Shrimp boats, their crooked arms resembling origami cranes, motored by, and always a few john boats, crab pots banging against their hull.

Now, nursing a warm Diet Coke, I sighed loudly and wondered how to make sense of the last forty-eight hours. Did I really try to kill myself, or was I just tired of living? There was a difference, I thought. Being so tired I wanted to go to sleep and not wake up didn't mean I wanted to stop living, or did it? Deluded and numb, the darkness always seemed like a dear friend ready to protect me from the abyss, then her mask slipped and I saw the evil bitch for what she was. The problem was in trying to see it before it was too late, and last night was much too late. All of this was just too damn exhausting to decipher. I knew I was so very tired, and I was tired of my life. But, I didn't think I wanted to die, not really. I needed to escape, from the pain and loss, find somewhere I didn't feel empty, alone, and sad.

Ian. My husband would never understand what I did last night. I didn't understand last night. How could I explain years of darkness? How did two people live together, but become strangers? He was too much for me. For now, I would hide at the beach house. Besides, it would take him a week to realize I was gone.

The ocean swells were soft today, the breeze easy and gentle. The gulls swooped and swirled on the currents dropping to strut on the glistening sand. I watched as a laughing gull abruptly landed, flapping its wings a few times then it speared the wet sand with its beak. Joining a few more, they emitted a high-pitched chorus, shrill and loud, like a nasally laugh. Their gray wings darkened into black tail feathers. I lost all time watching them preen and pose, their funny gait, slow, slow, quick step, like ballroom dancing, but a little less graceful and indelicately loud. Hearing their raucous calls to each other, I imagined lively conversations between gossiping church ladies at morning Bible study.

My thoughts returned to Ian. The last time I saw him was nine days ago when he left for Chicago on business. After a week of sleepwalking around our lovely and lonely two-story colonial in south Charlotte, I couldn't take the sham of my life anymore, so I drove five hours to the island and walked into the Atlantic. I didn't even leave him a note. There was nothing to say. What was I leaving behind? My counterfeit existence? I didn't belong there among the mothers and toddlers busy with music lessons, birthday parties, and life. Soccer goals in the green space, lawns crowded with bicycles and Little Tikes toys, all daily reminders that it wasn't my world and never would be. I didn't belong there. I didn't need a minivan full of car seats. I had miscarriages. I was good at those.

My third one happened just seven weeks ago. Everyone assumed I was fine, like the more babies I lost the more desensitized I became. No one realized I was dying inside. Pieces of me became the beginning of a family, a child, my future, my purpose. Then it was gone, taking fragments of me with it. How could I get used to that? How could anyone think it was getting easier to accept? Each miscarriage left deep cracks in my heart and crevices in my psyche that would never heal. With each baby I lost, I withdrew, turning away from reality and away from Ian. He became less visible in person, and in my heart.

Lately, he needed to be out of town on business more than usual. When he was home, he watched television, sports, any sports, and sitcom reruns, anything to keep from engaging with me. He slept in the leather recliner, clutching the remote, apologizing each morning for falling asleep in the den as he stumbled to the shower. Why should he come to bed? We barely talked. Our nights of lovemaking, cuddling, and dreaming of a family were futile. We produced nothing and now our love meant nothing. After the second miscarriage, I worked to summon the desire for sex, made gourmet dinners, and wore uncomfortable lingerie. I really tried for a while, but I never felt it and I was sure Ian knew. He went through the motions, he was a man, but it was just sex. We never looked at each other and when it was over, he mumbled *I love you*, and rolled over to sleep.

Jarring me from the past, honeyed giggles swept along the surf. I looked down the beach to see a young couple, a little girl running ahead, her auburn curls bouncing. She held clumps of wet seaweed in each tiny hand. Pure, sweet delight touched my heart. I cradled my empty stomach as fat tears pooled in my eyes. Spilling onto my cheeks, they dried on the wind. How had I gotten here? Did I cause this? My world was so ugly. Bitterness reigned, dominating a place of screaming despair, where souls self-destruct when the world becomes too much, where those things that will never be skulk in the shadows. Mean and vicious, they lay in wait for my flayed soul to be exposed, like flesh from a battle, to chew and mangle what I'll never have.

That was the thing about final endings. They made no concessions, offered no comfort, and ironically gave no closure. They just ended, like my chances for bearing children. I loved children, babysat as a teen, and earned an early education degree in college. I looked for a husband who would make a great dad. I had been pretending, just waiting for my happy ending. I longed for a home filled with the sweet laughter of children, Legos underfoot, and cardboard and popsicle-stick ornaments on the Christmas trees. Now, I could see the absurdity of my illusion, it looked like a Norman Rockwell fantasy. It lacked even a shred of reality. How could I mourn what I never had?

Who even plans for fertility problems? The tests, treatments, and drugs, each failed attempt draining to our relationship as well as our bank account. Give it time, all the doctors concluded. Regroup. Relax. They said to settle down, we were too anxious. Then it finally happened. We celebrated like we had won the lottery, holding each other at night, and trading baby names in the soft darkness. We designed the nursery, and told relatives and friends. Our happiness was ebullient and infectious. Then it ended. The cramps contracted in my abdomen, hot, searing pain, then blood gushed from me. Our dream ended on a cold table as my cervix was surgically dilated, my uterus scraped and scoured, sterile instruments eradicating its contents. We held each other in the quiet of the night as I cried into the dark curls of Ian's chest. But each day, I slipped a little deeper, and stayed in bed a little longer.

Trying to recover, I realized I blamed myself. Committing to heal my body, I tried all kinds of folk remedies to ensure a healthy pregnancy. I ate microgreens and super foods, drank smoothies while walking on the treadmill. I replaced all of Ian's underwear, consulted astrology charts for lovemaking, and began each morning with lit candles and chants. Ian was bemused, but I knew I could will it to happen for us. The universe would answer.

The second miscarriage was devastating. After that pregnancy ended, I surrendered to a dark place that terrified my family and required therapy. Ian couldn't do anything right. He needed to be away on business, and I found projects around the house. I was planning a life around a baby, but it was like living in a snow globe. My life was a still-life of perfection, but every time the scene settled an invisible force shook my life apart. Give her some time, the doctors told Ian. So he gave me time and space, and more time and more space, and nothing was ever the same.

The third pregnancy came as a surprise to us. Sex wasn't a frequent part of our marriage anymore and when it did happen, it was because I had too much to drink at a cocktail party or neighborhood barbecue. Only then could I escape my mantra of "what's the point?" I pitied us both. He deserved a better wife. I shut him out when I should have been reaching for him.

We celebrated the news with a date night, smiled at each other and touched intimately, all the while secretly terrified of what would happen next. Our marriage was strained at best. We seemed desperate. We clung to routines, our robotic behavior exposing the chasm expanding between us.

The familiar cramping began on a Tuesday morning. Already expecting the inevitable result, I called the doctor. Bed rest, he prescribed. Within fifteen hours the garish, red blood began, and by Thursday afternoon I was in the hospital having the third, and most likely last, remnants of my hope sucked into a machine.

The beach was quiet now. I was relieved I didn't have to see the happy families anymore. Watching the world continue to revolve was just too much, too hard. Was it supposed to be? Ian and I used to be really good, great with planning for the future. It's a shame we couldn't see that future, wasting so many days and opportunities clinging to our make-believe destiny. I wished I could have reached for him, let him in to see my anguish and agony. After the misery of the first loss, I hid my pain, throwing myself into body repair, as if a few mechanical tweaks would fix the malfunction.

When that didn't work, my stability ripped apart, raw and ragged, and I curled into an emotional fetal position. I needed Ian to wrap himself around me and shut out the world, but I didn't have the strength to reach for him and was incapable of asking. It was a paralyzing situation. I loved him. We had wrapped our bodies around each other and created miracles, yet I couldn't make myself need him enough to say the words. Needing him, wanting him, I longed for him to share the hurt and loss; instead he fixed the stair rail that I had nagged him about for years. Couldn't he see my flesh tearing apart, the hormone rampage that followed, my raging guilt and inadequacy? Why couldn't he save our doomed pregnancies?

Why couldn't he hold my heart together? He never even tried. I was alone with my demons.

Other times I had tried to show him the darkness, describe the unbearable misery. I really had. Sleep evaded me. I listened to his muffled snores against the backdrop of a television crime drama. Eventually, I would rise and searched for chocolate-covered cashews and vodka, waiting for the sun to light another dismal day. My therapist said to assign the loss a color, personify it, so I could name it, confront it. That never worked for me. Colors were beautiful. This feeling was a vile predatory force that invaded my body, stealing my children. I refused to even waste brown, a throw-away color to some people. Brown was for fall leaves in autumn, decadent dark chocolate brownies, soft, fuzzy puppies, and twelve-year-old scotch. There was no comforting kaleidoscope, just a greedy monster, its ruinous perversity contaminating my life. Ian barely flinched at the third loss. Numb and forsaken, it was too late for tenderness and unity. The last cells of our love had washed from me in a bloody escape.

Small, cool drops of rain surprised me. I must have been sitting for hours. I stood, and drug the weathered Adirondack chairs under the overhang. The ocean was fuming. Strong waves pummeled the sand, shifting it submissively. The breakers, turbulent, spewed salty foam into the air. Dense and oppressive, the humidity foretold of bad weather and the menacing gray water concurred. A solitary gull was lifted in the updraft, but the brown pelicans held firm and flew in formation north to the safety of the maritime forest.

"Storm's coming fast. Need to wait it out here." Startled by the voice that preceded the head of cotton curls, I peered over the rail as Agnes pulled herself onto the porch. I spit out a stilted greeting and motioned to the second chair. "She's throwing a tantrum today," Agnes said, nodding toward the breaking waves. Laughter peeled like crystal bells as amusement flashed across her pixie face. "She won't be coy tonight." I wasn't sure what she meant by that, only that she was referring to the ocean. The confusion must have shown on my face.

"The ocean's like a woman and the beach, a man," Agnes explained. "Haven't you ever noticed how the waves caress the sand, stroking and soothing, advancing and retreating, it's like a comfortable waltz between an old married couple? They know each other, their slope and curve, rhythm and timing."

"I haven't paid much attention to the sexual nuances of the ocean," I said, not sure if I could even recognize a sexual nuance. Agnes gave me a deep, pensive look.

"Look at her now. Storm's a coming and she's ready to tango," Agnes said. "That's a Latin beat, passionate, demanding and yes, aggressive, like two lovers. Definitely a force of nature." I didn't know how to respond. It had been a long time since I tangoed, and I wasn't sure it was ever a force of nature.

"I guess there's a lot about the ocean I don't know. I like it here. Always loved the island… it's comforting."

"Well, honey, that's a start," she said. "You have to know yourself first to really feel the ocean's call, or it's impossible to understand anything else. You know what I mean by that?"

I gave her a noncommittal nod. We sat in silence, experiencing the storm, the beauty of the summer lightning, the unrestrained wind followed by the crescendo climax of thunder, and a drenching downpour. I felt voyeuristic and flushed, like when I walked in on my college roommate having sex. Charged, as if an electric current connected parts of my body and mind I didn't know shared feelings. As suddenly as the squall blew in, the rays thrust through the cloud cover spilling sunlight onto the water. I exhaled sharply and relaxed against the chair. "What a storm," I said. "That was different. I've never looked at a storm like that."

Agnes smiled and stood to leave, the glint in her blue eyes connecting with mine. "You should change the way you look at things," she said. "Never know what you might see." Seeing the animation in her face, I gave her a slight grin as she skipped down the stairs onto the sand.

Our weathered cottage on the overgrown sandbar of James Island had been a place of solace my whole life. My parents bought it long before the island construction exploded. There between the marsh grass and sticky, black, pluff mud of the canal and the gray blue Atlantic waters, I felt affirmed as if I belonged. I didn't question. I didn't doubt. My spirit breathed amid the intoxicating essence of pure, undiluted life. I was ashamed about tainting my sanctuary with my attempted suicide, but in a weird way I knew I could rest here even if it was a permanent slumber.

Over time storms and wind changed the beach, so sand had been added to fortify the dune stability. Our one-story cottage was built on stilts and painted sea turtle green, light like its underbelly. The porch wrapped around three sides and extended beyond the roof's oceanfront overhang, forming a large sun deck. Mom and I argued about whether to make it into a screen porch. A walkway extended over the dunes then a flight of stairs cut through the sea grass to rest on the ground. The bottom ones were partially covered by sand and crushed shells, slender pickets separated our lot from next door. The house sat taller when I was younger. Now it looked slumped and tired like me. Maybe I could do some renovations. A project could benefit us both.

After Agnes left, I relaxed in my chair and studied the twilight sky. Pin pricks of silver stars were barely visible. The clouds had moved on and so had some of the heat and humidity.

The impudent ringing of the telephone violated the velvet hush. Who even knows I'm here? I wasn't going to answer but realized that if my mother was checking in and didn't find me, she might come looking. Facing her today would be unbearable. I mumbled a forced hello expecting her barrage of intrusive questions. Instead, a voice much too boisterous boomed loud enough for the neighbors next door.

"Oooh, Jade, you're back. I saw your mother at the museum exhibit in Raleigh and she said you were on the island. I just knew you wouldn't forget our reunion. So, so, so glad you came early."

Like an obsolete PC with too little RAM, I tried to process the words. Who? What? Suppressing my urge to scream in anger at my mom for compromising my privacy, I tried to figure out who it was. To be fair, the vague message I left on mom's answering machine days ago didn't mention keeping my location a secret. I just wanted to tell her goodbye and where I was, as inane as that sounded. What reunion?

"Jade? Jade? Are you there? What's wrong with you?" The voice continued. "It's me. Penelope. Penelope Prince. Were you resting? Anyway, I'm heading to Wilmington to visit my cousin. We must get together this week for tea. It's the hottest thing now. Oh, I made a funny. We have to go to Miranda's Tea Room. She just reopened. They've been closed for remodeling and it was none too soon. Those chintz curtains were beyond tired. How's your schedule?" Not pausing for an answer she continued like a hummingbird on a three-day nectar bender. "We have a reunion to plan. I can't believe it's been twenty years already. I'm just so excited. Jade?"

"I'm not feeling well, Penn," I said finally. "Have to talk later."

As I was hanging up, I heard her say, "Please call me Penelope…" I never heard the rest of it, too stunned by the realization that the watery voices that saved me last night belonged to the same girls who pledged to return to the island twenty years after our college graduation. That was this summer.

CHAPTER THREE

Twenty-four years ago
University of North Carolina, Chapel Hill

A MIXTURE OF FEAR and elation swirled around me as I watched my parents drive away from my dorm. Eighteen years old, away from home for the first time, I was jubilant about beginning college. The ancient, red-brick dorm was behind me, and the whole university was in front of me. I had waited my whole life to be a Tar Heel.

I grew up in a suburb of Winston-Salem, a small city that pre-dated the Revolutionary War. A defiant little bastion of patriots in the early days, Winston was now a thriving community highlighted by Bowman Gray, the medical school of Wake Forest University. A tradition of research and innovation was attracting new people to town, but my little suburb was still quite sheltered.

Life was so different here, fraternity parties every weekend, political demonstrations that expanded my mind, and the library, nine stories. I wanted to drink it all in and swallow, digesting every exotic taste. Exotic wasn't a stretch, not for me anyway. The smells and sounds of campus permeated my body. The chiming of the bell tower sounded like tradition, the heightening hum of the football fans moved through the trees surrounding Kenan Stadium, and music came from every direction. It floated through dorm windows, echoed across the quads, reverberated over frat court, a mixture of classic rock, Madonna's dance beats and throwback groups from the 1970s.

I loved the energy pulsing through the air. It smelled like spicy pepperoni and alcohol, fruity, sweet, red wine and the yeasty, bitter, floral notes of beer. The earthy, pungent odor of musk and hormones caused my belly to tingle. I wanted to hold onto the intensity, shrouding myself in the feeling. It was addictive. I wanted more and more, savoring every larger-than-life moment.

Sitting in the Pit one day, I looked across the broad, brick depression where students socialized between classes. I saw a booth advertising sorority rush. Maybe, that's just what I needed. On this campus of 30,000 people, this fish was going to need an estuary to survive in this ocean of higher learning. So, this small town girl decided to join the most elite social organization on campus. I was going to pledge a sorority. Good manners, which fork to use at dinner, yeah, I knew all of that. Soon, I discovered I was clueless about the social graces and intricacies of rush. This was a cattle call, the scrutiny, pretentious rules and attitudes. It was overwhelming. I had to visit each house on campus and make small talk, hoping to make a positive impression that gave me an edge over a thousand other women. What did I like to read? Hobbies? Favorite vacation spot?

I wasn't sure I had the right clothes or great conversational skills, but watching the classic, *Animal House*, as a teen had lit a fire to join that just wasn't going to be extinguished. I never realized how unprepared I was until I was hooked, and hoping to discover the experience of a lifetime.

The next few weeks were filled with lectures and essays, and I scrambled to keep up, learning to scratch out my own version of shorthand. I had gigantic assignments every week. To read and analyze entire books in a week and write papers with word counts that exceeded literary journals. I was lost. In addition, I had managed to hurl myself headfirst into a social arena where I felt more than a little anxiety. In a succession of rounds, the house choices were narrowed by the sorority or me, and after the fourth round, or Pref Night, I might receive an invitation to join one of three houses, if I had that many choices remaining.

Hurrying home from a late afternoon class, I had to change clothes, redo my hair and make-up, and sprint back through campus past Morehead Planetarium, cross Franklin Street and find Rosemary Street where most of the houses were for the first round of rush parties. My wardrobe, an explosion of rejects, covered my bed and floor, matching shoes were impossible to find, no selection of lipstick was the right color. Then I was running, like a wild filly through the social elite of Carolina's version of the Kentucky Derby. The Indian summer humidity was causing my make-up to slide south and the abhorrent sweat stains blooming through my silk blouse and wrinkled linen skirt told me they were clearly the wrong choice for my cross country trek. I had never felt so far from home.

"So what cities in Europe did you visit this summer?" asked a perfectly-manicured blond, who, of course, had no sweat stains.

"Well," I began. "Actually, I would love to visit Europe sometime, but this summer I worked in a hardware store." I could have proudly explained the difference between a kotter pin and a hex bolt but by then I knew it didn't matter. Those fake smiles let me know I was way out of my league. My best quality was being genuine. Thank god I had only one more house left in this social labyrinth. I couldn't wait to be in my air-conditioned dorm, wearing a t-shirt and shorts, a cold beer in my hand. I walked along the walkway and sat down in the shade on the porch swing. Ten degrees cooler, it was a nice private little spot, an orange clematis vine wrapped around the lamp post and somewhere behind me in the hedge, I could smell honeysuckle, the sweetness hanging in the late afternoon humidity. I didn't care if they asked to which country clubs my parents belonged, I was going to say the first thing that came to mind.

Suddenly, the swing chains rattled and a breathless voice asked, "Mind if I sit down?"

"Sure," I said. "I'm Jade Wolfeson from the historic town of Winston-Salem. I'm an education major."

"Is that a recording or do you just talk that way?" The newcomer laughed, tossing her chestnut hair over her shoulder. "I'm Penelope Faulkner from the historic city of Asheville and I'm an art history major," she added, mocking me. But the gleam in her hazel eyes teased a smile from me. "Ya know, sitting over here alone, is not how this game is played."

"I'm not very good at this game," I confided. "In fact, I think I made a huge mistake thinking this was for me."

"You're just not doing it the right way. First of all, you look way too serious and uptight. You're not having a pap smear, this is a party." Penelope grabbed my hand, pulling me from the swing. "Stick with me, kid. We'll get through it together."

Weeks later, I waited all Sunday afternoon for a knock on my door. It was Bid Day, the finish line, when sororities hand out their invitations to join. For me, it was all or nothing. Of my three possible choices, I wanted only one house. I twirled my hair absentmindedly around my index finger thinking about last night. Pref night. I had three houses to rank in order of interest then the Panhellenic Council would match my choice with the house selection. But I suicided. I chose only one. If they didn't want me, I had nowhere to go. It wasn't the idea of being a sorority girl that captivated me anyway, it was truly belonging somewhere, having a place to call home. I wanted a place to be myself. I knew I needed to feel like a part of something, not just look like it. The only house for me was Delta Xi Theta. If not there, then it was nowhere.

It was nearly six, the deadline, my whole day spent waiting. Frayed and frustrated, I threw my composition notebook at the wall and opened a Diet Coke, probably not the best drink to take the edge off. I wondered where my roommate kept her bourbon. I had been unable to write two coherent sentences all afternoon, and now I would have to re-think my social identity. I had a damn plan. I just needed others to do their part. I guess my bitching muffled the rattle of the suite door, but the pounding on my room door was unmistakable. I was afraid to hope, probably a lost pizza delivery guy at the wrong door. I was running through pessimistic scenarios when the loud bang prompted me to answer.

"Jade! Jade! Open this damn door," they shouted. "Delta Xi Theta wants you!"

The house loomed three stories into a blue velvet sky. Strands of multi-colored lanterns swung from the front porch to the wrought-iron lamp post. *Carolina girls, best in the world, Carolina girls, sweet southern pearls...* the sugared lyrics of the beach music song spilled from an upstairs window. I smelled barbecued meat, sweet and peppery with hints of smoke and more than a little alcohol, even though I learned during rush, sororities aren't allowed to have alcohol on the premises. Eye-roll. Standing on the sidewalk looking at the Greek letters above the archway, was powerful. Then there were the women, dancing on the manicured lawn, sitting on the porch rails, laughing, calling to each other. Oh my god, I was going to be a part of this. Elated and hesitant, I couldn't believe this was real. Flanked on either side by juniors and seniors wearing lettered shirts, I felt I had boarded a carnival ride as they whirled and twirled me through introductions and conversations. Sisters hugged me and shouted greetings. Someone gave me a Carolina blue shirt with the words *Delta Xi Theta* spelled out in white script. I was officially a pledge and right now that felt fabulous.

My new sisters were going to be my family. I was exhilarated, then terrified. What if they don't like me when they get to know me? They're strangers. What if I'm not exciting enough? What have I done? All my insecurities twisted around those questions, and I just stood on the walk, staring. Anxiety saturated my skin as I shivered in the September twilight.

"I'm beginning to think you don't understand the concept of a party." Hearing the familiar voice of Penelope Faulkner, I turned to see her wearing an identical shirt. Never had I been so happy to see anyone.

"Thank god," I said. Just her presence was reassuring. Everything was going to be fine, better than fine. College was going to be outrageous. The party went way into the night as similar encounters took place all along Rosemary Street. I would never remember everyone's names, but hallelujah, who cared? I belonged. Tonight, I had become part of something bigger than myself. I had four years to learn names, and that started tomorrow. Tonight was just for me. I felt alive.

As the beauty of fall exploded in a blaze of color, burgundy and burnt orange maple, golden poplar, and purple hues of autumn leaves swirled around the historic campus, and fell to red brick walkways. I swished through them walking to class and crushed them under my loafers. Carolina was iconic. The first public university was founded in 1789, just after the American colonies declared their independence. I marveled at the tradition surrounding me as I walked through campus. Three-story red brick buildings stood like sentinels around the grassy quads where walkways criss-crossed like giant 'X' formations. College was everything I dreamed, from lectures about art and archeology, to philosophical discussions that stretched my brain, and Latin lessons that made me feel scholarly. And sweet Jesus, there were the weekends. I loved those two days, sleeping until noon then waking to the sounds and smells of the alumni tailgating around the football stadium. We could see them and smell their picnics through the screened dorm windows. From the backs of luxury cars, they erected card tables with gourmet delicacies, from pungent, marinated mushrooms, crispy, fried chicken legs, red skin potato salad with fresh dill, to silky pates and creamy, exotic cheeses. Wine glasses sparkled in the sunlight as the voices of tailgaters, ripe with laughter and excitement, mingled with music, and the aroma of pre-game pizza from the dorm. The whole campus pulsed with the electricity of people having fun. My friends and I shared take-out and cocktails, rummaged through each other's closets and usually made it to the game by the middle of the first quarter.

My phone rang and I stepped over the pizza boxes, rushing to answer it.

"Can I wear your royal blue sweater?"

"Who is this?" I asked, stifling a laugh.

"Dammit Jade, I don't have time for your shit. There's a make-up stain on the one I was wearing and nothing else goes with these pants."

"So change pants," I offered, as our friends exploded with laughter. Before she stopped sputtering, I finished my sentence. "Get over here. This beer is disappearing faster than your virtue."

"Bitch," she said, and the line went dead.

"You're going to pay for that," Carey said. "Hand me a beer," she called to no one in particular.

Wearing my blue sweater, Penn walked to the stadium outlining our social agenda for the evening. "*Cream of Soul* is playing at the Omicron house. We'll go by there for a while and end up at the Sigma Rho house. Those boys can dance and I feel like a party!" She shouted the last sentence loud enough to make heads turn.

We sat in the bleachers with the sorority block, watching boys, and cheering. The fraternity boys looked delicious in their khaki pants with pleats and cuffed hems, oxford button-downs and colorful ties, their hair still wet from the shower. They yelled at the referees, joked and passed monogrammed hip flasks of Jack Daniels down the row. Yeasty beer and the potent essence of dark bourbon intoxicated the crisp autumn air and seeped into our pores. Football season was always a feast for the senses. But as much fun as the games were, the after-parties were legendary.

Massive stone and brick fraternity houses sat like ancient gargoyles perched on the edge of campus. The Greek revival and antebellum giants, aristocratic with columns and balconies, were remnants of the Neoclassical architectural movement of the late eighteenth century. They represented old money, privileged connections and ego, lots of attitude, but those boys could throw a party.

Clearing the main floor of furniture and rugs, local bands played at the wealthier houses and stereos at the others, going past midnight while couples danced on the well-worn hardwoods. Dancing, drinking, and socializing were new behaviors for me, and I embraced the experience with wide-open arms, reveling in the expansion of my mind, the pleasures of my body, and the freedom of my soul. Life had never been like this. It was glorious.

"Wake up sugar." Penn bumped her hip against the sofa jarring me from sleep. Slightly hung-over and a little disoriented, I slung my hair from my eyes and squinted up at her.

"What?" I wailed. "I just went to sleep."

"No, you went to sleep five hours ago after you staggered home from the last frat party. I know, because I was with you." Trying to hear above the clanging cymbals in my head, I assessed the situation. Penn sat on the arm of the sofa. Her pants were creased perfectly and she was wearing a thin cotton sweater the same olive-hazel as her eyes, an expensive houndstooth blazer was folded over her left arm. "Get up. Pledge lunch, remember?" she said. "You look like hell, and have about twenty minutes to get presentable."

What kind of wonder woman was she, I asked myself, stretching my leg muscles. They were cramped and sore from dehydration and dancing, the residual effect of too much partying and too little sleep. Recollecting vague portions of last night, I remembered Penn shagging, a regional beach dance, on the ancient pine floors of the Sigma house, balancing a rum and Coke without spilling a drop, and flirting her ass off. We came back to the Delta Xi house together, microwaved some popcorn then my body met the soft upholstery of the seafoam green sofa in the living room. The tan ones were scratchy.

"Sunday afternoon pledge lunch, the get-to-know-your-sisters requirement. Get moving Jade. You will not make me late." I rose with a grunt in her direction, wondering if I could get across campus to my dorm, change, then get back to Franklin Street in fifteen minutes. No way. As usual, I was flying by the seat of my pants. Borrowing toiletries found in an upstairs bathroom, I washed my face, swigged some Listerine, brushed my black hair till it was silky then applied a swipe of lipstick. It was a little darker than my shade but looking in the mirror, it worked. I thanked the universe again for my clear skin and reasonably good looks. My residual summer tan and light-olive complexion diminished the need for many cosmetics. Navy blue eyes framed with black fringe stared back at me. The subtle dark smudges underneath hinted of my late night, but they were still my best feature, besides my hair. I had gorgeous hair and I took care of it.

As a little girl, my grandmother brushed it one hundred strokes before bedtime and that became a ritual for me. It had great body, lustrous color, and the casual, carefree swing cut gave me a healthy appearance. Knocking on a senior sister's door, I borrowed a wraparound sweater of soft gray that fell mid-thigh on my long denim-clad legs, straightened the neck of my black turtleneck, and fished the silver and black pledge pin from my pocket. Pinning it over my heart, I look just like a proper pledge, I thought.

Upon returning to the living room, Penn gave me an approving look, and slipped into her jacket. Penn knew she looked good, I thought. Always fashionable in styles from the exclusive women's boutiques, her soft curls with thin copper strands fell shoulder length around her delicate face, accentuating her China-doll skin. It all looked effortless as casual elegance is supposed to, but I knew Penn worked to choose flattering styles for her curves and perfected make-up trends.

"You bitch," Penn said, rolling her eyes. "You crawled home drunk in the middle of the night, slept on the sofa, borrowed clothes and now you look like a runway model. You have no idea how hot you really are." I took Penn's arm through mine and escorted her out the door, flashing a white-teeth smile at her.

"We can't all be me, now can we?"

We were meeting at The Ram's Head Rathskeller. The restaurant was down an alley off Franklin Street. We called it The Rat. Passing through a thick castle-like door, we entered the cavernous collection of caves carved from limestone a century ago. Washed in amber hue, brass sconces adorned the walls, providing just enough light to navigate. The food was cheap and plentiful, two essential elements for college budgets. Pasta, pizza, salads, and sandwiches with savory sauces and herb-infused dressings, were so popular waiters rarely brought menus. Penn and I always ate spaghetti, which came sizzling hot in a shallow cast-iron skillet with a salad featuring spicy house vinaigrette dressing. "I'm ordering lasagna," I whispered to Penn. "I don't want to look cheap." The lasagna, known as a "bowl of cheese," was an individual crock bubbling with rich, basil tomato sauce, laden with pepperoni, Italian sausage, smoked ham, and flat noodles covered with fresh mozzarella cheese. A chilled mug of sharp ginger ale completed my meal.

The waiter motioned to a back room where a gathering of pledges talked in groups. Penn and I were two of the eleven first-years in the forty member class. There were times when we still felt like bystanders trying to take in college as well as the Greek traditions. Penn fared a bit better than me. Her parents met at Carolina in the 1960s, and were both involved in Greek life. She grew up attending football games and hearing stories of bygone glories. I still couldn't believe I had taken this gigantic social leap. I was not all together comfortable yet, but was thrilled by the prospect.

Finessing our way to a back table, we took the last remaining seats near some older pledges. A few were discussing midterms, two more oogled the waiter. He smiled a crooked grin at them, but focused his gaze on another first-year at the end of the table. Her name was Emerson Beckett. She was something of an enigma, and we had found it difficult to get to know her. Irresistibly beautiful, a natural blond with vivid blue eyes, she was from New Bern, a small city at the confluence of the Trent and Neuse rivers. We heard she was raised by her grandparents. A marine biology major, she was usually talking about a save-the-whales or sea turtle campaign. At first glance, she looked like a California beach babe, carefree and confident, with big breasts, an empty head, and a luminous smile. But I was rapidly getting the impression I had seriously misjudged her. Emerson may have spent her childhood frolicking in the Atlantic waves, but her knowledge of marine life was astounding, and she made a perfect 1600 on her college entrance exams. So much for bubble-headed, damned if she wasn't stunning, stacked, and smart.

The adorable waiter returned with a tray of frosty mugs, soft drinks and water for most, beer for a few of the juniors and Emerson. With a wink, the waiter set the beer down, spilling froth over the edge. How did she get beer? I wondered. She's not legal, there's no way she's twenty-one. Bitch has a fake ID. That's why the waiter winked at her. That and she was crazy beautiful. I opened my mouth to ask, but Penn jumped first.

"Where did you get the fake?" Penn asked.

"Fake what?" Emerson answered.

"Your ID, the fake ID. I've been looking for one." I laughed at Penn's bravado as if fakes were hiding in the shrubbery like Easter eggs. Emerson drew her brows together.

"This is my real license." She seemed annoyed by the question.

"Oh sorry, thought you were a first like us," Penn said.

"I am."

With that definitive and dismissive answer, Emerson began to eat her salad. Penn stared a few seconds as if deciding whether to comment, thought better of it, and shifted her eyes to me. I nodded slightly, understanding we'd beat that dead horse later. I sipped my ginger ale, quietly waiting for my lasagna. Lunch was an eternity. Topics ranged from classes to boys and back but no one seemed confused about Emerson, except me and Penn. Where had she been the last few years? Did she transfer? No, she would have college credits. Peace Corp? Anti-hunting whale boat? We'd see about that.

CHAPTER FOUR

Present Day
James Island, North Carolina

THE LIGHT COMING THROUGH the window blinds created crisscrossed patterns on the floor. I could tell it was late afternoon by the orientation of the shadows. Propping myself against the wicker headboard, I smoothed the crocheted bedspread around me. Absently, I fingered the knobby edges of lace and pondered if I should even get out of bed. What was the point? Did it really matter? I was beyond tired and felt utterly useless. What comes after an unsuccessful suicide attempt? Talk to a therapist or lay in bed until I evaporated into dust? I felt that my suicidal moment had passed, but I couldn't see the future either.

I watched the changing shapes on the wall as shadows wiggled and squirmed trying to escape. They too, could feel the despondency wafting in the air. Instead of making choices, maybe I should eliminate them. The fewer options, the better, maybe then I could focus. I was not going to kill myself nor was I going home. Those were the only two things I knew for sure. Gulls cried outside, desolate sounds that carried on the wind, mourning, maybe for me, but I wasn't dead and that was my starting point.

I didn't have clothes, food, or even a toothbrush, only the clothes I was wearing when I walked into the ocean day before yesterday, and a few things I found in a gym bag in the car. Among the motley assortment of canned goods in the pantry was some tuna, sliced water chestnuts, a very large can of creamed corn, and yes, cherry pie filling. Yesterday I consumed two bottles of water and some Tylenol from an outdated bottle, and slept for the better part of the day and night.

Since I was going to stay here, I needed to shop, but just getting out of bed was too much. Get up. Confront myself, I thought. I couldn't think of a single reason to move. Waves of emotions drifted over me, sadness, loneliness, exhaustion, but nothing settled around me. I think I was just numb. The tears came again, it was useless for me to do anything but curl onto my side and cry myself to sleep. Living was hard and my strength was slipping away with the tide.

The sunlight shadows were gone when I woke later twisted in my sweaty sheets. It wasn't dark yet but certainly evening. The bed looked as if I had wrestled with demons. From the stench, I determined I really needed a shower. The hot water tank drained before I felt I had successfully washed away the layers. My feelings were a mixed bag. I had planned to die. It should have been easy, but I screwed that up too. With a heavy sigh, I searched for my shoes.

Keys and purse, where are they? I found the apple Agnes had given me. I was pretty sure I had invented her, like an imaginary friend, but the apple seemed real as I bit into it. My keys were in the ignition and my purse on the floor of the passenger's side. An hour later, I returned with a few apples, baby carrots, shrimp, pasta, a case of Diet Coke, three bottles of wine, and a three-layer double fudge cake with sprinkles. Sprinkles were festive. They screamed stay alive. At least my sick sense of humor was still intact.

At the beach store connected to the grocery I bought a few pairs of shorts, some tank tops with sandcastles and tourist phrases on them, one bathing suit, one pair of flip flops, and a blank journal. These provisions would be enough until I decided what to do with the rest of my life, or at least until next week.

If I wanted much more, I would have to go off island. There was only one stoplight at the two main streets. Radiating out from it was a tiny bank, connected drugstore and doctor's office, and a specialty food store attached to a gift shop. There were several restaurants, a couple high end beachfront and fine dining, a family diner, and on the pier, a collection of food stands including a grill, ice cream shop, and a taco booth. The Seaside Pier stretched 900 feet into the Atlantic. Wooden benches were spaced at intervals near the rails for fishing and people-watching. Unique to the area was a summer kid's program where they learned about indigenous marine life, and preservation of the ocean and marshes.

I grabbed my bags and the journal. All my therapists recommended keeping a journal. It seemed like a waste of time but I bought one anyway. I didn't want to record my feelings or get in touch with them. I wanted to be happy and have a baby. Without that, I didn't need to be reminded in perpetuity of my failure.

The cottage phone was ringing as I entered. One plastic bag snagged on the screen door and groceries scattered across the porch. Exasperated by the mess and intrusion, I ignored it, but it continued to ring.

"Where have you been?" Ian thundered into my ear. "I've called your cell till the message box was full, called home and finally your mother. What the hell are you doing?"

Sweet Jesus, now Ian, what was I to say? His tone angered me, but his concern sounded genuine. I couldn't tell him what had happened over the last few days. "I came to the beach to get away."

"Get away, from what? Me? I'm not even home."

"Just to get away Ian, I needed to be alone. You know?"

"No I don't know. What does this mean? When will you be back? I mean just how much time do you need?" His voice was snappy and petulant, like an over stimulated toddler. I sat my remaining groceries on the table and sighed.

"I don't know. As long as it takes."

"Takes to do what? Leave me, run away from us? Is that what this is about, you can't even face me to tell me it's over?"

"Calm down Ian." As usual, this was all about him and his needs. "I'm not leaving you, not tonight. Right now that's all I can promise. You never understand and I'm tired of trying to explain. I can't do this right now." He tried to interrupt, but I continued. "I'll call you in a few days." I heard the hurt in his voice and I wished I could tell him I was sorry, but the words evaporated on my tongue. So, I gently placed the receiver in its cradle. He was a good man and I thought he probably still loved me. I just didn't know if that mattered anymore. All of this felt beyond saving.

I shoved the groceries into the pantry and manhandled my produce into the refrigerator. My mind was spinning like a hamster wheel, and my limbs were tingling and spastic, I needed to walk. My footprints pushed deep into the damp sand, hard and angry, grains flying out behind me. I passed under the north pier before I slowed down. My chest contracted and then the crying began. Fat tears streaked down my wind-burned face, salty streams ran along my cheek to the corners of my mouth and neck. I couldn't stop. My despair, unleashed, was roaring like a tornado. I sat down in the loose sand and propped my head on my elbows and knees, and cried the tears of my life, for my lost babies, my husband's pain, my near suicide, the Christmas cupcake I dropped in the third grade, and much more. My well opened and emptied. I let it all go and held nothing back.

"Are you done?"

36

I whipped my head around, seeing Agnes sitting above me at the base of a dune.

"I didn't want to bother. It's best to get it all out while you can."

I rubbed my raw eyes on the tail of my shirt and looked out over the waves. As one wave crested and washed into the sand, another took its place. No hesitation, no interruption, just waves, one after another, over and over into the sand. I felt really small. I could lose babies, leave my husband, and even end my life, but those waves would break and cascade, disappearing into the sand forever. The ocean was endless. I was not. I was finite and I could disappear and the waves wouldn't even stop to acknowledge my passing.

I turned to Agnes and said, "I'm sorry."

"Sorry for what?" Agnes asked. "I have a feeling you say that too much." I didn't answer, but nodded vaguely at her comment. "What are you doing tonight?" she asked.

"Nothing," I laughed. "Not going swimming, if that's what you're asking."

"No, I want to take you somewhere. You know the crab shack, before you get to the bridge?" I nodded. "There's a little foot path through the beach grass that comes out at a small dock. I have a little roundabout tied up there. Meet me at eleven tonight."

I shifted my eyes and bit my lip. "Yeah, I know that's a strange time. Trust me." I knew I had nothing else to do but continue my downward plummet and pity party for one.

"Okay, I'll be there. Do I need anything, are we going fishing?"

"Sort of, you can call it that." She disappeared over the dunes, before I could rise. She's a spry little thing, I thought. I felt like road kill and she was scampering like a rabbit. I brushed the sand from my sweaty legs and headed home.

CHAPTER FIVE

Present
James Island

A LITTLE AFTER TEN, I knotted the sleeves of my sweatshirt over my shoulders, cajoled the antique bike from the crawl space under the back porch, and left to meet Agnes. I took the loop around town bypassing the pier where the teenagers congregated, flirting with each other. From personal experience, I expected there were others under the pier making out in the cool sand. The road around the outskirts was darker, with deeper sand trenches. I lost control a few times but never fell, and soon was walking the path past the crab shack.

The shack, an open-air arbor with wooden tables, opened each spring weekend then expanded through the summer months until late fall. Local fishermen and farmers rented space to sell clams, mussels, shrimp, crab, fish, and a variety of vegetables. The larger boats had their own docks or seafood stands. They sold their own catch and imported delicacies like Alaskan king crab legs, lobsters, and Pacific Ocean fish. Phenomenal restaurants lounged along the coast but tourists seemed to enjoy cooking fresh seafood. It made them feel special to serve their friends broiled sea bass with crab stuffing. The popularity of food shows convinced many they were gourmands. That had caused the restaurants to step up their game, improve their quality. I knew from waitressing summers at a pricey seafood place, I earned more when people couldn't cook what they ordered.

Reaching the end of the walkway, I leaned the bike against the pickets. Maybe I missed her, I thought, but then her cotton ball head appeared above the beach grass and she motioned for me to follow. The small foot path was barely visible through the tall grass, but I hurried after her as she disappeared from view. The brackish water assaulted my nose, but the sharp salinity and decaying smell was oddly comforting. It was natural and primitive, remaining constant for thousands of years. The sulfur odor let me know I was approaching the north end of the island, almost a half mile past where the bridge connected the island to the mainland. I could see the silhouette of Agnes' lithe body untying a small, white outboard. The fiddler crabs scattered for safety as I navigated the narrow pier and stepped aboard. Not exactly an ocean-going vessel, I hoped we weren't heading out to sea. So far she had not spoken a word, only nodded as she busied herself with the motor. Not sure about the reason for the silence, I decided it best to stay quiet.

Agnes was a strange little woman, quirky and perceptive. She waved me to a seat in the bow and adjusted the choke before pulling the starter. We motored past the docks of the canal townhomes and headed for a small land mass adjacent to James. It may have been a part of the bigger island once, but erosion, tropical storms and hurricanes, and just the passing of time changed the boundaries. Barrier islands were living entities, constantly shifting with the influence of the tides and weather phenomenon. This extra piece of land may have separated decades ago or just after the last storm. I couldn't remember from my summers here. I never ventured this far north. The undeveloped parcel was covered with maritime forests and live oaks. I thought it to be an overgrown sandbar with a center of marshy swamp land, but as we got closer, I saw the land was denser than I realized. The ground had some elevation and was larger than it appeared from the causeway.

Suddenly, Agnes pulled the rudder and maneuvered with precision around a jagged jetty, into a small cove hidden from view. Even though I was looking directly at the shoreline, I never saw the obscure spot. In one quick movement, she cut the engine, hopped overboard and looped a tow rope over an iron stake protruding from a block of concrete on the beach. She removed a small bag from the dinghy and flicked a crooked index finger at me. Taking that as a signal to follow, I hurried after the sure-footed woman into the forest. It was like Agnes never touched the sand or disturbed the branches. One second I caught a glimpse of her, the next, she had vanished without a trace, like a wisp of smoke. To the contrary, I was traipsing like a buffalo through an English garden.

I hoped I was going in the right direction. The trees slanted toward me, so I knew the ocean was somewhere ahead. Maritime growth on barrier islands grew away from the ocean, leaning toward the sound. Decades of wind and salt spray stunt their development, giving the whole land mass a permanent windswept appearance. Live oak branches lunged with gnarled knuckles to pick at my jacket. Sticky loblolly pine needles peppered my hair. Catching my sandal on a wicked root, I stumbled into a stand of yucca plants, causing multiple pricks to my hands. The whole experience was beginning to feel like being bullied on the playground, frustrating and frightening.

Where was Agnes? I slapped at giant mosquitoes, my anger rising like steam from my sweaty skin.

"Who invites a person on an excursion and leaves them in the goddamn forest?" My vow of silence long abandoned, I was cursing loudly as I floundered and stomped. I should return to the boat, but I didn't know where that was either. This was getting me nowhere. Standing motionless, I evaluated my options. Head back toward the sound and walk the shore until I got anywhere familiar, or sit my exhausted ass in the sand and wait for Agnes to find me. Then I could tell her exactly what I thought of this outing. Between my ragged breaths, I heard a soft sound floating through the trees, a voice singing or chanting. It was hard to discern the words. Carefully, I picked my way through the waxy leaves and followed the lilting voice. Approaching a clearing, I saw a staggering vision. Holy shit.

Naked as a newborn, Agnes stood in the center of a sandy circle, palms toward the stars, chanting the words I had heard through the undergrowth. The petite woman's skin looked like the peel of a peach left too long in the sun. Not affected by my approach, she continued her ritual, turning in four directions, each time changing the cadence of her song and motioning with her hands. Speechless, mortified, and paralyzed, I could not look away, nor step through the camouflage leaves. All I could do was take in the bizarre scene, some combination of a religious service and a Stephen King novel. The trees in the clearing arched like a cathedral and Spanish moss hung like tapestries along the outer sides. What the hell was she doing? And where did I fit into this ordeal? Questions flashed through my brain as I gathered myself for a terrified retreat. Before I could escape, Agnes focused her piercing blue eyes on me and spoke the first word of the night.

"Strip."

CHAPTER SIX

Twenty-four years ago
University of North Carolina

"STRIP."

I heard the command, but it didn't register.

"Strip."

No louder than before, not rough nor sexual, not even threatening, the word was spoken simply in a woman's voice as a one-word instruction. Looking around at my fellow pledge sisters huddled in the enveloping darkness of the forest, we shared an identical panic-stricken look, eyes wide, mouth ajar.

Awakened at two in the morning, we had been collected from our dorms, marched beyond the outskirts of campus to an abandoned outdoor amphitheater, and now in the frigid January night were being told to take off our clothes. I had wanted to join a sorority, capture a sense of belonging, the echo of tradition, a hint of privilege, and all the socializing. Truly, it just seemed fun. Standing in the woods in my bra and panties was causing me to re-think my decision. I was sleepy, bewildered, and really cold. A little hazing was fun, scavenger hunts, light housekeeping and errands for the sisters, a few pranks. So far, pledging had not involved anything degrading or dangerous, until now. This seemed wrong. Disappointed and a little scared, I felt foolish. Bonding with these women, sharing trust and respect, was it going to decline like this? Maybe they were just strangers, friends you bought.

Suddenly, there was a rustling nearby. From the dark shrubbery, emerged an initiated sister to stand before each pledge. Each one held a white satin robe with a gold corded belt. We slipped into the robes wordlessly, the only noise, the fabric. I held my breath in the darkness and dared not look around, for fear of being singled out. My heart beat like a Japanese drum, soon someone would hear it and come get me. The robe tempered the cold air and felt sensual on my bare skin as it draped across my midriff, blowing gently over my thighs. Sensuality was unfamiliar to me, but I had always been fond of the possibility. Ecstasy and sisterhood aside, I was trembling with cold, way past cranky, and tired enough to make the dorm room mattress seem desirable.

Twinkling flames sparked like fireflies in flight. Then delicate breaths of candlelight exhaled, illuminating the faces of the sisterhood. Wearing black robes and conspiratorial smiles, they gathered in concentric circles around the pledges, an unwavering formation of light separated the initiates from the darkness. Candles extended beyond the stone archway of the outdoor theatre, and I perceived a couple hundred women in robes in the surrounding trees. Who were all these women? There weren't that many active sisters. Alums? When they said for a lifetime, they meant it. This must be something spectacular.

I let go of my frosty apprehension, and watched it dissipate on the breeze. No longer aware of the cold, I heard feathery voices lightly singing around us as the circle parted. Six women in black-hooded velvet robes trimmed with gold satin filed through, and took places divided equally on either side of a rectangular table. It reminded me of the church altar for communion sacraments. Each woman carried items. The two nearest the table held large pillared candles with trailing ribbons. The middle ones held boxes draped in silver silk. The outer woman on the left held a carved silver chalice and the last one an old leather-bound book. While I assessed this ornate display, one last woman stepped from the darkness to stand behind the table. Dressed in a silver velvet robe with black velvet trim, I recognized the sorority president, Claire, her amused blue eyes reflecting the dancing flames. This would be more enjoyable next year when I knew what to expect.

Previously arranged in groups of eight, we stood five rows deep awaiting instruction. The two innermost attendants placed their candles on the table and came forward for the first eight initiates. Claire's lips moved but I couldn't hear her words. She spoke only to the ones kneeling before her. After a few minutes, they rose and faced the rest of us. Claire came around the altar and stood between us and them, nodding for the chalice bearer, one box holder and the book holder. Those three stepped forward and began their part of the ritual. Offering the cup to each initiate in turn, the sister moved along the row and returned to her place beside Claire. Next, each one took the carved ivory fountain pen, and entered her name in the ledger. Finally, Claire and the box holder stepped to each initiate. The president affixed a jeweled pin above their left breast, embracing after. When Claire returned to her original position, the attendants wordlessly escorted those to the back of the initiates, returning for the next row. The series was repeated with each group.

I was in the third group, anxious for my turn. Excitement pulsed through my blood. What an amazing experience? I listened carefully to the ritual words of sisterhood and loyalty and vowed in response to always pledge my support to these women. I drank from the chalice, contents which tasted like fortified wine with bitter, pungent spices. It warmed my throat like whiskey and whatever was happening, I was shivering with emotion, not cold. My hand shook slightly as I signed my full name. Claire affixed my pin, we embraced, my breath in my throat. I don't remember the other turns, but instead reveled in this magical world, inhaling the clear, crisp air of winter. When all of the initiates had returned to their original positions, Claire spoke to us of responsibility to each other and about honoring the sanctity of the sisterhood. We were linked together for a lifetime, she said. While her words still echoed through the circle, we were tapped on the shoulder and led silently away. Candle lights flickered and twirled among the trees, like tiny, illuminated fairies, and still the only sound was the rustling of robes on the wind.

CHAPTER SEVEN

Present
James Island

AGNES NEVER REPEATED HER command to strip, merely waited for me to process the direction and react. Why on earth should I take off my clothes? To chant with an old woman? This was crazy, yet I found myself thinking, why not? Glancing around for onlookers, I dropped my clothes into a clump of grass. Other than my dignity, I had nothing to lose. I was doing terrible on my own.

Wary, my body approached the sand circle while my mind stared in disbelief. The out of body experience was just beginning.

"You are out of balance," Agnes said. Not waiting for my response, she continued. "Your mind is not in harmony with your body, and neither is connected with the spirit. You are broken, my dear, and I can help." I only nodded at the woman. I did feel broken, fractured from everything that used to make sense, and disconnected from everything I loved. The fragments of my life had been collecting at my feet for some time, burying me in rubble. "It is my calling to heal. Turning my back on one who suffers will break me." She picked up a feathery branch beside her feet and walked in a circle, waving the branch in the air.

"When we lose ourselves, as you have, we are not whole until the pieces are balanced, each in harmony with the next." She walked to a large, flat stone I had not noticed, and kneeled in the sand. Removing items from a bag, she lit a yellow candle, tilting it so the melted wax formed a puddle on the stone. She sat the candle firmly in the sticky wax. Noticing similar wax formations around the altar rock, I could tell this was not a new practice for her.

She poured water from a blue glass bottle into a clay chalice, laid an iridescent purple quartz crystal beside that, and lastly placed a dainty and deadly dagger to the left of the candle. She's some kind of witch, I thought. Agnes motioned for me to kneel next to her. "We'll start from the beginning."

"Our world is composed of four elements," she said. "We must acknowledge and honor each of these to balance the spirit within us." Passing her fingertips through the flame, Agnes explained that fire represents will and desire. Water represents emotion, she said, picking up the chalice. After drinking from it, she passed it to me, indicating I take a sip. "The knife is air. It is intellect and communication. Finally, the quartz is earth, formed by the pressure and energy below our feet."

Agnes took my hand and laid it on the altar holding it tight. "You must understand the connections between these elements and yourself. Feel the energy radiating within you. Only then will you begin to heal." I looked at her face so earnest and sincere, the blue eyes reflecting the single flame of the candle.

"So, which part of me needs healing?" I asked.

"That's for you to answer."

Frustration echoed in my voice. "Where do I start? How will I know if I find balance?"

"That, my dear, is your journey."

Grabbing her hand with both of mine, I pleaded to her. "I don't understand what you want me to do. I need answers, directions, advice, not this crazy voodoo crap." Agnes sat quietly, still kneeling. During my tirade, she closed her eyes, and spoke words under her breath.

"What? What do I do? Just tell me. You tell me I'm broken, but don't fix me. I can't have a baby. My husband doesn't want me and I tried to, well, you know what I tried to do. Obviously, I don't have any fucking answers." Making gigantic gestures during my tirade, my fists now fell to my sides, defeated like the rest of me.

"I feel like I'm dying. My insides are rotting." My tears of grief mingled with the sand and dust on my cheeks. Agnes embraced me with her sinewy arms, holding me as I trembled with exhaustion and grief. I shuddered one last time and wiped my eyes with the back of my hands. "What's wrong with me?" I whispered. "Please help me. You may be the only one who can." Agnes took my hands as if talking to a young child.

"There's nothing wrong with you, my dear. It's how you're looking at it. And, you're not dying. You're living, and living is harder. Dying is much easier." Piercing me to the core with her bold stare, she said, "What you're doing is grieving. You're mourning the life you planned for yourself."

Never had I heard more profound words. Agnes was like a deity come to life before me, an apparition surrounding me with her omniscient wisdom. Oh my god, she's so right about my life. It was all devastating. Nothing was how I wanted it to be. In that instance, the reality of my pain slammed into me. Then our nudity became obvious. The only thing more vulnerable than a sobbing woman was a naked sobbing one.

I reached my bedroom in that reticent hour just before dawn. A time of purgatory, holding between darkness and day, when decisions can go either way. Where shades of gray overlap and I can slide into ambiguity or embrace the hint of pink, promising dawn, and a new beginning. Expecting more tears, I was stunned that none came. My body was empty. I had nothing left and yet I had never felt more aware, as if every nuance was explosive, every detail magnified and my clarity explicit. I could hear my heart hammering and feel the blood pushing through my veins. I was completely alone in the universe, surrounded by stillness, but aware of every emotion and movement.

Then my second epiphany of the night shredded my senses. I was awake. I was awake for the first time in years. I was alive and responding to my pain. I had never let myself experience the emotions of my devastation, never allowed the raw debilitating agony to ravage my senses, never surrendered my body to unleash the fury raging within my flesh, and most importantly, I never encouraged my soul to grieve.

Agnes was right. I had to let it out, purge myself, get rid of this toxicity that was killing me. I needed peace. The last thought I had before exhaustion claimed me, was Agnes repeating her plea to find balance, her plea to survive.

CHAPTER EIGHT

Present
James Island

SUNLIGHT SCRAPED MY EYELIDS as the new day toppled into me. Pressing my palms to my temples, I squeezed my head hoping to lessen the pounding. My cathartic release of anguish from my experience with Agnes last night should have made me feel better, but I felt hung over. Two Excedrin, a cold, caffeinated Diet Coke, and a lengthy hot shower coaxed the tension from my shoulders. I was wringing the water droplets from my hair when the phone began to ring.

"Jade? Jade?" Ian's fury assaulted my fragility. "Where were you last night? Avoiding me or maybe you went out?" he accused. "I need you to come home today." And just like that, all the progress I made last night fell away against Ian's demands. He would never understand and I didn't have the strength to explain. I barely had the ability to breathe.

How could I explain that sitting naked in the moonlight had changed my life? Agnes had forced me to look at myself, under my skin, and in my heart. I had permission to feel my pain for the first time. Many parts of me needed to come together for me to be whole but at least I was awake. My time in the clearing had given me a starting point. I now knew I wasn't dying, I was grieving.

The silence nudged me back to the phone in my hand. Did he hang up? "Ian? Are you there?" I reached to turn off the phone then heard his ragged voice.

"I'm here," he said. I inhaled and let out a passive sigh. What should I say to him? My thoughts were worlds away from what Ian could comprehend, but I was tired of hurting him and he deserved some explanation. All I had done for most of our marriage was to disappoint him.

"I don't know how to make you understand what I need right now. I just cannot come home."

"So you're leaving me?" His voice cracked like a broken limb.

"No," I answered. "I don't know. I don't think so, but I've got things to sort through before I can be in this marriage."

"Shouldn't we do that together or don't I have a say in my future?"

"Please, just give me some space. I'm not trying to hurt you. I don't know my future or yours. I just know I can't be what you need right now." His hesitation gave me a sliver of hope that he might get it or at least respect my request.

"You got it. I'll give you all the space you need." His angry response oozed with bitter sarcasm, a tidal wave crashing my hope into grains of sand. Then the line went dead. What did I expect? Imagine if he knew about my midnight swim. He knew I was depressed, but I had tried for years to hide how bad it really was for me. I just wanted to protect him. The miscarriages were my responsibility, my body, my failure. I wanted to blame myself for all of it. Yes, he was grieving too, through each loss, but he withdrew. He blamed me. He wanted me to pretend, pretend I wasn't devastated, and pretend there wasn't a gigantic void in the middle of our marriage. He wanted too much. I couldn't give him what he wanted. I had nothing left for either one of us.

My tears returned, fat droplets of guilt mocking me, a pity party running down my face, reminding me that misery was waiting to bitch slap me down every time I discovered a moment of clarity. Everything I had in this life was gone. As the physical remains of our love were washed from me in sterile coldness, our marriage became the collateral damage.

From tiny heart beats to a suicide attempt, could I have reacted differently, my world might be intact. According to my collective therapists, the "coulds" and the "shoulds" didn't matter. It was only what I do after that, that defines me, they said. Agnes told me in our midnight session I had to love myself before I could share love with another. When had I stopped loving myself? How did I get that back? The first step to loving me, she said, was to be willing to change. "If you choose life, you take energy from the universe," the wise woman explained. "With energy comes responsibility. You must do something purposeful with it. A life is a blessing from the spirit, your chance to learn, grow and improve the world."

It had been a couple of hours since Ian's call when the phone rang again. I steadied myself for another round, but it wasn't him. "What a glorious day. Penelope here, how are the preparations coming?"

"Oh, Penn, it's you." A spark of disappointment stung me.

"Yes, silly, it's Penelope. Are you ready?"

"Ready?" I didn't know what she was talking about, and I was still thinking about Ian. God, I didn't want to hurt him. I didn't want to sabotage myself either. There's no answer for us.

"Where is your head? For our reunion, that's why you're in town, right?" Jesus was she still talking about a reunion. I tried to kill myself a few days ago. They could have been planning my funeral instead. "Your mother said you came down from Charlotte last week. I assumed to open the house and finalize our plans," Penn continued without a breath, much less noticing that I was clearly not with her. "I need to get out of town like you wouldn't believe. My schedule is killing me, you know what I mean?" Oh yeah, want to know what almost killed me? I couldn't imagine a worse time to get sucked into a weekend of superficial reminiscing.

"This really isn't the best time for me, Penelope." That pompous name stuck in my throat. "It sounds like you're really busy too. Maybe, we should postpone." Please let this work. I could not tell her the truth and I could not have this reunion.

"Nonsense," Penelope said. "My suitcase is almost packed. I've written the instructions for the housekeeper, and cancelled my book club meeting. I'm yours for the week."

"The week?" I lost my balance on the bar stool.

"Sure, it's the third week of May, twenty years since we graduated. We made a promise, remember?" She didn't pause for a reply. "I've been looking forward to this for the last year. Only heaven knows the time I've had making sure my family can manage without me for seven days." I sat dumbfounded, searching for a solution. I tried a different angle.

"Have you talked to Em?" I asked. "She's probably somewhere in the South Pacific stalking sea turtles. I'm sure postponing would work for her."

"No, not at all," Penelope said. "She's in Charleston working on a marine science grant at the aquarium. She was stunned it had been twenty years."

"So am I." Just my luck Emerson was just a little down the coast in South Carolina and not in some foreign ocean. "It sounds like she has a lot on her plate. We've barely heard from her over the last decade."

"Em said it was a great time. She's waiting on some turtle guy to finish his research project before they start the grant proposal. She's got plenty of time."

"Splendid," I said. It was all I could manage to say.

"Don't worry about groceries, sugar. We'll shop when I get there. I've done the menu planning. See you Friday." Like a tornado, Penn had stormed in and was creating chaos in my world. Like it or not, I was being pulled toward the widening abyss. Friday was only four days away. It would take that long to open the house properly.

Looking around, I saw sheets on the furniture and spider webs on the ceiling. The musty closed-house odor had settled in the corners along with a science project collection of dead bugs. Accepting my fate, I opened the first window and checked the screen for rips. I dusted the ceiling fans and hung the rugs outside to air. After scratching my thigh jumping from a rat under the porch, I wrestled the beach chairs from the crawl space, and opened the valves for the outdoor shower. By that time the sun was flaming out on the horizon, and my headache had returned. After some cold shrimp salad on rye bread, I washed down two Tylenol and an Ambien with the last dregs of the fruity moscato and crashed.

How could it be Thursday? I made myself a peanut butter and blackberry jam sandwich for breakfast with a cup of hot tea. Tea was supposed to be relaxing. Time really flew on by while I was mopping, dusting, and changing beds. The linens were washed and line-dried, the sweet smell of lavender wafting from the beds. Mattresses aired. Regardless of Penn, or Penelope, whoever the hell she was, wanting me to wait to buy groceries, some provisions could not. Besides I knew that was her way of gaining the upper hand, putting her in charge of the reunion. Paper goods, toilet paper, hand soap, and other essentials were needed including a stop at the liquor store.

I hated crawling into my airless car, but the basket on my bike wouldn't hold the bourbon I needed. The interior was a furnace, but I found an old towel to put between my legs and the leather seat. Friday night dinner was first on the menu, sautéed shrimp or snapper, Charleston red rice, salad, crusty sourdough bread, and several bottles of Pinot Noir, maybe a case. Penelope could do that to a person. What was with the formal name? Penn was a riot, daring and flirtatious, loyal, beautiful, and crazy artistic. Penelope was a stuffy Protestant waspy name given by pretentious parents to create a pretentious person.

Pulling into the outdoor market for fish and shellfish, I saw Miss Maggie and her flower display. Perfect for a musty cottage, I would get a few bundles. The large woman had looked the same for three decades, shiny black as patent leather shoes with hands and breasts like hams. She grew the most radiant flowers and had a regular table on the weekends. She pulled her converted Radio Flyer red wagon with built-up, plywood side walls, from her house on the mainland across the bridge to town. She also grew fresh herbs, rosemary, dill, lavender, parsley, all kinds to cook with, and other aromatics, like mint and lemon balm, to use in medicinal preparations. Miss Maggie crossed over the canal about an hour after daybreak and stayed until her bouquets were gone. Always wearing the same beach grass hat which she adorned with bits of ribbon, wildflowers or feathers, depending on her mood, and what the wind blew her way, she would say.

Bringing a paper sack of beach grass, she worked magic with her knotty calloused fingers, making baskets. Afterwords, she soaks her hands in a little paste made of baking soda, stinging nettles, eucalyptus and a smidgen of snuff. It takes the ache out, she said. Could you even buy snuff anymore, I wondered. My great grandma Bessie kept the powdered tobacco product in tiny, tin cans with a blue label, in her apron pocket. It was widely used by older women when I was a kid, by those women of a generation whose grandfathers fought in the Civil War.

The cut flowers resembled a box of Crayola crayons, the giant box of sixty-four. I didn't know where to start. I liked mixing colors and varieties, but Penn, the artist, would make some comment and re-arrange them. A better idea was to have Miss Maggie make me three small bouquets for the bedrooms and two larger for the dining table and family room.

With my errands done, I was home packing my seafood in ice to refrigerate when a voice from behind startled me. "Save some ice for these mussels," Agnes said. "I heard you were having company." I whirled to face the woman, a large smile lighting her face.

"You're like a damn ninja the way you creep up on me."

"It's not my fault you can't hear me," she said. She swung a bucket of wet shellfish on my newly-cleaned counter, scattering grit across my fresh mopped floor. "How long are they staying?"

"Too long," I said, searching for a plastic bag. Glad I bought some herbs from Maggie. The dill and parsley would make a nice white wine and butter broth for the mussels.

"What is it they say about fish and houseguests? After three days, they both stink." Agnes laughed at her joke, helped herself to a bottle of water, and hopped on a bar stool. I would have offered her a drink, but she had no qualms with making herself at home. "I didn't think you'd mind if I helped myself," she flashed a quick dimple. "Seeing as how we've been naked together and all." How do you respond to that? The flush began at my shoulders and rose to my cheeks.

"You said that was necessary for our nature ritual."

"I'm teasing you, my dear. That's part of your problem. You need to lighten up."

"Since you brought it up, why did we need to be naked?"

"Sometimes, you have to get back to basics," she said. "What's more natural than bare skin? Besides clothing can block your energy, in more ways than one, if you get my meaning," she winked.

Still laughing at my red face, she grabbed her bucket and headed over the dune. I couldn't remember the last time I shared my energy with anyone, except that weird little woman with her weird rituals.

After purging my tears with Agnes in the moonlight escapade, I had stood with her in the clearing, feet rooted in the cool sand, palms toward the stars, my eyes closed. Pretend you're a tree, Agnes said, her voice smooth and slightly hypnotic. Regardless how absurd her directions seemed, I followed them. There was no turning back.

"Imagine the energy of the earth is flowing into your feet. It's warm and rich, like golden honey spreading through your core, melting your misery, flowing from your hands, taking your anguish with it. Release the negative and cradle the positive. Let the sensations thaw your senses. Awareness is everything." Initially pessimistic and appalled, I tried my best to concentrate on feeling the warmth. Nothing happened. My body shivered from the evening chill and the strange circumstances. I squeezed my eyes tighter and tensed my muscles. The honey feeling was absent.

"Jade, you have to let go." She continued coaching me, the lilt in her voice caressing my torment. "You can't hold it in anymore. Let it go, Jade. It's toxic. Feel the energy radiating. Awareness is everything." It started like a vague tingling in my ankles, and grew, swelling and circulating, like blood rushing through my veins. Then a tantalizing fever ignited, possessing me, liberating me as the fever raged. I felt it rush from my fingertips into the dark night. Shuddering and weak, my knees wilted, and I knelt on the ground still in spasm from the sear. Satiated and hungry, I felt devoured and starved at the same time.

"What was that?" I whispered, between breaths.

"That, my dear, was awareness."

CHAPTER NINE

Present
James Island

FRIDAY BEGAN WITH QUIET rain consoling the dawn. Mourning dove gray and barely-blue merged like watercolors, spilling tranquility across the walls of my bedroom. It felt good to lounge under the quilt while the peace of morning awakened me. The feeling was contentment, I realized. How long had it been since I wanted to greet a new day? Penn and Emerson were arriving by late afternoon. I didn't have a clue how this reunion would go, but I wasn't worried. I felt peaceful, for now. That might all change after the first night.

Sipping peppermint tea and eating the last apple walnut muffin, I watched the gentle swell of the water and thought of Ian. I wanted to hear his voice, not the angry one, the sweet, sexy one I used to know. Impulsively, I dialed our number. "Hi Ian," I said.

"Jade?" He sounded sleepy. I imagined his caramel colored curls tousled from the bed, and for a moment, felt their silkiness between my fingers.

"Yeah, it's me. I thought I would check on things."

"Oh, I was still asleep, got in late from a business trip and was sleeping in."

"I didn't mean to bother you. Go back to sleep. We can talk later." I was nervously pacing around the coffee table. What was I expecting?

"Yeah, okay," he hesitated, and I held the phone, not disconnecting. "Hey, are you all right?"

"I think I'm moving in that direction." I closed my eyes, imaging the stubble of beard along the line of his jaw, his soft full lips parted slightly as he breathed in his sleep. My mind lingered on his mouth remembering what it felt like on the creamy curves of my skin. It was a glorious diversion until reality bit. I was so confused, fantasizing about my husband, yet hiding from him at the same time. Can I go forward without him? Can I go back without dying?

By midday, the rain had cleared, and soft pastels swept the seascape. It wasn't the clear, crisp color that followed a thunderstorm. Still a bit cloudy, the sky was a tender touch of rose, delicate lavender, and smoky blue, colors that yielded to each other like in a Monet painting. By mid afternoon, the deck chairs had dried enough to lay out the cushions. I remembered from years past, the hours the three of us had spent looking out over the ocean. Sometimes, contemplative or hung over, but mostly chattering like squirrels about boys, school, and life. Then there were the angry words, and the ones we left unsaid. It was those unspoken secrets that finally fractured our friendship.

The summer after our first year, the three of us stayed in my family cottage. My parents had purchased a second house to use as rental investment property. It was bigger than the first one. Three stories on tall stilts, painted a subdued mango. It reminded me of a flamingo preening and posing for tourists, and stayed occupied from March to December. Our island was getting more crowded each year as vacationers discovered our quaint little seaside secret.

I loved the early spring and fall days when the weather required fuzzy sweaters and cozy interiors. The little house was still my favorite, despite the majesty of the other. The older house had a homey appeal and a stone fireplace, very rare for a beach house. It was squatty, steady and solid with only one floor and a wrap-around porch. We had replaced the windows over the decades and opened up the walls to increase the ocean view.

Our waitress salaries paid the utilities, and we had to clean the other house between guests, but for a chance to spend the summers on a barrier island, we would have done anything. How different those girls were from the women I expected to arrive within the hour. Instead of being nineteen with the whole world to spin, we had moved through our thirties to the permanent life-dictating decisions of our forties. We were on the edge of the halfway point of our lives. The age when we realize some goals will never be achieved, some dreams will never be fulfilled, and that who we are right now might be all we'll ever be.

CHAPTER TEN

Third summer of college
James Island

THE ORANGE GLOW OF his cigarette was visible before he was. I saw him sitting on the north pier rail the first Saturday night of summer break. He was about six feet, a little thin, but muscled through the shoulders and chest, a little fuzz of hair peeked above the vee in his shirt. His body was still wrestling between youth and manhood, but manhood was winning. The fringe of his cut-off shorts blew against the bronze muscles of his thighs and his feet were bare and propped on the middle cross piece of the fishing pier.

As I walked closer, the lights from the structure illuminated his face. Sun-streaked hair fell across his tanned cheekbones. He tipped his head down and slightly to the side. That's when I saw his eyes. They were the color of the Caribbean Sea, the blue-green that pools beside a white sand shore. I gasped as those eyes flicked down my body and back up to hold my gaze. It was an embarrassing little sound and he smiled. I smiled back and knew my life was going to change. He took a drag on his cigarette and nodded his head slightly to the space beside him. So slight a movement, I wasn't sure if I had imagined it. Did he want me to sit or go away? Penn nudged me forward and stepped away, announcing she saw some friends.

"Uh, hi," I said. "Nice night." Great, I sounded like a weather girl. He grinned, making me think I must have rolled my eyes. It was a bad habit and I mentally chastised myself.

"My name's Zeb," he said. He had a warm, sweet tone but he didn't look like a choir boy. He didn't look like an altar boy, college boy, or any boy at all. He was a man. Not so much in age, but in his attitude and the vibe surrounding him.

"I'm Jade."

"Nice to meet you, Jade." He took my hand and brushed it lightly with his warm lips. In the movies it was a silly dramatic gesture, but the charge sizzling up my arm didn't seem so funny. I climbed up beside him and tried to think of something to say. I thought and rejected so many questions and comments. Are you on vacation? How old are you? Are you in college? Do your eyes make all women feel like they've had too much champagne? I was so bad at this. I envied Penn, who could flirt madly and Emerson, who was so beautiful she didn't need to speak.

Zeb was quiet, staring off into the ocean, watching each crest fall and roll steadily to shore. He didn't seem to be bothered by the silence, so I stayed still trying to think of anything to say. Envisioning him cupping my face with his strong hands, I saw the colors of our eyes merge before he took my lips with that sweet mouth. "Are you okay?"

"What?" I realized he was talking.

"You were leaning over. I thought you were going to fall." I stammered some excuse about seeing something on the beach below, but I knew I had been leaning toward him pantomiming our kiss. If I wasn't rescued soon, I was only one more weird action or comment from hanging myself. This guy wasn't some frat boy. He was mysterious and aloof. I had sorority sisters who could toss their hair and smile, brush a hand lightly over a knee, stare into a guy's eyes and boldly lick their lips. I just wasn't good with all that flirting. He was so damn fine I needed to learn.

"Are you on the island for the summer?" I finally managed to speak.

"Maybe." He ran a hand through his hair and it fell tousled and wavy to his shoulders. "If I find anything interesting." I explained how Penn, Emerson and I were on our third summer break from college, living in my parents' rental house and waiting tables. There was a semi-regular crowd that returned each year, mostly working as wait staff and hanging out together after hours. We'll be seniors in the fall, I told him.

"Have you seen much of the island?" I asked. Not commenting on my summer break story or offering anything about him, Zeb pushed himself off the rail and turned to face me. With me sitting and him standing, we were eye level. He leaned in slightly and my pulse roared. His eyes sauntered from mine down to my mouth and back to my eyes without ever moving his body.

"I've seen enough," he said. "For now."

I sucked in my breath as he smiled at me, and parted my lips delicately. "Later," he called over his shoulder and strolled down the beach never looking back. Holy shit, I thought. What just happened? What the hell? He didn't kiss me. I was incredulous. Why didn't he kiss me? Couldn't he see I wanted him to… God, that was hot. I had been imagining a kiss for the last twenty minutes and it was all I could think about right now. Half a dozen college boys would have tried something, anything, with much less invitation than I gave Zeb. Who did he think he was? Wait until next time. I tightened my jaw and pushed off the rail. Like he was the only guy on the beach, I fumed.

"So who is he?" Penn said, approaching from behind.

"He's a cocky ass," I said, drawing my hand through my hair. "And smoking hot. He's hotter than a habanero." Penn smirked at my admission. We laughed all the way down the beach about my tongue-tied flirtations.

"I'm sure Em can give you lessons when she gets here," Penn said.

"There's no one better." Emerson was exotic and beautiful. Guys were naturally drawn to her, but it was more than her looks. She was book smart and street smart. She knew just what to say and when to let him talk. Easy to be around and although she didn't act or look cheap, Em knew how to please a man. You could just tell. She was spending one last weekend with John before break began. Her college boyfriend of three months was going north for the summer for an internship. Penn and I spent the next few days opening the house, stocking up on supplies and lounging in the sun. I had been back to the pier a few nights, but Zeb wasn't there. Maybe he moved on, I thought. Emerson came and we began our third and final summer in paradise.

By the next Saturday, we had served more Neptune platters than Neptune himself had eaten, and smiled sweetly, making small talk with patrons. Tired of waiting on people, we each grabbed a six-pack of beer and headed toward a friend's party. As we passed under the north pier, a slow whistle got our attention. Catching sight of Zeb on the rail, I stumbled and rammed my bare toes into Penn's heel. I screamed, bending to the sand to grab my foot.

Within seconds Zeb was at my side, taking my elbow in his hand to support me. Damn, I looked like a buffoon. My big toe throbbed but I was hopelessly lost in his eyes. My trance was broken when I heard Emerson and Penn's introductions. Zeb gave them a polite greeting but returned his attention to me. I noticed he didn't kiss their hands. Could I bear weight, they asked. My foot stung and I quickly lost my balance. Zeb caught me in his arms and carried me to the sea wall a few yards away. "Can you walk Jade?" Penn asked. "Jade?"

His hands, on me, tingling body parts, fluttering in my core, he could carry me anywhere. He had a quiet strength, not bulky brawn, but real muscle from hard work. I could feel it under my hands. "Are you going to let go of him?" Penn asked. Jesus, I was still holding his arms. I didn't normally lose control over a boy. But hot damn, he was a man.

"How far do you need to go?" Zeb asked. All the way, I almost said out loud. Em smirked over my shoulder, making a noise in her throat. They assessed where we were going and determined it was too far, while I stared at his mouth. Em and Penn discussed logistics until Zeb interrupted, making a suggestion. "You two go on to the party and I'll sit with Jade until she feels better."

Before they could dismiss his offer, I found my voice and my wits and agreed it was a great idea. With hesitant looks and rushed promises to just make a quick appearance, they hurried eagerly into the dark. Penn had her eye on a waiter and Em just needed to relax. Now that I was alone with him, I didn't know what to say again. All I wanted to do was look at him and feel his arms and silky hair. Touch his lips. Have them touch mine. His shirt matched his teal eyes and was frayed at the neckline. I wanted to nibble the skin around his mouth and taste the edge of his jaw. His shorts hung lightly on his narrow hips. How could a man look so good in worn-out clothes? They weren't the latest styles but they were clean, he certainly wore them well.

We had nothing in common but the attraction was flammable. I was going to combust if he didn't kiss me soon. I tried to breathe and nod occasionally while Zeb explained he worked in construction. I envisioned him leaping around the steel skeletons of the massive beach structures. We laughed about the strange requests the restaurant customers made to the wait staff. Then the small talk was over and I felt awkward and boring. Why didn't I ever know what to do?

Different scenarios played like movie trailers in my brain while Zeb sat quietly on the sea wall. The moonlight was playing on the water, swaying in an enchanting waltz of waves. What would it be like to dance with him, his hands on my hips, my hands in his hair, our eyes meeting, lips together. I could feel the softness of his mouth brush mine, barely a whisper. Then I realized it wasn't a fantasy anymore.

His fingers, calloused and strong from hard work, stroked the hair from my face, his eyes held mine as he leaned in again. This time it was all very real. I felt every sensation, his lips soft and seeking, skimming the edge of my mouth, drifting along my cheekbone and back to my mouth. By then, I was responding. His hair felt like it looked, thick and glorious in my fingers. My other hand fell to his chest, partly to keep from falling into him, but mostly to feel his granite muscles straining against his shirt. One of his hands kneaded the small of my back above my hip, the other caressed my neck.

Zeb pulled his lips from mine with a tiny tug and nip. It took me a second to recognize we had parted. I would dream of that kiss all night. Kissing wasn't new to me, but holy shit. I forgot where I was. Zeb leaned in again taking his time with my mouth. He tantalized and savored, tasting me like a decadent dessert. That was the difference between Zeb and other guys, I thought. He made me feel desirable. The others worried about pleasuring themselves. How far could they get? What could they touch? Zeb wasn't pushing or rushing. He was teasing and enjoying my reaction.

It was working, I thought. I wanted more. Waging a war between giving in to temptation or restraint, I pressed my curves against his hardness. For the first time, I wasn't thinking like the conservative girl I was. I wasn't thinking at all, just responding. Zeb made that easy. He was controlled, casual, sexy, and different from any guy I had ever touched. Even the way he embraced the stillness was unusual, not trying to fill every moment with conversation nor groping and grabbing. Others fumbled and felt, hoping to wear down my resolve or touch something, even if accidental. Zeb's actions were purposeful.

"How are your toes?" he asked. I couldn't even feel my feet.

"Great."

"Great?" he raised one eyebrow. I laughed and leaned into him.

"Okay, the truth is you made me forget all about my toes."

"Let's walk." We strolled quietly. Zeb absently twinned his fingers with mine. Before too far, we reached the beach party.

The sparks from the bonfire crackled and exploded into the wind. Somewhere a radio played and silhouettes moved and merged in the shadows.

"Want to stay?" I asked when we stopped. He looked at me, composed and pleased. No need for awkward conversation. He held my hands loosely, not clinging or sweaty. I wondered how he was so calm. I felt like I'd run a triathlon, cuddling, caressing, and kissing. Sign me up again. My pulse, rapid, my breath scarce, my body needed more of him.

"I need to go," he said. He pulled me to him, still holding one hand. He traced a fingertip along my chin, gentle and deliberate. No movement was wasted, not the way he stroked my face, held my gaze, or teased my lips with his. It all made me want more. Wrapping both arms around his neck, I molded myself to his body, fisting my hands in his hair. I pulled his head to mine, needing him with an appetite that ached within me. I wanted it all, to taste him, explore him. Intensity flamed through me. I was in deep and didn't care. This was too fantastic to mess up by engaging my brain.

When we finally separated, Zeb gave my hand a squeeze, flashed a sweet-dimpled smile and headed toward a path in the dunes. I watched him walk away, nice shoulders, tight hips, a primal need firing through every cell of my body.

For me, passion had been elusive, scarce as a liberal in church. With every guy, I expected the earth to stand still, sun beams from heaven to come forth and illuminate the chosen one. Tonight it happened. The planets aligned, the moon found the right house, and I ignored the little voice instead embracing the whole evening with reckless abandon. I was always looking for the fantasy, a starring role in a romance novel, and a leading man to match. It was the plot I never thought through, always expecting too much, and never being satisfied. Right now I didn't care if this was impulsive, it felt fabulous. Passion was addictive and I wanted more.

CHAPTER ELEVEN

Present
James Island

PENELOPE ARRIVED FIRST, ZIPPING in and out, from her Mercedes to the kitchen, unloading salad greens, a crate of fresh vegetables, smoked turkey breast, fresh bread and wine bottles, so many wine bottles. She paused and pecked me on the cheek, smoothed her periwinkle linen top and matching capris then straightened the loose-weave sweater around her shoulders. Who wears that to the beach? She looked like a catalog model for senior fashions

"You're looking well, Jade," Penn said. She was being polite. I dragged myself out of the Atlantic just days ago. I had seen the bags under my eyes and felt my protruding cheekbones.

"Looking great yourself," I countered. The small talk began. Penn talked about her busy week, the bucket load of commitments, her husband's dental practice and then she brought out the photographs, one perfect boy and then another perfect miniature of the first, in perfectly-pressed, private school uniforms. Both were spending the summer at an honors arts and science camp. That they were gifted didn't surprise me. Penn was brilliant. The disconcerting part was how perfectly predictable and dull Penn's world seemed.

It was shocking. Sure, Penn could be proper when she needed to, but she was happiest when she was immersed in the art studio. She was an artist, a double major in fine arts and art history. Her fingers always stained with oil paints, her sun streaked auburn hair escaping from a loose pony tail band, her studio clothes, Bohemian bum artist, and all of it was wrapped up with her sly grin that leaned a little to the left. This woman barely resembled the younger version. She kind of resembled the very first version of Penelope I met at the beginning of college, but that was so long ago. Now her hair was in a perfect bun, almost severe, with not a single strand loose, her casual attire, designer, and a slight polite smile stretched over properly-drawn lips. There was no light behind that smile. She was a mannequin and if she didn't come to life soon, it would be an impossible week. She had reverted back to that pampered princess she left in the dust post high school. All the while she was chatting about her book club, the museum benefit, her house, and other nauseating details of her conventional existence.

I interjected the appropriate response here and there. Penn was so consumed she never noticed how little I contributed. The crunch of shells in the driveway was the sweetest sound I'd heard in months. Emerson. We greeted her at the doorway, Penn and her plastic persona and me, skittish and wary. She was still beautiful. Chic honey-blond hair, stylishly-faded jeans, and a coral scoop-necked tee that complimented her tanned toned body. Still proportioned like a pin-up girl, big breasts, small waist, sparkling blue eyes, and manicured nails that matched her toes in coral. I could not spend the next week listening to Penn and looking at Emerson. I was going to need more wine and plenty of Xanax.

I took a few minutes to style my hair and put on a little make-up while they unpacked. Could they see my depression? Did the dark circles under my eyes betray my desperation? Could they smell my fear, my terror of surrender mingling with the empty despair of living? My biggest worry was that they would discover my secret from last week. I needed my girlfriends for support and counsel. We had solved the problems of life throughout college, all of our coming of age issues. Nothing was off limits then. There were no secrets between us, not until that last summer when everything imploded.

"Shall we start dinner?" Penelope crossed the floor from her bedroom to the kitchen and filled her wine glass. "Not a bad year," she said. When did vineyards and harvests matter to Penn? In college, we drank green stuff made in trash cans by chemistry majors at Venable Hall. A person could drink it or use it to refinish furniture.

"I've made a chilled green salad, summer veges are marinating, and I'm waiting for word from you to start the seafood. I have fresh fish and mussels in white wine broth. Can you slice some bread?"

"Impressive," Penelope said. "When did you learn to cook? The only thing I remember you making was instant mac and cheese and butterscotch pudding."

"It's been twenty years, Penn. Don't you think I've learned to cook in the last few decades?"

"Oh please call me Penelope. I don't use that ridiculous nickname anymore. Brian says it's not very refined."

"What's not refined?" Emerson asked, emerging from the bedroom. "Where's the wine?" Not waiting for either answer she located the wine and poured a very full glass. "I've got six bottles in the car. Should I bring them in?"

"I was asking Jade to refrain from using that nickname. I go by Penelope." Em snorted and glanced at me.

"Even your parents call you Penn," she said.

"Well, I can't do anything about them, but I expect you to respect my wishes."

"Are they your wishes or Brian's?" Em asked, the twinkle in her eye taunting Penelope.

"It's the same thing," she said. "Brian and I are a team. He's the front man and I play the supporting role. We reflect on each other and Penn just does not behave like Penelope does." She tucked an escaped curl behind her ear and refilled her wine glass. "Brian is very particular about image and how it reflects on his work."

"His work, my god, he's an orthodontist, not a Nobel Prize winner," Emerson joked. With that sarcastic spike hitting home, Penelope began to rearrange the flowers.

"Where did you get the beautiful blooms?" she asked. "I doubt you grew them." I overlooked her jab. She looked as prickly as she sounded. Her lips tucked in, working intently on the arrangement. I explained about Miss Maggie and the fish market.

"You mean that large, black woman from decades ago?" Emerson moved back to the wine service. "I can't believe she's still alive. She was ancient then. Oh, and ya'll can call me Em." Taking our plates outside, we sat down at the table and I adjusted the umbrella. After finishing the excellent meal I prepared, we settled in as the evening dwindled away.

From the deck of the beach house we could see the sun setting over the canal side of the island. I loved looking at the sun as it slipped through the lower horizon. It energized me, causing warmth to radiate through my chest, like I was inhaling inspiration. Smears of orange, purple, red, and pink melted together over the royal blue waters of the salt marsh, like a toddler finger painted the sky. Herons and kingfishers caught their last fish of the day before bedding down for the night. Tucking their heads under downy wings, they slept scattered in shallow depressions through the marsh grass. The electric orb hung suspended just over the horizon while the colors deepened and ran toward the water. Slow, slow, then quick and it was gone. Awash in a gray haze, the coastal basin settled into darkening silhouettes.

"I forgot how beautiful the sunset was here," Penn said. "All the colors." She looked wistfully out over the view. She seemed sad, I thought. And distant.

The softening twilight seemed romantic and tranquil but darkness wasn't always peaceful in the tidal flats. Nightlife thrived under the veil of darkness. The day sounds of beachgoers, sea gull cries and marine traffic gave way to deeper, darker, primitive sounds. The crickets rub their legs together in a lusty call for companionship while the deep bass of the tree frogs call for mates. Raccoons prowl for oysters and mussels at low tide along with long-legged egrets. The night makes beings want to be satiated and warm and not alone. Humans were no different, I thought.

As shadowed arms wrapped around the cottage, I felt alone, stuck on an island with two strangers. We had changed. I had learned to cook. Penelope knew about wine and was in a team with Brian. Emerson looked even better older and had a very successful career. We were different, not the girls we once were. We had agendas and secrets. I needed familiar, not strangers here with me. Ian never wanted to come with me, always too busy at work, no time for vacations, he said. No time for me either. Why would he want to spend time with me, I was a miserable shell of myself. Well, he has time now, all he wants. I kicked the rail in frustration.

"What's with you?" Em asked. She and Penelope, startled, sat up abruptly in their lounge chairs.

"My foot slipped. I didn't mean to scare you. I guess I dozed off after our big dinner and barrel of wine."

"Dinner was really good," Penelope said. "I guess I never knew you could cook."

"There are many things you don't know about me," I said. Penelope let the remark go unchallenged and shifted her attention to Em.

"So what are you working on?" she asked.

"Not much." Em was noncommittal.

"Oh, tell us about that fascinating life you have," Penelope begged.

"Just doing some grant applications between projects. I finished the sea turtle rehab program down in the Caribbean and I'm working on some funding options with a colleague at the Charleston aquarium. He's a marine biologist I met in Mexico a couple of years ago."

"A romantic prospect?" I comically raised an eyebrow at her.

"No," she laughed. "He's just a guy, a very handsome guy with a well-built resume and a wife."

"Well, I'm sure if you wanted him you could have him," Penelope said. "We've seen it before dear, other women have never been an obstacle."

"I've never broken up a marriage either," Emerson said. I lit the outdoor torches and we emptied another bottle of wine, making small talk and avoiding real topics. We were jungle cats circling our territory, waiting for the first one to be exposed and vulnerable. It was disgraceful that three women once closer than sisters had come to this. I wanted it to be like college, like long ago when we could talk about anything and still feel safe. Now guarded, I couldn't let them know how bad my life had become. I was a train wreck. A failure as a wife and a mother. I couldn't carry a pregnancy much less a relationship. I was a waste of a woman and they would be disgusted by me.

The strangeness of our unfamiliarity and the abundance of wine had put me in a melancholy mood which just exacerbated my depression. This was a bad idea. I needed to crawl under my comforter and hide or sleep, whichever took me away from this hell. We agreed to an early bedtime, promising we would feel better after a night of beach rest, that peaceful place between tides and dreams, salt air and simplicity. I tucked myself under my eyelet-trimmed sheets and suspected tomorrow would be no better. None of us knew what to say anymore. Reminisce about college days or keep making genteel small-talk, either way, no one was telling their real story, I thought. It might have been decades since we spent quality time together, but I was smart enough to know we were all pretending.

Something that smelled a little like bacon woke me in the early morning hour just after dawn. "Wake up sleepyheads," Penelope called from the kitchen. I heard totally impolite words coming from Em's room, followed by a thud against her door, maybe a shoe. Pulling a sweatshirt over my thigh-length t-shirt, I side stepped a perky Penelope and groped for a cold Diet Coke.

"Those things are not good for you." She geared up for a lecture, but the look on my face must have changed her mind.

"Neither is waking me up at this hour on vacation." Ten minutes later Emerson entered the kitchen, mumbling about coffee as Penelope extolled the virtues of breakfast.

"The damn queen of England better be here since you woke me before daybreak." Em's demeanor seemed similar to mine, but it didn't stop Penelope.

"I've prepared a high fiber, low fat meal for us." Penn talked while Emerson nosed around the kitchen.

"I smell bacon," she said, searching for a salty bite.

"Oh, bacon is so bad for you. I've baked us some turkey bacon. Can't tell the difference." She placed three plates at the table. "It tastes just like pork bacon. I've paired it with a probiotic yogurt and granola and half a grapefruit." Emerson and I groaned in tandem. "Then we can have a brisk walk on the beach," Penelope continued, paying no attention to the eye-rolling and sarcastic looks we exchanged. It's going to be a long, damn week, I thought for the tenth time.

I remembered when Penn's breakfast consisted of one of those dreadful Diet Cokes and a Butterfinger candy bar. Or on a football game Saturday, we would wake at noon after a Friday night frat party, grab day-old pizza, spike a drink with bourbon, and head over to the stadium. This woman in her matching jogging clothes with the old lady breakfast could not be the same person I knew. Somehow this week I was going to find out what happened to my best friend. I really missed her and I needed her more than ever. I was so lonely. I felt a physical pain where Ian used to be and had realized I had no female friends beyond a casual lunch date.

All my energy the last decade had been focused on starting and losing a family. I used to meet my fellow teachers once a month for dinner and drinks, but after the depression invaded, I made excuses and rarely went out with anyone. Then six months ago, during the Christmas break, I took a leave of absence. One more holiday with no children, no Santa to prepare for, no need to bake gingerbread, no peace on earth, no joy in my world. I couldn't go back to work after the holiday. Teaching and loving other people's children was breaking my heart. I didn't have the strength to let my co-workers see my decline, give them a front row view to the guilt and inadequacy that strangled the last of my dreams.

How much of this could I show to these women? They were as much strangers to me as the people at work. What would I tell them? What remnants of my life were up for analysis? Should I flay open my chest, exposing the pathetic wounds of failure that scarred me? Would they rub salt? I didn't know these women anymore and I didn't think I could trust them with my devastation. Penelope was the overbearing, condescending mom us teachers despised, the ones at school monitoring my job performance and running the parent teacher association like a corporation with acquisitions and mergers.

Those who don't have enough personality and buried their identity in their children, they compared square footage, designer labels, and destination vacations hoping to outdo each other. They made me sick. Maybe, I was just jealous. Somewhere under that polished Stepford wife I might still find Penn, the nonjudgmental free spirit, who held my head when I was sick, cried with me as my young heart broke, and loaned me her best cocktail dress.

Then there was Emerson, the beautiful one. Boy, she was living the dream, pursuing a thrilling career, traveling to exotic places, no one to be responsible for or for whom to be accountable. The same body she had as a coed, and her face, made more gorgeous by her confidence and self-reliance. Em was a cool woman, a marine biologist saving turtles. I also knew she was beautiful on the inside. She had a radiant personality, enticing wit, and loyalty that surpassed a golden retriever.

"Jade? Jade, honey? Where are you?" Penelope knocked on my door. "How about that walk?" After thirty minutes of dressing and hygiene, we finally made it to the beach. I was distracted. Em was examining shells and Penelope seemed like a ventriloquist on speed making enough nervous small talk for all of us. She outlined lunch and planned our afternoon.

"So where are you, Jade? Not at home with me. Call me. I've had enough of this. Jade?" Ian's husky voice filled the small living room. Penelope's manicured finger froze above the play button of the answering machine. She and Emerson turned to me as I emerged from the bedroom. I stopped midway, a flush the color of ripe watermelon rose from my neck past my hairline.

"Oh, Jade, honey, I didn't mean to intrude," Penelope said. "I gave my kids this number for emergencies." They heard, I thought. Now what? Now they knew. How to spin this? My god, how hurt Ian sounded. And angry. Hearing that little boy tone, I wanted to cradle his head on my shoulder. How dare he call here and berate me. I replayed his words in my head. What could they glean from his message? Maybe, it wasn't so bad. I could say we had a little spat about him working too much or something. I knew they could hear my heart beating and the denial screaming in my head.

"Don't mind him." I concentrated on keeping my voice from faltering. "We had a little misunderstanding. I've been on his case about working too much and when he finally took a few days off, I was leaving for the beach. I told him about our reunion months ago." I crossed to the kitchen and poured myself a glass of wine. Could they see my hands shaking? "You know how men are." I kept talking because I was afraid to stop. "He's just pouting because I didn't change my plans. The whole world revolves around a penis." I laughed, a little too shrill. "It's like the axis of absentmindedness." I wasn't even making sense anymore. I took a large gulp of wine and refilled my glass. "Anyone want some?" I turned to them, forcing a light smile.

"You do know it's not even lunchtime," Penelope said, shifting her eyes to Emerson.

"What the hell? Pour me some," Em said. "Aren't we on vacation? We can call it a juiceless mimosa," she continued. "Besides don't your country club friends start drinking after a morning tennis match, Penn?" Em's smug smile showed more amusement than concern. "Penn will have some too."

"Sure, sure." Penelope skittered around the counter. "But, please call me by my given name. I find it difficult to answer to Penn."

By mid afternoon, empty wine bottles littered the counter. We had lunched on brie and water crackers, bread and butter pickles, crab dip, and double fudge ice cream, basically anything that looked good in our drunken state. The conversation had moved beyond reminiscing and our protective layers were thinning. As we chipped away at each other, our irritability bled to the surface. I was restless and shifting in the chair, wearing my vulnerability like outgrown shoes, pinched and worn.

"So, Em, you haven't mentioned your latest love interest," Penelope said. "You've always had a stringer full of them, like fish. You keep some, you throw some back."

"I haven't had much time for a relationship." She twirled the stem of her wine glass. "I'm usually moving around too much."

"Whatever happened with Andy?" I asked. "I thought you were engaged."

"We were engaged, but there was always an ocean between us. Eventually, one of us needed to give, and he was too stubborn."

"It's not thumb wrestling, Emerson." Penelope uncrossed her feet and straightened her back. "You make sacrifices when you're in love. You have to give a little. Be a team player."

"Why should I give in? My work is just as urgent as his. It's crucial to the survival of a species."

"Of course your work matters, Em, but you can't expect a man to follow a woman around," Penelope said.

"Are you kidding me?" I interjected. I had stayed out of their volley until now, but that was just too much.

"You're one to talk." Penelope turned to me. "You followed Ian to Charlotte and never looked back. When did you ever want to live in North Carolina? You used to talk about teaching all over the world before you settled down."

"That is so different. I had just graduated. Ian was already there. I wanted to see if we had the real thing. I didn't care where we lived. I wanted to be with him, and when I was offered a teaching job in Charlotte, it worked." I put down my glass. "How can you say Em should be the one to give?"

"You two are acting like that's a crime," Penelope said. "It's the natural order."

As Em and I sat open-mouthed, Penelope, definitely not Penn, continued her sermon. "I'm sure Emerson could find sea turtles in the same ocean as Andy. Men need to know their women are supportive."

"Their women! When did you become a cave woman?" I was on the edge of the ottoman, my eyes fiery and combative. Penelope knew that look, and should have avoided the bait. I'm sure it was apparent since Ian's message that I was just waiting for a spark to ignite. I was ready to blow.

"Let's change the subject," Emerson interrupted, always the peacemaker, level-headed and balanced.

"I'm not a cave woman, nor am I ignorant." Penelope stood, as if to emphasize her authority. "I am happily committed to fulfilling the needs of my family. Nurturing a man and children doesn't make me prehistoric. It makes me a woman, a real woman, who makes babies and satisfies her husband. You're just jealous." Penelope looked at me, horrified for a split second, but she couldn't control her mouth, and the words spewed like bile from her black core.

I breathed in the filth of her betrayal. How could my friend, my Penn, say these things to me? It was devastating, demoralizing, tormenting. My eyes stung and my body pulsed with my pain. A breakdown was coming. It was just under my very thin skin, and the eruption was going to be volatile. Penelope walked brusquely around the kitchen cleaning up dishes and wine bottles. I wondered how she could be so mean. She was brutal. I realized this wasn't my Penn. She would have never hurt me like this. Turning to face her, I spoke.

"The Penn I knew was never cruel. You've sold out. You're nothing like her, just a sad imitation. A goddamned fake!" Penelope slammed her glass to the counter, shattering the base and stem on the ceramic tiles.

"What do you mean I'm a fake? I'll have you know I've always been authentic."

"You were once, but you ain't now," I said. Emerson rose from her chair and stepped toward me. We were too far gone now for her intervention. This was going to end very ugly.

"The hell I'm not," Penn said. "And you're drunk."

"Maybe I'm drunk, but nothing out of your mouth this weekend has been real." My slurred words of anger scattered over her like the glass shards in the kitchen.

"I have always known who I was and what I wanted," she said. "I'm a creative, giving person. I'm a mother and a wife. I take care of my home. I volunteer at the museum and I chair fundraisers for the hospital." She stabbed every "I" statement through my heart. "How can you call me a fake? I'm living my life."

"No, you're living the life created for you, but not by you." Emerson spoke softly, never looking away from the window.

"Yeah, Em's right. That's what I'm trying to say. You don't do anything for you. It's all about what everybody else wants and needs." I stumbled forward. "What happened to Penn? This Penelope's a damn robot, always smiling and flitting around like a neurotic dragonfly, landing here, there, making sure everything is perfect. You never slow down to really see anything. Our Penn used to see everything, savor the moments, treasure creativity." I reached for the door frame to steady myself. "When did you lose yourself? You threw yourself down a rabbit hole years ago." My scowl screamed disgust and pity. "Why did you give up?" Slowing down to focus, I could see her mortified expression.

"Give up!" Penn screeched. "You're a good one to talk. At least I am someone. I know myself. But you, you've never known who you are, always caught up in some idealistic dream world waiting on your fantasies to come true, never living in the moment. The present was never good enough for you, always waiting for the future. How's that working for you by the way? Where's your husband? No children, I see, and I hope you've got some other friends because you sure don't call us." Her posture was defensive, hands out in front of her, eyes penetrating.

I moved into her face, so close she should be able to see the mascara clumps on my eyelashes. Speaking low and threatening, I said, "You don't know anything about me anymore. You can't begin to know my hell and what I've lost. You'll never know how dark my world is. As for keeping up with you, why should I? You're a plastic bitch!" With that, I slung open the screen door and walked to the deck railing. I could hear Penelope opening a new bottle of wine.

"We should have these little reunions more often," Em said. "This is better than an episode of *Desperate Housewives*. Oh wait, Penn, that's what you are."

"Emerson, you've always been a sarcastic bitch."

I wanted to run. I wanted to scream. I wanted to slap Penelope after our fierce argument. I settled for crying. Crawling into the chair with the faded cushion, I wrapped my arms around my knees. Plump, salty, tears melted from my eyes, blurring the waves that broke before me. I was numb. Those women inside were strangers. What did they know about my pain? My life? I couldn't give my husband a child. Lately, I couldn't give him a wife, and I hated myself for all the things I couldn't do. I couldn't even kill myself. This reunion had been a terrible mistake.

It was quiet inside. No one spoke. All we heard was the wind teasing the screen door as the tide retreated to the sea.

CHAPTER TWELVE

Third summer of college
James Island

I STOOD AT THE deck rail of the beach cottage taking a Marlboro Light and a Myrtle Beach souvenir lighter from my jeans pocket. My hand trembled with anger and I could barely match the flame to the cigarette between my lips. Smoking was a nasty habit and I didn't care for it, but it made me feel independent and reckless. Penn and I had had another argument about Zeb. Once again she warned me Zeb was a bad influence and that I was spending too much time with him.

I took a drag from the cigarette and turned my head away from the wind to exhale. Zeb smoked. I didn't care if he did and I didn't care if Penn was right. She was. I had done what was expected of me my whole life, what everyone wanted me to do and thought was best. I was so tired of others dictating my life. This summer was different. Zeb was different. I wanted to give in to temptation, taste real life and savor the thrill. Zeb was an exotic sensation, nothing like the college boys at Carolina. He was a man. Muscled and hard from his construction job, I loved tracing the sinews down his forearm to the wide palm and long fingers then feeling those same hands as he pulled me to him urgently kneading the flesh of my hips. I was lost in my passionate daydream when the screen door slammed behind me.

"I don't care if you want to hear this or not, but I'm going to say it anyway." Penn walked to the rail and pulled my arm to face her. "You're in over your head. This is not a clumsy frat boy you're leading on. This is a man, a stranger and he is going to annihilate your heart."

"You don't know him at all," I said. "You're not giving me much credit either. Did it ever occur to you that I know what I'm doing? I don't have to consult you every time I make a move."

"I don't think you have a clue as to what you're doing. You meet him at midnight in the dunes for a quick roll in the sand. He's taking what he wants from you, and you're just giving it away."

Crushing out my cigarette, I took a breath. "When did you become so smug and superior? You don't exactly have a pristine reputation. You think because you only do college boys you're better than me?" I kicked the Adirondack chair to face the water and sat down. "Besides there's been a sexual revolution, it's okay for me to take what I want."

"No, I'm not better than you, but I am realistic. What are you doing with this guy? Are you going to dress him up in a tux and a tool belt for the sorority formal?"

"Why do I need a plan? I always have a plan and goals. Can't I just have fun? Zeb is freaking fun. He doesn't analyze me or make demands, and he doesn't care what anyone thinks." Penn perched on the rail turning to look at the ocean.

"You didn't answer my question, Jade. Are you going to take him home to meet mom and dad? I bet they care what people think and you care what they think."

DRAWING DOWN THE MOON

"Why do I have to take him anywhere? We're just fooling around, no plans, no complications." Finally, Penn turned to look at me.

"What about Ian?"

"Ian? Why bring him into this? We've only been out three times. I haven't even kissed him. He graduated and moved to Charlotte in case you've forgotten." I pulled the band from my pony tail and let the wind toss it around my shoulders. "You're just making up reasons now."

"I know what your face looked like when you came home from those three dates," Penn said, just as Emerson stepped onto the deck.

"What's wrong with you two? People on the beach are starting to stare. This isn't improv theater. It's embarrassing." She moved a seat near me. "Get a grip and shut up."

Penn took a seat while Emerson put three shot glasses and a fifth of bourbon on the side table between us. "You're bringing out the hard stuff," Penn said.

"We're going to talk this out," she said. "The bourbon just speeds up the process. Okay, Jade, pour." After a few shots for each of us, the rough edges were smooth and the anger was subsiding. The hurt feelings slipped away and we began to talk. Sometimes, it takes an inebriated conversation to get to the heart of the matter.

"I know y'all don't like Zeb and generally he's not my type, but this summer isn't about you. It's not about Ian and whether we are a possibility. It's not even about Zeb. It's about me. I need something different right now. I've felt restless lately." I threw back another shot and took Penn's hands in mine. "Can you just let me do this? I know you want to protect me, but I need to make these decisions and learn to trust my instincts. I'm suffocating. Being with Zeb makes me feel liberated." Sufficiently drunk, we reclined in our chairs and watched the sun set over the canal. Nothing was perfect, but for now it was good enough.

CHAPTER THIRTEEN

Present
James Island

Penelope's Point Of View

MY SUITCASES WERE PACKED last night after my fight with Jade. This was not going to work, and I would not tolerate being treated like that. I planned to grab a quick yogurt for breakfast and say goodbye to Emerson before heading back to Asheville. We didn't last two days together. This was breaking my heart.

I looked through the screen at Jade curled into herself on the porch. She was obviously in pain. Her attitude was more than anger. There was something physically happening too. Now that I really looked at her, there were dark circles under her eyes that a good make-up concealer had been hiding. She was skinny and her hair was thin with broken ends. She looked tortured. All this misery couldn't be the result of our argument, I thought. Jade and I had legendary arguments, sometimes just to push each other's buttons. No, there was much more to this, I concluded.

Somewhere deep inside the uptight Penelope, a tiny voice named Penn whispered to me, begging me to listen. Jade always lashed out when she was afraid. What was she so frightened of? It must be terrifying. I regretted letting our argument get so nasty. What was it that set her off so bad?

I know I've changed. Life and family does that to a person. It's been twenty years. I made choices. Decisions that weren't easy to make regarding what I wanted and what others needed. I made sacrifices. To me, choosing my children over my career was right for me even though I had never anticipated giving up my dreams. There would be time for me when my kids were older. I still paint-ed occasionally in the corner of the garage. There was a skylight in the utility room and a window. Both focused natural light on my easel. I painted between morning carpool and soccer practice a few times a month. No one saw them. I wrapped the canvases in paper and stored them in the attic. Every time I painted, I craved it more. It awakened a feeling in me, a tingling in my belly. For a few days, I would notice the details of my day. The way rain splat-tered and raced across the window panes, how the daybreak colors swirled and faded into the morning, busy people rushing to work and school, phones ringing, chores calling, but it all slowed down like a slow-motion recording when I painted. I was so aware I could see the flowers open to bloom and the bees suspended above them. I could appreciate the architectural structure of a bird's nest and hear the peeps of the babes calling mom.

There was some validity to what Jade accused. I had lost part of me, most of me. That's what happened when a woman has a family. I lost who I was and became what was needed. Most women with a family live lives of requirement. If those two had children, they would understand. I couldn't do what I wanted all the time, hardly ever. Emerson sailed across the seas and explored beaches on every continent. Jade taught school. She shaped young minds. They both had careers, respectability, and identities. I had a husband and children, and I would not apologize or be made to defend my choices.

Why didn't Jade have children? That was so important to her. Her plans always included the right husband, a houseful of kids, tennis lessons and ballet classes, finger painting and Halloween costumes. Replaying our fight in my head, I heard myself insinuating none of her plans came true. Husband issues, no children, that's when it had gotten ugly. She charged me, and I thought she might hit me. She scared me. The fire in her eyes was volatile and her body was shaking with rage. How could I have said those things?

Jade said some really mean things too, but history told me she was panicked about something. I hit a nerve with the family remarks. I put my suitcases back in the bedroom and changed my clothes into a t-shirt and shorts. It felt really good to leave it un-tucked and have my feet bare. I woke up Emerson and sent her out to the deck. I grabbed cinnamon rolls, a pitcher of orange juice, a bottle of champagne, and three wine glasses.

A drink would help us talk this out, but I hadn't lost all sense of decorum. I had not drunk bourbon at ten in the morning since college, and I wasn't going back now. I sat the tray on the table and walked toward Jade. I moved a chair alongside the deck rail and faced the ocean. Emerson was on the other side of her. "Jade, I didn't mean to start anything like this," I said. "But you did provoke me," I added, in a subdued whisper. Em glared at me over Jade's head. I knew that attitude wasn't going to help. "What's wrong honey? We want to help."

Her reaction was not at all what I expected. Jade leaned forward and laid her head on my knees. "Please help me," she said. "I've lost everything and I'm too tired to go on."

PART II

CHAPTER FOURTEEN

1944
James Island

Agnes

IN THE BIBLICAL SENSE, I had never known a man. My first time was not at all what I imagined. Then again, I had very little frame of reference. Between what I witnessed animals doing in nature and what my mother told me, I didn't expect to enjoy much about the process. Women endure this, my mother said. Eve's shortcomings caused God to curse women forever, lying with the husband to bear children is a marital responsibility, just another chore on the list between washing clothes and cooking breakfast, she told me.

Watching female deer chased down and assaulted was not any more encouraging nor was overhearing my sister screech like a stray cat while her husband panted on top of her. No, I wasn't in any hurry to be with a man, until now.

Jackson Ross landed on my island and changed my life. He was a young army pilot participating in Operation Bumblebee, a secret operation that prompted the United States government to commandeer the south end of James Island. The southernmost eleven miles were restricted from the public. Square concrete towers had been erected at intervals along the coastline.

He wasn't my idea of a soldier. He was gentle and inquisitive, talkative and awkward, with a sense of humor that was odd and self-deprecating. He told me he loved to fly, soaring among the clouds, teasing the edges of heaven he lost himself in the blue beyond. It was the military part that didn't suit him. Not aggressive nor combative, Jackson wasn't instinctively strategic or militant. But he was honorable and patriotic, and took his obligation seriously. I was fascinated by him.

When he was off-duty, we were rarely apart. We talked and explored and absorbed the energy our relationship created. He had never pressured me to make it more sexual. We kissed and caressed tentatively in the beginning, then ardently, over the last few days our touches had become willful and delicious. We were hungry for each other, and my lack of sexual experience was no obstacle. I had never done what was expected, instead preferring to follow my instincts, letting the energy of the world guide my actions. What I desired now was Jackson.

I knew this night felt different as he and I puttered my roundabout around the north end of the island and slipped gently through the surf to moor on a secluded stretch of sand. This was our special place and we visited often. By the time we finished the crab salad and tomato sandwiches I packed, the tide was easing into the Atlantic and the moon was just above us cavorting with the waves. The air stirred by the breeze was sultry and heavy. Lying back on the quilt, I felt the cool softness of cotton on my skin. My body felt warm and tingly like I was floating in carbonated water, effervescent bubbles rippled over me and Jack had barely touched me. The stars were brighter, the tree frogs more symphonic, the honeysuckle sweeter and Jack's lips so tender I melted into him. By the time his mouth trailed down my neck, reaching the hollow above my shoulder blade, I knew I would be different by morning.

"Are you sure about this, Agnes?" Jackson's green eyes matched the green of his uniform shirt. I never verbalized an answer just nodded to him with an intake of breath as he kissed me.

He took his time, his long fingers, calloused, but not rough, touched like a whisper over my skin. Then he teased me, the tip of his tongue tickling the corner of my mouth, moving along the bone of my jaw until he nipped the plump lobe of my ear. He sucked it slightly in his mouth and a quiver shuddered in my center. I giggled with delight.

Loosening the ribbon holding my hair, he smiled as the blond curls spread in an unruly mass over my shoulders. They blew across my face alive on the ocean wind and covered my eyes like a blindfold. "Close your eyes," he said. His touches were tantalizing, surprising, brushing the side of my breast, the slight swell of my hip, cradling the back of my head, tracing circles along my thigh. When I could stand it no longer, I brushed the hair from my face responding to him with deliberate eye contact and searching hands. I loved the lean hardness of him stretched beside me. His thigh muscles hard as stone against my own, his shoulders, not bulky, but broad with the promise of maturing manhood. His fingers were warm as he unbuttoned my blouse pausing to pass his lips across the flesh above my bra. Sensations sizzled, connecting forbidden fantasies with erotic impulses, and I shivered with anticipation.

"Those Sunday school teachers were wrong," I said. "Or else they weren't doing it right and sweetness, you are doing everything right." That was the last coherent thought I had before the fever overtook me. His caresses became bolder and my clothing was falling away along with my inhibitions. Taking his initiative, I removed his shirt and fumbled with his belt until he stood and removed the remainder of his clothes. I gasped at the sight of a naked man. He was the first one I had ever seen, and I was surprised by the beauty in the hard lines of his body, the muscles taut and ready. He lay down with me and pulled me to him wrapping his arms around me. The small, sweat beads evaporated as the night breezes skimmed our skin.

"I hope you're still okay cause I don't think I can stop now." Jackson's breath was ragged with readiness.

"You better not stop."

The next morning I knew I had changed, I just didn't expect the rest of the world to be so different. I walked around like I had a secret. I did. I was in love with a man who loved me. Sex wasn't the unspeakable wifely duty about which women complained. I thought about this discovery as I gathered mussels in the salt marsh.

Collecting shellfish to sell to Charlie, all I could think about was Jackson. I was grinning like a circus monkey and I couldn't wait to be alone with him again. Charlie and his sons owned two boats and fished and shrimped. Mostly, I sold what I collected in the open air market, but I didn't have all afternoon to sit behind a table. Charlie would buy what I collected to sell in his building. I made less money selling to him but the prospect of sex with Jackson was far more appealing than profit.

My attitude toward sex didn't surprise me. I loved it and couldn't get enough. We had done it three times last night. Jackson's fingers, his lips warm on me, the sturdy feel of his weight and fullness of him as we found a matching rhythm. Maybe that was the big secret about sex. Everybody liked it but didn't tell anyone. I found myself staring at women, tourists, my sister, the quilting ladies, and even Miss Maggie, the flower lady, wondering how they liked it. Jackson said men love it. He explained how some women didn't get that shuddering, fluttering release like I did. He called it an orgasm. I felt like I had butterflies vibrating in my delicate parts. My flesh throbbed and pulsed until I could hardly stand the delirious sensations. I grabbed Jackson's shoulders as it increased, a moan of pleasure slipping through my lips. That made Jackson laugh and he nuzzled my neck in response. Those orgasms are addictive, I told him. It seemed to make him happy. "You know I love you, Agnes. We're going to be so happy together."

By the time I realized I was pregnant, Jackson was in Europe.

CHAPTER FIFTEEN

1944
James Island

Jackson

THE ONLY TIME AGNES and I were apart was when I was on base. Pilot training was intense but it didn't last all day. Other than my flights and target practice, I had very little to do. We flew night missions and patrolled the coasts for submarine activity. As an officer, I didn't have barrack chores, so I had free time most every day. The secrecy of our operation kept our base contingent small and we weren't very regimented. The men fished, body surfed, played football and cards. And we waited. We waited for our turn in the war.

I knew I wasn't just seeing her to pass the time, nor was I using her for sex. I was in love. She fascinated me. She taught me to catch shellfish and harvest herbs that she sold for cooking and medicinal uses. We sat on the beach talking for hours about my world and hers, and when we could mesh them into one. Sometimes, we didn't talk at all, just watched the waves, our easy silence another layer of pleasure for us.

Agnes explained how to track the swooping sand fans left by female sea turtles coming ashore to lay a nest. That was a calling for her and to be able to share her enthusiasm was fantastic. She searched every morning for new nests, marking them with shells and rocks, making sure they were beyond the high tide line. Otherwise the breaking waves would flood the nest and destroy the incubating eggs, as many as eighty to one hundred and twenty. If it were near a public beach access I helped her surround it with wooden stakes and string and hang handwritten *Do Not Disturb* signs. Her eyes were fierce and spirited when she talked of sea turtles. Her breathing shallow as the words tumbled out about hatchlings and moonlight, and their precarious journey to the water, how they returned thousands of miles to the beach of their birth to lay eggs, and continue the cycle of life.

I wanted nothing more than to wake each day naked next to her and to end each night with the taste of roasted oysters and her salty skin on my mouth. I knew my training could end anytime and my overseas assignment was imminent. I dreaded leaving her or the barrier island, each so alive I could feel both move under my body. Their wildness stimulated my senses with a fiery passion. Their earthy smell intoxicating and sultry, their taste, rich and wanton, their touch, bountiful and yielding, their sight, primitive and fresh, and their sound, delightful and perpetual. Both the island and Agnes satiated my soul.

Would she go with me, I wondered. She loved me, but this island was the only world she knew. We could come back when my tour was over. There were bases all over the Carolinas. I could get stationed at one of them and we could build a little cottage on the island for vacations, later make it a permanent home. I had been thinking about this since the first day I saw her exploring the salt marsh at low tide, her blond curls falling over her inquisitive blue eyes. Her lithe body, tan and healthy, shadows playing in the shallow curves of her hips and breasts so much a part of the virgin landscape it took my breath.

The army had built a runway and a small collection of buildings at the south end of the island. One day, I borrowed a jeep and journeyed several miles off base past the center of town where the swinging bridge connected. North of the square, the area was untouched, a savage wildness of maritime forest, protected tidal flats on the sound side, and barren beaches on the Atlantic side. I didn't know if the land was government or private, but it didn't belong to the town. A buddy saw me reading a book about sharks and told me it was a great place to look for shark's teeth. I parked in town and hiked along the main road then waded across a shallow inlet at low tide. I never saw any posted *No Trespassing* signs but I was wearing my military identification and knew I could talk my way out of a problem.

Walking with my head down, a Yankees cap shading my eyes from the sun, I was searching for the ebony black teeth that glimmered in the wet sand when I tripped over a piece of driftwood and fell sprawling. Spitting grit from my mouth, I looked out in front of me and saw her. Inhaling sharply, I sucked in sand and coughed loudly. Then I was choking and fumbling for my canteen when she noticed me and walked over. I scrambled to my feet wiping sand from my fatigues as she approached.

"I'm Agnes. It's an old woman's name but I'm told I have an old soul."

"You have a what?"

"An old soul, when you're wise beyond your years or smarter than you should be for your age."

"Well, you're certainly beautiful." I realized I sounded like an idiot and never introduced myself. "I'm Lt. Jackson Ross. I'm a pilot stationed down at the south end of the island."

"You don't say," she said, her stunning blue eyes sparkling with merriment as she gave my standard-issue fatigues and combat boots the once-over. I smiled at her, displaying my darling left dimple.

"I hope I'm not trespassing." I wiped my hands across my pockets bulging with shells and rocks.

"As long as you're not taking anything," she said. I plunged my hands into the oversize pockets bringing out handfuls of my collectibles, and exclaiming apologies to her. "Whoa, I'm just kidding." Agnes reached for my hands to stop me, but she was laughing so hard she could barely stand. Finally, in a fit of breathless giggles, she fell to the sand looking up at me standing motionless and confused. She patted the sand next to her and I smiled again and sat down on the beach, dropping my shells into a pile between us.

CHAPTER SIXTEEN

Third summer
James Island

"ARE YOU MEETING ZEB tonight?" Penn sat on her beach towel staring at me. She didn't expect an answer to her question. "Three days ago you told us he might be seeing someone else." I didn't have an answer for Penn. I had some suspicions about Zeb, but I couldn't stay away from him. Penn, Emerson, and I were sunbathing, the sun overhead and blistering. It was midday and the ocean breeze was barely breathing over our sweaty skin.

"Maybe I overreacted," I said. "He's just been a little distant." Penn swallowed a long drink of water but continued to watch me.

"You know if you're not going to be honest with us at least tell yourself the truth. He's no good for you Jade."

"Okay, I've heard this before. He's a little rough and maybe I don't trust him entirely, but he makes my body feel things I didn't know it could." I laughed, trying to keep the mood light. Penn was tenacious about Zeb and how wrong he was for me. "Hand me a Diet Coke, Em. Are you worried about my virtue too or is Penn the only one with a halo?" Before Emerson could answer, Penn interjected.

"He's going to hurt you. If you can't see it then know that I'm just trying to protect you. It's like seeing a car wreck in slow motion."

"Then you should look elsewhere." I jerked my towel, scattering sand over everyone and started toward the cottage. "Besides, I didn't ask you to watch." We avoided each other the rest of the afternoon, showering and napping before our wait shift at the restaurant. It was a busy Saturday night, the peak of tourist season leading into the July Fourth holiday. I avoided Penn and Emerson until closing. Penn's stressful night got worse when she realized I was leaving with Zeb.

"When will you be home?" she asked. "The last time you didn't come home until three in the morning. We were going to look for you."

"What difference does it make when I come home?"

"Why is it a problem for you, Penn?" Em asked. "You do know Jade's not a virgin right?"

"Do you always have to be so crass and sarcastic, Em? I'm worried about her. He's not like those white bread boys at school."

"Maybe that's why she wants him," she said. "But there's more going on here. I think you're threatened by Jade's behavior. Does she need your approval? She doesn't seem to want it, so why are you hell-bent on causing trouble?"

"I don't need anyone's approval," I said. "You two are discussing my choices and behaviors like I'm the family dog. I'm just having a good time."

"As long as you don't have any expectations, Jade," Emerson said. "This is a summer fling, a beach tryst, a little sex in the sand, that's all this is, you know?"

"I know exactly what this is," I said.

"You seem to have it under control," she said. "Penn and I just don't want you to romanticize this. We're going back to school next month."

My resentment of Penn's intrusion only made me more reckless. They had been all over me lately and I didn't need any more parents. What I needed was cold beer, hot sex, and a break from judgmental roommates. Why was everything so complicated with them? Being with Zeb was so easy. He didn't expect anything from me. It was all about the moment and unlike any experience I ever had. I was rarely spontaneous but when I did allow my spirit freedom a feverish power ignited. I loved the euphoria.

"You know where I like your hands," Zeb said, as I straddled the motorcycle seat behind him, wrapping my arms around his waist. He popped the clutch and spun sand from the back wheel as he left the parking lot.

"Where are we going?" he asked.

"Your place." Minutes later, we crossed the bridge to the mainland and Zeb maneuvered the bike down a sandy lane nearly hidden with overgrown hedges and drapes of Spanish moss. When the brambles quit tugging at my clothes, we slid into a clearing where a depressed-looking house stared vacantly over the marsh. Several guys were renting the place and Zeb's room consisted of the screen porch with a pull-out sofa bed and wicker furniture unraveling slowly in the perpetual ocean breeze. He kept a cooler on the porch and grabbed us a couple cold beers. The icy water ran down the brown bottle and dripped into my cleavage as I tipped it to my lips.

My senses were manhandled by Zeb's energy, all I could do was absorb his heat with my hands, mouth, tongue, my body wrapped around him like summer sunlight. Later, we lay together under the ceiling fan, the air of the rotating blades tantalizing the moisture on my skin. Tree frogs sang to each other while other primal screeches of nocturnal creatures erupted in the dark. I loved the afterglow of sex, especially outdoors cradled in nature. It felt provocative and elemental. Far away lightning flickered out over the ocean as if winking at me.

I know your secret, it said. *You're not even ashamed of your brazen behavior.* It mocked me from its heavenly station. I closed my eyes to the judgmental flashing screaming like a neon sign to my ego.

"Go to hell," I whispered ferociously to the sky. Zeb snorted in his sleep, satiated and oblivious to my inner struggle. Am I ignoring the warning signs, I wondered, only just pretending I was comfortable with the arrangement? Casual sex wasn't usually casual to me. I had waited until college to lose my virginity to my high school boyfriend. Am I expecting too much from myself? So what if Zeb was seeing other girls. We had never discussed being exclusive. Truthfully, we didn't discuss much at all. Talking wasn't our preferred pastime.

I listened to Zeb's steady breathing beside me and heard the sounds of his roommates talking inside. Wonder if they watched us? The images of us together flashed through my brain. The house was empty when we came in. I didn't notice anyone arriving while we were involved. I blushed at the memory of my body, writhing astride Zeb's, moonlight illuminating my bare breasts and thighs, my head thrown back in ecstasy, my eyes sparkling with fiery passion. I don't know if the thought horrified or excited me thinking of the guys watching us. This was not a side of myself I had ever met. I never stayed the night with him and I wondered what the morning would bring. There was an addictive component that made our attraction surreal, but the reality was that the fall semester began in several weeks. Was I expecting something from him he couldn't give? Did I even want anything from him? My insecurity was exposed like skinned electrical wires. I was begging to get burned.

The sun looked like an egg yolk sliding through wet paint when I woke. Zeb left before dawn since construction started so early this time of year. Temperatures would pass one hundred degrees by early afternoon and the roof tops were scorching. I stretched, massaging a cramp in my left calf, and wondered how I would get home. I could call Penn or Em, but they were going to be so mad

I couldn't bring myself to request a favor. I wanted to turn over and sleep a few more hours and would have done so in the privacy of my own room, but there on a screen porch open to the canal and fishermen was a little too public. Looking for my clothes from last night, I found a note on Zeb's pillow and a miniature box of Fruit Loops.

Enjoyed last night. There's water in the cooler. See you soon, Zeb, it read. I smiled at my breakfast, thinking of Zeb's sweet smile and gentle attention. Penn wouldn't find his offering of dry cereal as romantic as I did. I could understand why Penn didn't think he was good enough for me. He was an uneducated, construction worker, a touch abrasive and raw, and poor, very, very poor. But he wasn't rude or dishonest and he never portrayed himself any different. I knew I didn't have a future with him but it hurt that Penn refused to respect my judgment. She needed to get laid, I thought, by someone as good as Zeb. It would improve her mood and soften her frustration. And put a big damn smile on her face. A great orgasm can mellow the harshest temperament. Penn needed a healthier outlook. Maybe I should loan out Zeb to my friends. I laughed as I pulled on my black shorts and searched for my bra.

Leaving my black tank un-tucked, I laced my tennis shoes, picked up my waitress shirt, the cereal, and water bottle, and exited through the screen door. I didn't want to go inside and run into his roommates or a collection of hung-over women they had brought home. I needed a bathroom but town wasn't a mile away and something would be open, surely.

After crossing the bridge onto the island, the open-air market was my first stop. It housed public bathrooms and drink machines. Before leaving the bathroom, I washed my face with water and disposable towels, ran my fingers through my hair and tied it back with a band from my pocket. I funneled two quarters into the drink machine and grasped the icy Diet Coke as it hit the chute, feeling the freezing burn of the carbonating bubbles exploding down my esophagus. God, I loved that burn.

I sat on the cool, cement block wall to rest before the two-mile trek down the beach and watched two older women talk. One was as black as diner coffee and the other was a slip of a woman with light curls and luminous blue eyes. Buckets of rainbow flowers flanked the one while the tiny woman unloaded smelly coolers from the back of an ancient pick-up truck with the strength of a longshoreman. She had a box of Ziploc bags, a tarnished measuring scoop, and a folding lawn chair. Probably a shellfish dealer, I thought. Tourists love to buy their own fresh seafood and the public marketplace gave the locals a place to sell. It was a great supply and demand situation and a brilliant marketing strategy by the tourism department. Easy banter floated across the tables and the two women gossiped about characters colorful enough for a Jill McCorkle novel. I could have stayed longer, delaying the inevitable confrontation awaiting me, but the sun was getting higher and hotter and those miles weren't getting shorter.

Penn didn't raise an eyebrow when I came in mid-morning. Em would be asleep a few more hours, but Penn was sipping coffee and reading the newspaper. Sometimes, she acted like a senior citizen.

After I showered, Penn was still reading the paper. I popped the top of my second Diet Coke and sat down without a word. I anticipated a scolding from her. Feeling like a teenager who had missed curfew, I realized I was defensive, rationalizing my behavior as not irresponsible. I was prepared to challenge Penn with her own sexual indiscretions, but she never said anything. I became even more agitated and anxious to have the confrontation over. I shifted in my seat, tapping my fingernail against the aluminum can while Penn sipped her caramel-colored coffee and rattled pages of newsprint. Distant shrieks of children playing in the surf, the monotonous breaking of waves against the sand, the cry of gulls, the daily white noise of island life was amplified in my ears. When would she start? I needed this to be over. The tension was atrocious. Let this be soon, I silently demanded.

Penn's silence was devouring my pleasure from last night's encounter. "Dammit, Penn, let me have it." I turned to face my friend, my damp hair slinging water droplets over the newsprint.

"What?" Penn's tone was as innocent as mine was incriminating.

"I know you're pissed and intentionally making me sweat."

"You're an adult. If you're sweating, it's because you jumped into the fire and are feeling the heat." Penn picked up her mug, said something about breakfast and went into the kitchen. Her behavior wasn't at all what I expected. It was oddly unsettling that I found myself dissatisfied with our verbal exchange.

CHAPTER SEVENTEEN

Third summer
James Island

WILMINGTON DAILY NEWS – James Island, N.C.-- The bones of a female infant were found yesterday morning in a clearing on the canal side of the island. Retirees, Mabel and Ed Houssard, were digging for clams in the marsh on the northern end of the island when they made the gruesome discovery. Pender County medical examiner, Dr. Bryan Edwards, believes the remains are from a female under the age of two. The bones seemed to be arranged within a circle of debris three feet in diameter. The cause of death could not be determined and the remains have been sent to Chapel Hill to the state medical examiner, Dr. Michael Sherrill, for autopsy and anthropological evaluation, he added. Police Chief Austin Howard, of James Island, did not elaborate when asked about the ritualistic aspect of the site. There is no criminal activity or determination regarding time or manner of death, he said.

"What do you know about Zeb?" Penn asked Monday afternoon. It was our day off and we were eating a late lunch.

"Not this again," I said, tossing a handful of Fritos at Penn. "Can't you let it go?"

"I'm not trying to start a fight. This is not about your relation-ship," Penn said. "I'm wondering how much you know about him. Where's he from? Who does he hang out with?"

I was so tired of defending my relationship with Zeb. "He's a construction worker, from somewhere in Virginia. He dropped out of college after one year. He's twenty-three, loves mint chocolate chip ice cream and barbecue potato chips, sometimes together. He's never played golf, has an older sister and likes to fish. He and his roommates are making repairs to their cottage in exchange for rent. Boxers not briefs. He wants a dog but it's not convenient and he's one hell of a lay." I made the last statement looking directly at Penn and finished with a contemptuous look on my face.

"You don't have to make me the enemy. Em and I are your best friends. Don't shut us out because we question your relationship with a stranger." I flopped back in the easy chair and slung my leg over the arm. Dropping my head back, I stared at the ceiling fan and started to speak, stopped, sighed, then tried again.

"Penn, I don't want to do this with you, again. I'm just having fun with him. Zeb's different and instead of seeing that as an obstacle I welcome it. Sometimes, I get tired of those frat boys spending daddy's money, immature as middle-schoolers, who are just trying to get into my pants."

"What's Zeb trying to do?" Penn asked, rising from the table and heading toward the kitchen. I ignored her and continued.

"What am I doing that's so different from when you trade in your frat rats for those artsy types at school? You know the ones, dressed all in black, with pony tails and a chip on their shoulder, because society doesn't get them." Penn reached behind her chair for the newspaper.

"Okay, I get your point, but I was asking those questions for a specific reason. Did you read yesterday's paper?" Penn laid the paper on the ottoman in front of me and tapped a small story near the bottom. "How about you Em?"

"No Penn, I sleep in the mornings," I said. "And Em sleeps through the afternoon."

"Read this article."

Penn uncorked a bottle of Zinfandel while Emerson and I sat together reading the account of baby bones found only a few miles from us. "It's a little gruesome, but why are you showing this to us? You think Zeb had something to do with this?" Emerson asked, moving into the kitchen to pour wine for us. She was probably waiting for me to explode on Penn for insinuating Zeb was a satanic killer.

"You've got a wild imagination, Penn," I said. Then I took my wine and went out on the deck. I heard them tidying the kitchen.

"I thought that would go differently," Emerson said.

The confrontation came at sundown. I was getting dressed for a date with Zeb and could hear Penn and Emerson in the kitchen. Penn was washing dishes, probably wearing those silly yellow rubber gloves that rose to her elbows. "Is he picking her up?" Penn asked. Em had cooked so no dish duty for her. Absently flipping magazine pages, Em answered without looking up.

"I doubt it. Has he ever? He waits down by the pier and who knows where they go."

"Well, I know what they're doing," Penn said.

"Who cares?" Emerson's sandal dropped from her foot to the linoleum floor. "Penn you don't worry about Jade like this at school, so why do you here? Is this just about Zeb? Or does it have more to do with you?" I moved to the door so I was better positioned to eavesdrop. Standing still, I could see them through the crack in the door. Penn wiped sweat from her face with her sleeve and slammed the sponge into the sink, sending soap bubbles skyward.

"Why on earth would you say that? This has nothing to do with me. I think Zeb is just a redneck and no good for her. I want her to wake up and see that. He's a womanizer and he's going to hurt her." She pushed the tendrils of sweaty curls back, and leaned against the counter.

"Jade's not a teenager," Emerson said. "She is twenty-one and we're getting ready to start our last year of college. Just let her have these last few weeks." With a raised eyebrow, Emerson looked at Penn. "Maybe you want to give Zeb a spin." I choked on my saliva behind the door and Emerson laughed at Penn's expression. Then the phone rang. "Hello," Emerson said in her best sex-kitten voice. "Ah, well, she can't come to the phone. Can she call you back?" She covered the mouthpiece and whispered to Penn. "Go see if Jade's out of the shower."

"Just tell him she's out with friends," Penn said.

She made a face at Penn and spoke into the receiver, "Sorry, should she meet you somewhere?" After a pause, she said, "Sure, I'll give her the message." Emerson hung up the phone. Zeb had to cancel, she announced.

"He's probably meeting another girl," Penn said.

"Probably, but Jade doesn't need you adding to this."

I stuck my head around the door frame. "Did I hear the phone?"

"Yeah, Zeb can't make it. Has another engagement." Penn made the announcement before Emerson could interject. "Probably a yacht party or a cotillion." Penn's devilish eyes snapped with energy. She relished getting a rise out of me, I thought. I glared at Penn and turned to Em.

"Did he really call?"

"I'm sorry, honey, he did. Said he couldn't make it and give you the message."

"Did he say why?"

"No, just that he couldn't see you tonight and wouldn't be at home."

"Sounds fishy to me," Penn said. "Another girl, maybe?" This time I couldn't ignore her jab. I squared my shoulders and turned on Penn. I was so mad I could feel lightning strikes in my eyes.

"What the hell is your problem?" Surprised by my fierceness, Penn took a half step back. "I have listened to you all summer make fun of Zeb and degrade me for seeing him. I've had enough. All I'm going to take. I'll drag him into the middle of campus and screw him at the Old Well if I want. And you can kiss my ass!" With that, I slammed the screen door and stomped off the porch, heading south down the beach into the dark.

CHAPTER EIGHTEEN

Third summer
James Island

Emerson

AFTER JADE LEFT, I looked at Penn standing in the kitchen, water dripping from the yellow gloves she still wore. "You two are crossing a line," I said to her. "It's one thing to fight like sisters but this is getting nasty. It's mean. I'm worried this is going somewhere you're not going to come back from. This is a very dark place y'all are going, all over a damn guy. What is going on with you? The truth, now."

Penn removed her gloves, took two beers from the fridge. She handed one to me and opened the other as she sat down across from me. "Things are moving too fast, Em. Everything is changing. We're changing, and this is our last year together. Jade's different now, she's changed this summer, doing things on her own, taking risks and keeping secrets. It's just..." Penn faltered, a tear rolled down her cheek. "It's just not the same anymore."

I shifted in my seat and put my hand over her hand resting on her knee. "Penn, we can't stay the same. Jade's just going through some growing pains. She needs to stretch herself a little, get her feet under her. Maybe you're just pissed she's not asking your opinion every time she makes a move. Maybe, that's what's changing and you can't handle it." Penn stood up quickly like she would challenge me, but turned abruptly, took a fresh six pack of beer and let the screen door slam behind her. I didn't know where any of this was going. We had buckled up on a rollercoaster and we were on it until it stopped.

CHAPTER NINETEEN

Third summer
James Island

"DAMN PENN FAULKNER." I stomped down the beach in the dark, away from the cottage and humanity, talking aloud to no one. "I'm so tired of being cautioned and mothered, told what to do and who to do." I exhaled with every footfall, leaving heavy-heeled prints in the damp sand. Of course, I couldn't stay with Zeb, and I wasn't taking him with me to parade through the sorority house. We had no future and weren't going to get married.

I just wanted to savor the last few weeks of my last summer vacation before adulthood claimed me. As different as Zeb was, this wasn't even about him. I was addicted to the way I felt and reacted when I was with him. I was different with him and would probably be different from now on. I had experienced my own sexual awakening. Alive with desires and fantasies, each cell of my body screamed to be ravished. I was a woman, instinctual, primal, passionate, and selfish. I felt invincible. I didn't care that I was all impulse, and no consequence, my behavior so radical and contradictory to my first two decades of life. My elemental strength had always been there, like a slow burning fire, smoldering under the roof before the house ignites. I was catching fire. Sexy, provocative and sultry, like Emerson, and flirtatiously wicked, like Penn, I was a sexual goddess. This summer had been the most liberating experience of my life, and would change me to the deepest core of my being. My confidence was greater, my actions self-assured, my ideas deeper, all from a well simmering with fervent potential.

I was nearing the end of the island where the canal joined the inlet, and flowed into the ocean. There were no houses, just beach grass and dunes sliding into the water. My muscles were burning and my mind was still raging, even though I had walked several miles. Flopping into the sand, I lay back against a dune. The moon was almost full, not quite round, but bright and the sky clear. The heat of the day had dissipated only slightly, and I was sticky with sweat, my t-shirt clinging to my back, my mini-skirt plastered to my thighs.

Already feeling disjointed and void of intelligent thought, I dropped my clothes onto the beach grass and waded into the ocean. Cooler than the air, sensations swallowed the beads of perspiration and the water wrapped around my body in a sensual embrace. My mind was calm and the waves came in placid and soft, undulating as my body buoyed in the swells. I floated on my back, mesmerized by the moon, her light gently illuminating my yielding limbs. I was sure the moon was female, I don't know why but I had always thought so. Tonight I felt her gaze, like she was studying or assessing me. Then she whispered to me. *Accept the changes, embrace your womanhood, spirit and body. But be cautious, with ecstasy comes responsibility. Be mindful of your strengths. Your spirit will tell you what to do, listen to yourself, to your inner core and you will be at peace.*

The words felt disturbing, like a warning. I didn't want warnings. I wanted bliss, rapture, freedom. I made my way to the shore and let the shallow breeze dry the sea water from my skin. Redressing in my damp clothes, I turned north along the beach for home as the tide crept toward the lonely dunes.

The cottage was empty but the cars were still there. Wherever they were, they had walked. After changing my clothes and fixing my hair, I grabbed a bottle of wine and walked up the beach toward our dune. A hollowed space, protected between several dunes, was the place Zeb and I first had sex. It was our special spot and we often met there after work. It wasn't always about sex, we talked a little too. Honestly, he was quiet and meditative. Still, I did enjoy our time together. Like him, it was simple and easy, unpretentious and genuine.

I carried my sandals in one hand feeling the deep sand shift under my feet. Near the dunes the dense sand was still warm from the sun, not yet cooled by the rising tide. The beach was empty and dark except for the moonlight. The full roundness I had basked in earlier was higher and pure white like an orb of selenite, called "liquid light," it was named after the Greek goddess of the moon, Selene. The translucent white crystals of gypsum, were believed to contain mystical and healing properties.

Maybe I would see baby turtles. Female loggerheads came ashore about three times a season during a nesting year. After sixty days of incubation during the summer months, the baby turtles broke through their shells and spent a few days digging out. Under a cover of darkness, they crawled toward the brightest light, hopefully the moon, to reach the ocean, and began what could be a seventy year life span if they managed to survive their precarious first year. To stop any confusion for the new hatchlings, beach dwellers were asked to dim their outside house lights so the turtles would not be confused.

Emerson was likely looking for hatching nests with a handful of volunteers led by a local woman. She was using the experience for an extra concentration she was earning about endangered sea turtles.

I passed the bed and breakfast inn, the wrap-around-porch dark, except for the flicker of candlelight, like shooting stars harnessed from the sky. The tinkle of glasses and soft chatter drifted on the breeze, making me wonder about the guests. A private game I played with myself, I would choose a couple or family and map out their entire past. I envisioned where they were born, their occupations, likes and dislikes, their fantasies and fears, the secrets they hid from the neighbors. Complex scenarios of passion and intrigue ran through my imagination.

Once past the inn, our dune was a couple hundred yards north. Zeb and I hung out together at the pier several times and once went out for a movie and ice cream. Then one night Zeb came to the restaurant after my shift with two bottles of wine, fresh flowers, and a blanket.

We walked together, laughing and talking, stopping midway between the north pier and the inn and spread the blanket in a sheltered spot in the dunes. Before the second bottle of wine was empty, we had lost most of our clothes and were passing a passionate point of no return. I wasn't a virgin, but I wasn't very experienced either, just my high school boyfriend during my first year at Carolina, then a ten-month relationship with a frat boy who was sweet.

Zeb was faster and slower than both of the others. I had known him only weeks before I slept with him, not typical for me, and as for the sex, he was slow, excruciatingly slow. Delighting my senses and teasing behaviors from me, his hands were magical, his mouth sensuous and alluring. His lips tantalized mine, his tongue playful and curious, nipping at my bottom lip. His kisses started at my neck, right under my ear lobe and moved to the hollow at my collarbone. He lingered, brushing his mouth downward. Just as he reached the rise of my cleavage, he changed directions and made his way back to the delicate spot just above the ridge of my shoulder. The hairs on the back of my neck stood. When he made it back to my mouth,

I was starving. I devoured him with startling aggression, both hands in his hair, the strands long and silky. His eyes, that seawater turquoise, dared me, provoked me, as if the seduction was all me. I could taste the challenge on him and the saltiness of his skin, the sweetness of the wine on his mouth. Taking the lead surprised me more than him. It was like he was willing my body to act and my mind was floating above.

"How do you do that?" I breathed. Zeb just laughed. "I'm never like this."

"Like what, hot, sexy, breathtaking," he mumbled, trailing kisses along my neck.

"Bold, oh my... what are you doing... to me." I wanted to say more, but my brain wasn't working.

"Just wait," he said. "I've got more."

His jaw line had just enough stubble to tickle when his face grazed the soft skin above my breasts. His lips nibbled and his tongue danced around my nipple. By the time he took it in his mouth, I was singing show tunes. I don't know why, I just suddenly heard happy, upbeat notes, soaring lyrics, and applause, so very much applause. I expected his finale would be spectacular. He took his sweet time with the performance. I had never experienced this kind of foreplay and was so ready for him. Anticipation, I had been there before, but this raging desire was erupting from every nerve.

"Please..." arching toward him, I pulled his hips with urgency, swinging my legs around him. I had never wanted anything more, and dug my nails into the flesh below his shoulder blades as he entered me. Bring on the encore, I thought.

I still didn't know why he cancelled our date tonight. He was working really long days in the brutal sun and could just be tired. Sometimes, I found him alone at our dune, just watching the waves. Contemplating my future, he said. He never elaborated and I never asked. Summer was ending and we both knew this was just a fling, but neither of us had said it aloud.

Pushing through the prickly sawgrass, I climbed the last few feet over the rise of sand, hoping he was there. I could probably count the nights we had left on my fingers, and I intended to take advantage of each one. This summer had shown me being depraved and reckless suited parts of my personality I had ignored too long. Safe, solid, guarded Jade was boring, and I was tired of her ruling my life.

Zeb's throaty voice rising on the breeze wrapped me in desire. I loved his laugh, carefree and resonant, like river water tumbling over rocks.

Then I saw him, on the blanket, shirtless, his bronze arm muscles taut, and wrapped around an unseen woman. Her fingers coiled in his hair, their bare feet intertwined as they lay kissing. When I screamed his name, Zeb whipped his head around, the girl grabbed her clothes and ran in the opposite direction. I felt sick, a burst of anger exploded in my stomach, my breathing shallow and rapid, matching my pulse. He tugged at his shorts with one hand, holding the other before me like a stop signal.

"What the hell!" I screamed. Zeb, dumbfounded and mute, looked from me to the fleeing body behind him.

"What the hell are you doing!" He tried to answer me and although his mouth was open, no sound manifested. "You son of a bitch! What the hell have you done to me!" I was screaming at him, and moving closer as he struggled with his shirt, so flustered he was trying to put his head through the hole in the sleeve.

"You fucking ass! I should have listened to them. I defended you, you fucking screw-up!" I swiped the back of my hand over my eyes, smearing black mascara and perspiration. I turned to go, but Zeb grabbed my arm and spun me to face him.

"Calm down, Jade. Listen to me."

"I need to get the hell out of here," I said, jerking my arm from his grip.

"You're out of control," he said, reaching for my hand as it ricocheted off his face. "Calm down and listen." I smelled beer and a feminine, floral scent in the night air. Enraged energy blazed over my skin. Shrugging my arms to break his grip on me didn't work, so I raised my leg hoping to hit his cheating parts, but he rotated protectively and my foot vibrated off his hip bone.

"Let go of me," I growled at him through clenched teeth. I sounded like a feral feline, flashbacks of tenderness and brazen wanton sex, followed by humiliation and fury. What I had done with him. How I defended him. How I had shared the private inner lustful part of myself, only to have the images shattered with perverted deceit. I pulled my hand free and slashed at his eyes, those eyes I trusted, and gave myself to. I had never given so much of myself to anyone. He grabbed a sweatshirt from the ground and tried to wrap my hands with it.

Shame and madness engulfed me, combusting with my newly discovered passion. That was a dangerous cocktail to mix with a cheating boyfriend. These volatile emotions were new to me and they hurt. Tormented by the look on his face, I lashed out as he tried again to subdue me. The restraint was profane and vicious, like a power struggle for the last dregs of my dignity. This relationship was shredded and having his hands on me was torture. In a move neither of us anticipated, I lunged down, grabbed a piece of driftwood, and hammered Zeb's left temple.

When darkness invades a body, it seeps in through the pores and sickens one's principles. I felt the evil breed in my cells, a degenerate disease that consumed rationality, leaving me corrupt and decaying with madness. I didn't flinch when the wood connected with his head and he went down. The blood trickling along his hairline, dripping into his ear, did not disturb me. His silence never screamed a warning in my mind. Lying beside his inert body was a Carolina blue sweatshirt. Emblazoned across the front were the Greek letters, Delta Xi Theta. Penn.

I walked away moving with cold deliberation, and never looked back. I didn't remember the walk home. One minute I was screaming at Zeb, and then I was at the bottom of the porch stairs listening to the incoming tide crash below my feet. My hands were shaking, perspiration trailed down my neck and between my shoulder blades. Tiny glimpses of the past hour flickered in the edge of my vision, Zeb, bare skin, a woman's leg, his twisted face, my wrists burning, hurting, blood.

I entered the cottage, still dark and quiet. I flipped on the kitchen light, poured myself a tumbler of bourbon and went to the bathroom. Rote memory took over as I washed and shampooed then packed my toiletry bag. In my room, I packed my clothes and belongings. I was calm, robotic muscle memory overriding my disengaged mind. I laid down on the bed watching the curtains ruffle from the ceiling fan and outside breeze, the cross wind prickling the hair on my arms.

When someone knocked on my door, I pretended to be asleep. When Emerson tiptoed into the edge of my room, I remained still, slowing my breathing to force my diaphragm to conform to my will. For the next few hours, I dreamed of giant fish that leapt from the waves and chased me down the beach. As I fled, I came to a staircase and climbed two stories before it ended abruptly in the air. Below me baby turtles scurried toward the dark water, a great yellow moon so close I could touch it. I needed to feel its texture. My hand disappeared into the liquid gold, but it was brutally cold, and I drew it out quickly, gasping as my fingers dripped with blood.

I left the beach as the first colored streaks stained the sky. The note on the table instructed Penn and Em to close up the house before they returned to school in two weeks. A family emergency had called me home.

We all have a dark side, if one is brave enough to look. Mine seemed tame and nondescript. I had never so much as stolen a candy bar. I gossiped and cheated at cards occasionally, but I never thought I could hurt someone. People who claim they could never kill someone, are the ones to never overlook.

Like having a wick inside the soul, down in the black vapid space, when it burns out, it's final, no more tolerance, no more forgiveness, no more restraint. When that wick flames its last breathe, anyone can commit any kind of atrocity. The crucial question, how long is the wick? I knew when I saw Zeb, that girl's legs wrapped around him, his bare, white ass in the moonlight, that I had enough dangerous rage to kill him. We weren't having a great love affair, but I did expect respect and honesty. I was a new woman with him. I had freed parts of myself that would never land again. I was like a great white ibis, with awkward legs and a gangly strut who flies majestic and fearless, wings spread and opened to the wind, unafraid and not ashamed.

My last carefree summer fell tragically from the bright sky, broken and wounded, as I crossed the bridge to the mainland racing the sunlight west before it caught me.

CHAPTER TWENTY

Present
James Island

THERE ARE POIGNANT MOMENTS in life when time has no relevance. Whether it's been twenty minutes or twenty years, when there is a crisis, all of the in-between falls away. Resentment becomes insignificant and we find those emotions and behaviors inside us to do what's needed for someone we love. The turmoil of our last summer on the island before our senior year at Carolina was obvious at every football game and alum tea since graduation. We all returned to school that fall dragging hurt feelings and suspicions.

Penn and I pretended our relationship was symbiotic as usual, but it was never the same. Emerson stayed for fall semester but left for an internship in the spring, returned for graduation then set sail on an international marine biology career. She attended a sorority Founder's Day luncheon here and there, and one football reunion weekend ten years ago but contact between us was artificial.

That's why I was stunned that night before graduation that we all agreed to plan a reunion for two decades into the future. I think it was our frantic attempt at salvaging what we once were to each other.

We planned it, knee-deep in bourbon shots, at our favorite haunt, Henderson Street Bar, for twenty years after our May graduation. Now, we were forty-two and very different women from those girls heading into adulthood. Was there even a fragment of our bond still intact?

Only the desperation of my suicide attempt permitted me to tell them my story. I was beyond vulnerable. With a last hope for a soft place to land, I told them about my miscarriages, my little lost children that became medical waste, my subsequent breakdown, and finally my self-destruction. I didn't know how they would react, but I was too tired to care about our painful past.

Penelope and Emerson responded with twenty-four years of love and loyalty. They wrapped their arms around me, cradling me as I sobbed. Hot, hopeless tears broke free and I couldn't speak, just cry. They didn't ask me for details, just let me fall apart and get it all out. They let me set the pace and unfold the trauma as I could manage. The little lives created with Ian eradicated, one after another, taking pieces of me with them. I will never be whole, I told them. "These babies weren't just cells and cytoplasm. They were my blue eyes and Ian's dimples, his passion for music and my love of reading." The tears continued to escape my swollen eyes. "This was my whole identity. If I'm not a mom, being a woman is meaningless."

I finally confessed my suicide attempt which made them cry too. Especially, after I explained how distorted visions of us together rescued me from my watery death. It was our bond that wouldn't let me quit, that made me fight for my life.

"I have chosen to live but I don't really know what there is left for me," I said. Emerson led me inside to the sofa and wrapped a blanket around me. Penn made tea.

"She needs more than tea," Emerson said, watching Penn fumble with the kettle.

"No, tea is exactly what she needs," Penn answered. "We need to dry her out, purge the toxic sludge in her system." Emerson rolled her eyes. "Look at her, Em. Does she look good to you? She looks like hell if you take a long look."

"Alright, sweetie, you heard the boss. Tea it is." Emerson propped my feet on the couch and pulled the coffee table closer to set my tea within reach. "But if we have to drink tea, we're going to do it the British way... with cookies."

"Biscuits."

"Shut up, Penn."

I don't know how long we sat there together or how much tea we had, but it was long enough to go through the last ten years of my marriage. "I think it's over," I said finally.

"Do you still love him?" Penelope asked.

"Does it make a difference," I answered. "He doesn't love me anymore. I've hurt him and shut him out. He couldn't share my pain and fear, and I couldn't look in his eyes anymore without seeing the disappointment I've caused."

"It does matter if you love him," Emerson said. "Because if you do, you have a starting point to rebuild, no matter how bad this is, if there is love, it can be fixed."

"Spoken like someone who's never been married," I said, then immediately apologized. "Em, I'm sorry, I'm just a bitch and you're trying to help. But love isn't everything, you know, it's only part of the equation. Can I give him what he needs? Can I accept what he can give?" Exasperated and tired, I wasn't sure I could talk about this anymore. I felt like I had vomited until there was nothing left, but the retching wouldn't stop. "I don't know if he respects me anymore, and I'm terrified he can live without me now." After my emotional catharsis, I must have drifted off to sleep. I awoke to the voices of Kevin Costner and Susan Sarandon. *Bull Durham.* What a great movie. We had seen it in college since the Durham Bulls baseball team played in the neighboring town.

Both women were quiet and watching me. I guess they were going to see what kind of emotional display I would make now, kind of like spinning a wheel or throwing darts. I had been a hot mess of random moods over the last twenty-four hours.

"Do you feel any better?" Emerson asked. Penelope jumped up to put the tea kettle on the heat. "Good god, Penn, she doesn't need any more tea." I knew Penn just needed something to do.

"What do we have to eat?" I asked, hoping that would give her a way to use the restless energy that buzzed around her.

"I'm thinking ultimate comfort food, tomato soup and grilled cheese sandwiches," she said. I didn't answer right away. "Or not. Maybe macaroni and cheese, but I'll have to run to the store."

"Penn, the soup and sandwiches sound perfect." I got up from the sofa and hugged first Emerson and then Penn before going to the bathroom to wash my tear-and-snot-crusted face. I had also drooled in my sleep, my shirt sleeve was damp. I cleaned up, changed my top and returned to the den.

It began to get dark soon after dinner. We moved to the porch, Emerson brought out the bourbon and shot glasses and we drank until I was numb. Then they put me to bed.

The sun was high overhead when I emerged from my bedroom. I looked and felt like road kill, some decaying carcass pummeled beyond recognition.

"Breakfast, lunch, coffee?" Penelope asked.

"Little hair of the dog?" Emerson suggested. "It's five somewhere and we can pretend that's here." I shuffled to the fridge.

"Maybe I'll start with a Diet Coke and some crackers. Then we'll work up to cocktails." I winked at Em. Sitting down in the family room, I stared vacantly out over the ocean. I didn't know what to say or where to start or how much I should reveal about the choices I had made.

I was going to have a few days alone to think about it. Deeming me desperately fragile, they were leaving to make arrangements to come back to the island and stay with me for a few weeks. They left after lunch and I napped most of the afternoon. I heated some soup in the microwave and sat on the porch watching the world fade.

The horizon was clear one minute. Then the fog was near and menacing. Fog didn't creep in on little cat feet, more like a snarling panther. It was stealthy and shrewd, waiting for me to be alone and exposed. Tiny water droplets converged, obscuring, restricting my visibility. The mist materialized and merged with the water offshore confusing my clarity. Like a paint chart at the hardware store, the changing hue began with Mark Twain Gray merging into a thin line of Winter Slate followed by Smoky Mountain Blue. Subtle and smooth, I was prey for the taking.

Standing on the porch, I felt I could walk straight into the ocean, like descending into the center of a storm cloud. How would that feel? Would it swallow me or shelter me, protect that fragile soul inside me? I wanted to leap off the deck railing into that bank of unrefined cotton and feel the microscopic droplets of moisture sponge my body. Fairly certain I was beyond another suicide attempt, but there was something so appealing about stepping off into that oblivion, like a soft flannel blanket waiting to swathe me in compassion. God, it was so much harder than I expected not to drift away, quietly evaporating from earth. Maybe the fog was a portal to the spirit world. Forgiveness might await me. Even empty nothingness was preferable to the abyss in which I wallowed.

Agnes would tell me to embrace the elements, air, fire, water, and earth. They each have a purpose. They reside within us all, she would say. Let them purify you, Jade, she would encourage. Feel them infuse you with positive energy. They don't want to claim you, only redeem you. I could hear her voice clearly in my head. I wasn't so sure about Agnes' ideology, chanting naked in the woods, lighting candles, and personifying the wind. Maybe she was some kind of witch, I thought. But I did feel stronger when I was with her.

The longer I sat there, the more the fog beckoned. Moist fingers curled around each wrist and tugged at my ankles. This was a trap, I could feel it. This voice wasn't part of a cosmic universe or from a white-haired witch. Like a horror flick trailer, the call was coming from inside, the voice was in my head. It knew I was fragile and unprotected.

I just needed to survive the night, I thought. Darkness would surround the fog and the morning sun would absorb its allure, dissipating my temptation. I could make it till the light returned. I repeated that mantra until sleep claimed me sometime after midnight.

Penelope and Emerson were returning in a couple of days. When they were reasonably convinced I was stable, they returned to Asheville and Charleston to make arrangements. Both were clearing their schedule and coming back to the island for the next several weeks. Penn's children were in academic summer programs and Emerson was going to telecommunicate via laptop about her grant project with the South Carolina Aquarium Commission.

The next little while was going to be brutal. They would dissect me like a biology class frog and study my parts. In high school science class, my lab partner had deposited a small bit of bubblegum into the giant bullfrog's filleted cavity. The entire class was hysterical as the flustered teacher failed to identify the spongy pink part. This examination wasn't going to be nearly as amusing.

CHAPTER TWENTY-ONE

Present
James Island

AGNES AND I WERE back in her special clearing. She summoned me from my stupor and ordered me to meet her like before, at the canal path a little before midnight. "Why do we do this in the dark?" I asked, doing my damndest to follow her quick little body through the thorns and stickers of the forest undergrowth. She didn't answer. "Agnes," I said again, my voice louder. At this, she whirled around and gave me some kind of weird hand gesture.

"This is not a time for shouting, Jade. This is a time for silence and reflection. We are doing powerful work here."

I crept behind her trying to float through the woods as she did. "But why during the night?" I whispered. "So no one will see us naked?"

"I explained the naked part before. As for the dark, we seek spiritual guidance at midnight. It is a time not of the past, nor yet of the future. Like a standstill, when the universe is motionless and thus receptive to our meditations."

I was afraid of her answer but I had to ask the question. "Agnes, are you some kind of witch?" She turned from me, continuing toward the clearing.

Finally, she said quietly, "Something like that." I never said another word as we walked through the thickets. What was there to say? I had a billion questions, was intrigued and oddly not afraid. I stood on the edge of the clearing, watching the woman disrobe and raise her arms to the sky. She chanted something I couldn't make out, knelt before her stone alter and began removing items from her bag. She lit a dark blue candle, dripped some wax on her rock and then positioned the candle on top. She motioned for me to kneel beside her. I took a step forward and she made a deep throated ahem, tugging at invisible clothing on her body. You're kidding me, I thought. Again, naked in the woods with a witch, but I did as she asked and knelt in the sand.

"Colors are representations of our energy, reflecting different vibrations. We use those vibrations to focus our intention which strengthens our meditation, and helps direct our power and energy for the outcome we are seeking." She passed her hand across the flame and lifted my hand to do the same. With only a split second of hesitation, I allowed her to guide my hand through the flame. I felt warmth, but did not burn.

"Do you feel the warmth?" Agnes asked. "That isn't the candle you feel, but the power of your own body, the energy pulsing from your core and circulating, gathering strength. Your strength." Who was I to argue with her? It sounded plausible. At this point in my life, anything anyone could do, would help.

"I chose dark blue for our candle because it represents forgiveness and healing, inspiration, communication, and happiness. It's time."

She motioned for me to stand and took a small dagger from her bag. What the hell, I thought. Knives and nakedness, not a combination I was a fan of. She took my hand, pulling me close, then bent and traced a circle in the sand around us with the point of the blade. She said a few unintelligible words pausing at each quadrant to make a hand gesture. Then she looked at me and said, "You are safe now."

Agnes placed her hands on my face and lowered my chin, bringing our faces inches apart. For a few moments, she only stared at me, using her blue eyes to penetrate my defenses and reach the vulnerability underneath. She opened her mouth to speak, closed it in a thin line of determination, let out a deep sigh, and began.

"You can stop running now. Your darkness has caught up with you. It's time to let the light in. Without that balance you will die." Her focus was intense and I tried to look away. Her words scared me. I trembled and tried to turn away, tears filling my eyes. Agnes held firm, such surprising strength for a woman her age. "There's nowhere for you to go," she said.

"How is being buck-naked in the sand chanting to the heavens going to help me." I clenched my fists, my hair blowing across my face as I grimaced at her. "I'm just getting sand in very wrong places." Agnes smirked, and continued to stare at me, not offering anything to this unbearable scenario. "Come on old woman, what are you telling me, that some spirit wants to help me? A goddess wants to keep me from drowning myself in the ocean?"

"Not any spirit or goddess but The Goddess and The Spirit, The One who gives life and sustains us. You're only a cosmic speck in this universe, but yes, She cares for you and in turn lives within you. It's time to meet them both. It's time to begin the search for Jade."

"What do you want from me?" I pleaded with her, agony and confusion explicit in my voice.

"Quit running. Stand still. Slow your breathing. Feel the sand on your skin. Let the rain run down your arms and drip from your fingertips. Let the sweet smell of honeysuckle spark a childhood memory. Feel something good, Jade. You haven't felt anything but pain for years. You've buried yourself in the dark muck and it's suffocating the life from you." She reached for me, laying her small hand against my cheek.

"An old friend told me that pain like this requires trench warfare. We've got to hold on to each other and fight. Fight like we are annihilating the greatest evil." She put both hands on my shoulders. "Do you hear me? Listen, all your energy, your enraged passion, it's misdirected. You've been feeding this demon a buffet, giving it pieces of you, because you don't feel like you're worth saving. Choose you. You. Quit giving body and soul to that darkness."

I listened to her words, they were heartbreaking. All the time I'd wasted, not knowing how to heal or if I even could. "Don't you deserve love?" she implored. "If you were Jade's friend, would you shun her, hate her, try to kill her, or would you wrap your arms around her and lift her up?"

I was openly weeping from her words. "Her tears are your tears. She needs your love." Agnes took both my hands in hers. "Let her live. You're blaming that girl for all your sins. That girl needs you to love her and you need to give love. That pain is festering inside you like an open wound, poisoning your heart and polluting your soul. You must exorcise it with the cold precision of a surgeon and the absolution of a priest."

The tears running down my face dripped onto our hands as I tried to breathe. A sharp pain knotted in my chest, the one that precedes the abandonment of control, when the sobs can't be contained and the rush of emotion is cataclysmic. I gasped for air and tried to pull myself away from her. I succeeded in pulling us both to the floor of the clearing. "I don't know what to do? How do you do this?" I cried. "How do I let go?"

"You first have to understand who you are and what you're not. Right now, you're fragmented. Shattered pieces of you are waiting to be rearranged, creating a true reflection, not that distorted image you've vilified for years." Her words struck me like her dagger. I had loathed and rejected so many parts of myself for a very long time. Such a sad existence.

"The Goddess represents three stages of life who reside within us. It's our responsibility, our purpose, to balance their desires, forgive their transgressions, and honor the essence of each."

I'm so broken, I thought. Just like a puzzle, I was missing pieces and forcing others to fit where they didn't belong. Avoidance had become my drug of choice, a way to anesthetize my grief, desire, hope, and my insanity. The wind from the ocean was intensifying, drying my tears and whispering through the tree branches. It was calling me, like a slow moan of desperation.

Agnes let go of my hands and we sat in the sand facing each other. "Can you help me?" I asked. It wasn't a plea or a cry. It was clarity. It was reality. It was the last lifeline of a drowning victim who has shut out the fear and doubt, recognizing there is only one way to persevere. Survival is instinctual if you just surrender control.

"Yes, Jade, I can help you. The woman you were two decades ago is still with you. She's never going to leave you. She is you. She is a natural part of your existence. She's playful and passionate, erotic and foolish. She is the maid and was just beginning her exploration as a woman when you met her. The maid wants excitement, fulfillment, but she doesn't understand her desire or its consequences."

I shifted uncomfortably as Agnes continued her explanation. "Next is the mother. This is where you are now. Her focus is creation, bringing new life, unity, two people building a home and family."

"But that's just it," I interrupted. "I can't build a family. That's why I'm a failure. I can't ever fulfill that part of me!"

"You need to love the woman you are and forgive yourself for having miscarriages. That doesn't make you less of a woman. Motherhood doesn't define you. Can you understand that? Giving life doesn't always mean giving birth." I stared at her feet, watching the moon rays shift and search through the pine boughs as if spotlighting me. Agnes tried to reach out, but I pulled away.

Looking at her, my eyes stung and my body shook with outrage. "It's my own fault I don't have children!" I screamed. "I know I caused it and I can't let go! How do I forgive myself for killing my baby?"

CHAPTER TWENTY-TWO

1944
James Island

Agnes

IT WAS ESSENTIAL TO place each bone in a particular way. The extremities must point outward to attract energy, the spine due north to call celestial intercession, and most importantly, the skull facing inward on a small stone altar.

Platinum moonlight dripped through the twisted branches and collected on my naked body. At least the weather was still warm, the last remnants of Indian summer resting on my bare skin. I was panicked. My best estimate made me about three months along, ironically the same amount of time I had been separated from Jackson. I received a letter last week, written six weeks ago, sent from an undisclosed location. I had no way to contact him. I was alone except for the tiny cells dividing in my uterus. Jackson would love us both, but without him I was just another unwed pregnant teenager, bringing shame to my family, ruining my future. How could I think of this pregnancy as anything more than biology until I knew what to do and how to find Jackson? I mailed him a letter about the baby, finally. I had made myself wait to share the news until I heard from him. A tiny part of me worried he might forget me.

He wanted to marry me, I knew that cause we had talked about it. He planned to send for me when he could. I hoped I could get to him before the baby came. So far I had hidden everything, including Jackson's existence. My family would never understand about the pregnancy and would send me away to one of those homes for unwed girls. I couldn't talk to my sister. Married now for three years, she was consumed with homemaking and wanted a baby desperately. Her husband worked up the coast at the army base, but wasn't a soldier. He had a heart defect, unable to enlist, he was sullen and resentful. I knew my sister was secretly relieved and couldn't wait to have children.

So here I was, seventeen years old, pregnant and constantly afraid my secret would be discovered, afraid that Jackson would forget me, afraid that I would lose the baby or have the baby. I didn't know what to do.

But I wasn't the only one paranoid and afraid. After the Japanese attacked Pearl Harbor, Americans realized that we weren't safe from assault. Europe was the war front, the zone of terror where bombing raid sirens screamed in the blacked-out cities and people stayed hidden indoors. Neighbors were suspicious of each other and terrified some family secret or bloodline would bring the wrong kind of attention. Living in cities where rationed food turned friends into enemies, Americans knew we could be in that horrible situation any day.

The horrors of war were quickly infecting the United States. Distrust and anxiety ran in torrents, picking up the sediment of dying young men and tortured cultures. Flowing west across the gray Atlantic, wave after perpetual wave of horrific inhumanity washed onto our shores. The black-out curtains became mandatory a year ago, and the ration list of food and supplies increased each week as bad news sputtered out of government-controlled broadcasts.

Jackson's small air base had changed since he left. Security fences were put up and military watercraft patrolled the coastal waters. Rumors circulated about German submarine sightings. Fishermen and locals analyzed every questionable object. Invasion was talked about at every weekend fish market and the town was considering closing the market a few weeks early instead of waiting until Thanksgiving. Most fishermen were making plans to take their catch inland, but for small-time gatherers like me it was going to mean a big hit to our income. The one thing I needed almost as much as Jackson, was money.

After saying my prayers to the goddess, and invoking the elements for guidance, I erased my circle in the sand and bagged the bones for a proper burial later. I always felt guilty when I needed the sacrifice, but the powerful energy I was calling on, required it. Usually my prayers calmed me, but this ritual had not given me the peace I was seeking or the balance I needed.

I never brought Jackson to my clearing on my tiny island. It was about a hundred yards inland from the beach where I met him for the first time. The beach was where we spent our time, languishing in the surf, and making love in the sand. I was part of this land, just another island dweller rooted in the sand, breathing sea air. Since the clearing wasn't yielding much solace, I gathered my cotton shift and leather pouch and scrambled over the roots and through the branches to the shoreline. Well after midnight, the moon had moved behind the island so I sat in the damp sand watching the black water slink onshore. What little comfort I had invoked with the sacrifice dissipated with the outgoing tide. I felt I was losing myself, so many things unsettled, the complications were suffocating.

The water was taking tiny pieces of me with each surge of foam. I watched them float to the surface and drift east. I imagined Jackson calling to me from England, rescuing each piece of me, collecting and cherishing them, until I was whole again in his arms. Maybe we were married, cradling the proof of our love between us as we strolled through Paris. Such an exotic life we would have exploring Europe before we settled back on my beloved island.

The tears dripped from my face dissolving into the humid sea air before I could feel them on my skin.

CHAPTER TWENTY-THREE

Senior year
University of North Carolina

IN THE WEEKS FOLLOWING my quick exit from the beach, I stayed in my bedroom sleeping or taking walks through the woods. Being outside surrounded by nature made me feel better for a little while; when the pain became unbearable I went to sleep. I wasn't sure about anything in my life. I questioned my instincts and judgments and had no idea what to do about Penn and Emerson.

Penn was the woman in the dunes with Zeb. How could she have betrayed me? No wonder she was always criticizing him. She was jealous. She wanted him. We were both living in the sorority house this year. Thank god we weren't sharing a room. I didn't want to go back to school, but I couldn't explain any of this to my parents. At least at school I could avoid their questions and strained looks. My parents were already suspicious about my shortened summer schedule. I told them I didn't feel good and needed to rest before this major year in my life.

Returning to Carolina was difficult. I waited until the last minute, swinging in late the night before classes began. After class, I avoided dinner at the house, staying in the library working on an assignment. Avoidance and hiding wasn't going to work all semester, so at some point I would have to face Penn.

I was reading in the living room when she walked in. "Move over," she said, swatting at my feet with her book. "Where have you been and why didn't you call? We've been worried sick about you." I didn't know until this very minute how I would handle seeing her. I had agonized for days, never reaching a solution. She doesn't know I saw her sweatshirt in the dunes. Would she pretend everything was fine or would she be honest and plead for forgiveness? I decided right then I would wait for her confession, and in the meantime, distance myself by staying busy. I wasn't good at confrontation and I felt like I could pretend better than I could stand the tension and anxiety of a broken friendship.

"My grandmother was sick," I lied. "She's still in the hospital and I'm worried about her." That would account for the aura of sadness around me.

"What can I do?" Penn asked. "How about we get some frozen yogurt?"

"Maybe later, I really have to finish this." Penn said she understood, but I could tell she sensed something had changed. I knew her brain was analyzing the situation. Maybe she would think it was residual angst from our beach fights. She had some gall screwing Zeb and acting like nothing was wrong.

"Hey, Jade?" Penn stepped back in the room. "Did you find an extra sweatshirt in your stuff from the beach? I lost mine."

Jesus, I thought. You bitch. "No," I answered, my eyes glued to my book. I tried to read, but the lines blurred and letters scattered, floating on the page. I didn't know how long I could act like nothing was wrong. Four days later, done with classes for the first week, I sat with some sorority sisters in our dining room. We had eaten a late lunch and were discussing weekend plans and the Saturday afternoon football game.

Emerson came in, pulled an extra chair to our table and laid a shopping bag in front of her. She turned to ask me about a frat party, but before I could answer, Penn joined us. She slid the bag over to Penn. "This is for you." Penn removed a new Carolina blue sweatshirt with our Greek letters on it. It was identical to the one I saw in the sand dunes that night in August.

"I lost this," Penn exclaimed. "Where did you find it?"

"Actually, that's a new one," Emerson confessed. "I borrowed yours at the beach and misplaced it. I felt terrible but I planned to get you a new one before I told you."

What the hell? I was so confused and flustered. So, if Penn wasn't wearing the sweatshirt then she wasn't sleeping with Zeb. Damn, that meant it was Emerson. I couldn't get out of the room fast enough. My world was spinning and I couldn't hang on tight enough. Any minute I was going to slip the pull of gravity and hurdle into the black void of madness.

I ran to the bathroom. I was going to vomit. Beads of perspiration broke out around my forehead. I wet a cloth and closed myself in the last stall of our multi-person bathroom. Sitting on the floor against the wall, I put the cold compress under my hair on the back of my neck. I prayed the dizzying nausea would pass and my lunch would stay down.

Eventually, I drifted off to sleep. When I woke, my shirt was damp on the shoulder from the cloth and wet between my sweating cleavage. Feeling slightly better, I pushed to my feet and went to the sink to wash my face. The girl in the room beside mine came in and began to rummage through her toiletries.

"Hey, Jade, you got any tampons?" she asked.

"Sure. Help yourself." She fumbled through my things.

"Thanks anyway, but you don't have any. I took one from Penn. Don't tell."

Tampons, the word was frightening, foreboding. I searched frantically through my belongings, the intensity escalating. When had I needed them last? My knees buckled when I realized I hadn't needed any since I left the island. Oh shit, oh shit, oh shit. This was not happening. I was always careful, took birth control pills. I could not be pregnant. The nausea, the exhaustion, the food sensitivity, all the cogs were in the wheel and it was turning out of control. I couldn't stop the rotation. Seven weeks since a period, seven weeks that I had been too preoccupied to notice what was missing. I grabbed my keys and headed to the back parking lot for my car. I had to buy a pregnancy test.

Half an hour later, my fears were confirmed in a McDonald's restroom as I stared at the stick, wet and smelly with my hormonal urine. Now what? I was single, pregnant, and stupid. I wanted children eventually, but certainly not like this and not with that cheating redneck. I would be a college drop-out and my parents' greatest disappointment. I couldn't do this, I wasn't strong enough.

There's another way, I thought. If the pregnancy just disappeared, nothing would change. No one knew or needed to know and I was going to be totally alone with this. I couldn't confide in Penn, she would never let up about my mistakes with Zeb, and her righteous opinions would destroy me. Oh, damn, Emerson, she had sex with Zeb. Only weeks ago, I would have trusted them with everything, now I couldn't turn to them during the worst crisis of my life. With this desperate secret, I was alone. There was only me.

Two weeks later, I had the abortion on a Friday afternoon, booking a motel room for my recovery. I told Penn I was going home and fortunately I hadn't seen Emerson. She was busy with school and rumor was, she had a new man. I tried to move on with life but it was so hard.

Regular nightmares disrupted my sleep. In one, I stood on an island covered with flaming trees. Everywhere I ran was scorched or burning. A baby was crying, but I couldn't find it, like so many atrocious video games where I was lost in a maze looking for the golden coin, only that coin was a pulsating part of me.

In another dream, a gulf of water separated me from a small land mass that slithered and swarmed with snakes, asps, adders, mounds of them, hissing, and striking. Inside a small circle was a crying baby, snakes encircling it. Using a long thin pole, I was attempting to snag a small hook on the infant's sleeper to rescue it. The dreams were relentless, always a baby and always me attempting an absurd rescue. I never saved the baby and before long I hated going to sleep. I couldn't bear losing that baby in perpetuity night after night.

I prayed for grace. I prayed for forgiveness. I prayed to be released from this unholy hell I slept in. After a while, I stopped sleeping, staying up most nights, sitting in the den watching late-night crime dramas. I slept only when my body collapsed from exhaustion. The nightmares didn't come as often when I was depleted and deprived. Finally, they faded away, but only after the total destruction of my normal sleep pattern and losing part of my psyche. An abortion, I never imagined to have, just another incident that would change me forever.

Every few weeks, I was experiencing something that altered my path. I was supposed to be finding myself, but I felt like I was losing myself over and over. Maybe it was the same thing.

CHAPTER TWENTY-FOUR

Present
James Island

"AGNES, WAIT. AGNES." I ran through the undergrowth, my shirt snagging on a stray branch. Not slowing down, I heard fabric rip and give away as I plunged ahead, thorns grasping at my bare legs. The low branches of the live oaks blocked my view, but I knew she was there, just in front of me. "Agnes." Maybe I should let her go, I thought, but I couldn't stop now.

Curtains of Spanish moss concealed my way. There was something lurid and illicit about the parasitical plant. Like intrigue and rough sex, shadowing and soliciting, summoning, just enough that curiosity got the best of me. So much more to excite the imagination when the path was hidden by a drapery of camouflage, secrets beyond, roads unknown, luring, leading, offering somewhere other than where I was. The truth was, the place I was seeking might not be better, but I couldn't stop myself. Surrendering to impulse, I pushed aside the veil and hurried ahead. Agnes was the key. She could unlock my heart, teach me to love myself. I needed her.

The last forest growth gave way and I fell into the clearing, sand spraying out in front of my splayed hands. I knew she was there. I could see her, catching glimpses of the over-sized pink shirt, a man's dress shirt, as she darted through the trees, elusive and quick. I got to my feet and looked around. No Agnes. But sitting in front of a stone altar was a pink rabbit staring into the flames of a burning candle. In disbelief, I walked toward the rabbit. I had never seen one that color, but it was as pink as an outdated bridesmaid dress. With an outstretched hand, I was within a few feet when a heavy gust blew out the candle and the rabbit vanished. Before I could react, the air around me began a circular swirl, a tree cried out, cracking as it was uprooted. The rain spat from above, massive drops pelted the sand, tempestuous and provoked. I turned to run back, retreat to the beach, but the swaying branches were wild, groping me, probing. The trees skulked inward, gnarled knuckles flexing in aggression. Nowhere to go, I knelt at the altar and curled into myself, arms covering my head in fear. The ground underneath me trembled, like a great heaving beast lurching and tumbling. I closed my eyes and prayed to a heaven I rarely acknowledged, and begged for deliverance. The storm showered me, soaking me in rainwater as the dark clouds thundered with vengeance and lightning bolts hit the clearing, causing my hair to sizzle and pop, rising on my head in an electric surge.

Abruptly the rain stopped and was replaced by snakes, so many snakes. I screamed in terror as they thudded into the sand around me, hissing and slithering. Leaping to my feet, I vaulted from the clearing, dodging stinging brambles and slicing grass blades. Ragged breathing, my heart thrashing in my chest, I was overcome with terror. The snakes writhing after me, I screamed for help until my throat cracked, raw with dehydration and terror. Bursting through the last thicket, I hit the beach and skidded to a stop before the ocean waves. Except the ocean was gone and the island hung in nothingness. No above, no below, just emptiness, bleak and barren. The misery and sadness rushed through me like a frozen blade. "Agnes!" I screamed in madness.

I woke, thrashing in the sheets, the blanket tangled around my ankles. My hair was wet, the nightshirt plastered to my torso. I inhaled short, broken gasps of salty air. A dream, my god, not a dream, a nightmare, that reached inside me and pulled my demons through my pores, the snakes, the pink rabbit, the storm, all of it. I stripped off my nightshirt and lay back on the bed letting the air from the fan blades cool my body. Eventually, a chill swept over me and I pulled the blanket over my nakedness, trying to regulate my breathing and recall the details. What the hell did any of that mean? It was so real, I was afraid to look over the footboard at the floor for fear that intertwining snakes were convulsing under my bed. Rolling over, I pushed the hair from my face and tried to sleep. An hour later I gave up, showered and fixed some hot tea.

Taking my tea and a sweater I went to sit on the porch, the dawn just beginning to fracture the horizon. I expected Penn and Emerson later today. I needed to explain myself to them and confess my secrets. I also had to find the courage to confront Emerson about Zeb, the betrayal, and the secrets that festered between us. I had crammed it all into a tiny compartment of my subconscious after the abortion. I couldn't let the rot destroy me. Somewhere through the years, I let go of what happened that summer night. I had seen her only a handful of times since graduation and there had been so many other troubles in my life to focus on.

After these years, I had made my peace with Zeb. That relationship did give me courage and allowed me to feel liberated. It also gave me a reality check about myself. The girl I looked at in the mirror at the beginning of that summer wasn't the same woman I was forced to see by autumn. I was honest with the girls about Zeb. They knew I liked him even though he wasn't the great love of my life. He wasn't even that special of a person, and in the end he was just a guy along the way.

After each miscarriage, I thought of that tiny life I disposed of. I told myself it was just a cluster of cells, but I had come to understand it was my only chance for children. I brought it all on myself, thinking of that pregnancy as an inconvenience.

I refilled my tea mug and took the blanket from the sofa and returned to the deck hammock. After my tea was gone, I curled up in the fabric nest with a fuzzy blanket and drifted off to sleep.

Later, I opened my eyes to see Agnes sitting in a deck chair, staring out over the ocean. A picnic basket sat on the table. Maybe another dream, I thought. "Agnes?" I asked, waiting to see if she would transform into a pink rabbit or green llama or some other strange creature.

"You awake?" She glanced my way briefly then looked back out to sea.

"I don't know, am I?"

"Are you talking in your sleep?" she joked.

I sat up, realizing I was awake, and Agnes was sitting on my deck. "I'm just a little confused. I had a dream, nightmare really, and I'm, well, I don't know what I am."

"Tell me about the dream. Maybe I can help," she offered. Reluctantly, I explained how I was chasing her, then the pink rabbit, the storm and snakes. "What does all this mean? That my sanity is slipping?"

"Well, rabbits come into your life when it's time to pay attention. Like a messenger from the spirit world warning you to take time to observe, examine your path, and follow your instincts." I fixed us a cup of tea and she continued to analyze my dream. "The pink color represents unconditional love and understanding." I nodded as she talked. "Dreaming of thunderstorms means you are struggling with a catastrophic event or unexpressed fears and emotions. Now snakes, most people think they are about fear or evil, but that's just nonsense. Snakes mean transformation, and a group of them like you saw, means abundance. An abundance of energy you have yet to realize."

"So what does all this mean together?"

"Kind of seems obvious to me," she said. "But I'll explain it to you. You are struggling with your past, the guilt of your abortion, the grief of your miscarriages, how to rectify that with yourself. The universe and your subconscious are telling you, you cannot stay like this. You must make changes to yourself, and in your life, to survive. It's instinctual. Recognize your own power and use that energy to change."

I didn't know what to say to Agnes. Letting her interpretation sink into my psyche, I rocked myself with my foot, pushing against the deck rail. She never prompted me or spoke another word, just let me swing and think. After a while, I wiped the quiet tears from my face and spoke. "I really have to do this. I have to save myself for myself, because if anyone else does it, or I do this for anyone else, I'll never survive."

"Now you're getting it. This is about you, about you as a woman, not a mother, a wife, or a friend. Come on let's have the lunch I brought." Agnes opened her basket and laid two cloths on the picnic table. Then she took out two sandwiches cut in half diagonally. She laid one of each half on the cloths, followed by two mason jars of lemonade with fat, juicy blackberries floating in the pale liquid, a bag of Cheetos and some brownie cookie concoction with pecans on top. "I never eat lunch without Cheetos," she said. "All we need is some ice for the lemonade."

I went inside, filled a cereal bowl with ice cubes then sat down opposite her. "Homemade pimento cheese in one and crab salad in the other." I tasted the salad, flavors of sweet crab, creamy mayo and spicy herbs, savory, and a tad sweet from the shellfish. The combination was delectable. I could have eaten a pound of the mixture with soft slices of whole grain bread.

"My god," I exclaimed. "This is fantastic. Where can I get this?"

"Only from me, I make my crab salad for special people and it's a limited commodity." Agnes looked over the horizon while I took two more bites and put ice cubes in our jars. The tangy lemonade was tart and crisp with a hint of sweetness.

"I suppose you made the lemonade too," I said. She never moved, mesmerized by the waves. "Agnes?" Finally, she turned her face to the side and wiped what could have been a tear from her cheek. "Agnes?" I said again. "You okay?"

"Instead of sugar, I mix a bit of honey into it. I keep a few bee hives. I caught the crabs, grew the herbs, also the peppers in the pimento cheese. What did you think of the cheese?" At the moment, I was licking the creamy cheese spread off my fingers, the peppery essence not quite mild but delicious in the balance. I think I moaned.

"Put the Cheetos on the pimento cheese sandwich and smash down the bread, it's my favorite way to eat it."

"Agnes, this lunch is tremendous. Thanks so much for bringing it. I could eat this every day." She smiled her sheepish grin. I didn't think she was used to compliments. I had wondered before about her home life, a husband, children, grandchildren? She never mentioned anyone. "Where do you live?" She laid her sandwich down and took a swig from her jar before she answered me.

"Over yonder," she said. I didn't know where that was and she didn't offer directions or seem inclined to continue the discussion so we ate in silence until she unwrapped the cookies from the plastic wrap and laid two on my cloth. Not as thick as a brownie but softer than a cookie, the chocolate melted on my tongue. I tasted butter, honey and a slight saltiness from the roasted pecans.

"You make these too?" I asked.

"Well, I pick up the pecans in the fall and shell them during the winter months when I can't get out so much. I didn't churn the butter though," she said with a smile. She packed up her basket and talked of all the stuff on her agenda the rest of the day. It exhausted me and I was half her age.

Her white curls blew playfully in the wind as she disappeared behind the dunes. Feeling satiated and blissful from lunch, I realized that I felt almost cheerful. I had not experienced anything close to joy lately, and while it was odd it also felt right, like perfectly fitting jeans that needed a few more washings to reach the ideal softness and faded color. I wanted to talk to Ian, maybe even wanted to see him. I missed the happy times, the comfortable times when we hung out in the den watching football and eating popcorn.

I called our home phone to leave him an upbeat message and was startled when he answered. "Hello, Ian Montgomery."

"Ian? Hi, it's Jade. I didn't expect you to be at home."

"That sounds about right," he said.

"No, that's not what I meant. I'm just surprised you're home in the middle of the day. I was going to leave a message asking you to call tonight." I twirled my hair around my finger waiting for his reply.

"I've been working at home lately."

"Well, that's different," I sounded surprised. "Do you like it?"

"Actually, I get more done here. No commute, no hectic rushing to work. I like having more time. I fixed the bathroom mirror and reset the stones in the walkway over the weekend.

"That's great," I said. Neither of us spoke for a minute and then we both did at once.

"Why are you calling Jade?"

"I miss you." There, I said it out loud and I couldn't take it back.

"Are you coming home?"

"I don't know how to answer that question. I'm sure none of this makes sense to you but I think I've made some progress. I've been working out a lot of stuff in my head, coming to terms with my life and how to make it work." Pausing, I waited for a snide comment or an expression of anger, but he was quiet. Finally, after a few minutes of us breathing I spoke his name soft and tender. "Ian, I'm sorry I hurt you. There's a lot to explain, but I can't come home right now. You need to know it's not because of you but because of the house. It's too much for me right now."

"What's wrong with the house?"

"Memories. It reminds me of loss."

"Would it be okay if I came there sometime?" His voice was tentative, with a slight quiver. I had not expected that, offering to come to me. Now what? "Or not," he said.

"No, no, not no, yes, I think that would be nice, really nice," I said.

"I'll look at my schedule, maybe toward the end of the week. You think that would work?" he asked.

"Well, I'm not going anywhere," I tried to laugh at my joke but ended up choking and made a coughing sound. "Yes, I would love to see you."

"I miss you." His words melted into me, warming me from the inside out like the hot buttered rum we used to drink at the ski lodge. I hung up, elated at our progress. I hadn't expected to have a conversation and wasn't prepared. Maybe that's why it was successful. I didn't think, I just felt my feelings and reacted, opposite behavior for me. The idea of seeing him created tingling sensations low in my belly. I needed to pull myself together before then, I thought. And more immediately, I had to prepare for Penn and Emerson to return.

CHAPTER TWENTY-FIVE

1945
James Island

Agnes

AS I TIED MY roundabout to the tiny dock, I saw a man in an airman uniform walk down the path. "Jackson!" I screamed, trying to hold my awkward pregnant belly as I maneuvered the bank of the canal. My sense of balance was shaky. I know my strange gait looked unusual to people, but so far I had managed to keep the pregnancy a secret. My increased size wasn't very noticeable with the baggy shirts I wore. "Jackson!" I kept calling his name as we moved closer together.

When I saw it wasn't Jackson, something dark detonated in my chest. I knew it was bad. The soldier's expression was blank, that told me everything. "You're Agnes, right?" He spoke quietly, his eyes focused on mine. I could only nod. "I'm Chris, a friend of Jackson's. He wanted me to find you."

For an instant, I let myself think he had brought a message from Jackson. Maybe he was sending for me, maybe he was being sent home, or discharged. I let the fantasy run its course through my brain but the rest of me knew he was gone. "I'm so sorry to tell you this but Jackson's plane went down..." He kept talking, I think, but I didn't want to hear his words. If I didn't hear what he said, then it didn't happen. Maybe none of this happened and I was lying on the beach in Jackson's arms, my head resting on the place right below his shoulder next to his chest. His heartbeat echoed in my ear. This was just a nightmare I could still wake up from.

"...pieces of wreckage...nothing recoverable..." I sank to my knees, desperate to put my hands over my ears like a child, and sing while he spoke. Finally, he either finished or realized I wasn't processing his words so he bent down, patted me on my trembling back and handed me a large manila envelope.

It wasn't within the first few hours or even days that I processed Jackson's death. It's a war, I thought. Soldiers go missing, especially pilots. Then they're found. Jackson could be anywhere in Europe, crawling through a field, recuperating in a stranger's barn, a prisoner of war. He could still come back to me and our baby.

It had been a month since Chris came to see me. The weather had turned cold but I was lying on the beach anyway. Dressed in a baggy sweater to cover my swelling belly, I watched the stars emerge into the black, varnished sky like a handful of scattered glitter. Then I felt it, tiny flutters in my midsection, like the wings of a dragonfly. I imagined it iridescent, wings of purple and teal, sparks of emerald green with a crystal body. It was lovely and tragic. I would never share this miracle with Jackson. I realized my beautiful dream was over.

The blinding moment hit my stomach and exploded up my throat. I can't go back. I won't go forward without him. The knowing changed me at the darkest part of my core. That's when I knew it was forever. The awareness stopped my heart and I prayed for release from this torment. I wanted to die. I couldn't inhale one more shallow breath, exhale the ragged remains, and struggle for another. My shock hardened into glacial numbness that froze my blood and turned my heart frigid and brittle.

With Jackson gone, the pregnancy was a mystery to me. I didn't know how to keep going alone. Where would we live? How would I take care of us? Ultimately, I knew there was only one choice. Reluctantly, I would have to turn to the only people I knew, the people responsible for me. My parents.

At best, I was an afterthought to them. My sister, Priscilla was the real gem. She did everything right, high school graduate, junior college, married a stable man and owned a small house. Her only shortcoming, she had yet to produce an offspring and the tension was killing them all. Priscilla's life was about to change. I knew they would want her to take the baby. Her bundle of joy was coming in the near future, sometime in June to be exact. I didn't know why I thought they would help me raise it. It wasn't their baby to give away.

Nothing they could do to me would make me feel worse. After Jackson was lost, I was dead. I was trying to get through my everyday life without calling attention to me, but I felt nothing, not fear or love. I was a hollow shell surrounding the quivering life inside me that I was merely a vessel for; it would never be mine.

It was almost time for the birth. I was approaching eight months. My belly was round and hard, smaller than I imagined it would be, but the doctor told my mother that we were healthy. I couldn't bear to think of Jackson. I collected everything that reminded me of him and put it all in a small wooden box under my bed, a silver bracelet he gave me for my birthday with a tiny turtle charm, special shells we found on our explorations, a cloth napkin from the picnic when we gave ourselves to each other, a few letters I had received from Jackson before he disappeared, and the manila envelope Chris had given me that I was still unable to open. I'm sure there was a letter from Jackson. Reading his last words to me would break my heart.

It had been a month since I told my parents; so much had changed in my world, my miserable, unhappy world. The first thing my mother did was take me to a doctor out of town. They were completely ashamed of me. A few days ago, we went to my sister's house. She showed us the nursery. Her husband, Henry, had painted the walls pale mint green and trimmed the woodwork around the windows, door casings, and baseboards with crisp white paint. The room was decorated with yellow accents and prints from the Peter Rabbit series.

Priscilla had tiny undershirts in the drawers and baby socks to put over plump wriggling toes. A soft yellow duck lay in the crib and my grandmother's quilt was draped over her antique rocker. I had planned to rock my baby to sleep in that very chair with that quilt around us. I thought she was a girl. I talked to her that way. Nothing about this would ever be mine. She was supposed to be mine, mine and Jackson's. I made this baby with the love of my life. In the end, I would have nothing to love and no one would love me.

I didn't even go into the house when we got home. I took off walking toward my island. I sat on the beach and cried until I ran out of tears. After midnight, when the moon was high, I walked toward the mainland bridge. My parents' home was on the canal side of the mainland facing the island so I needed to cross the old iron bridge. Looking down into the black water, I saw visions of Jackson swirling in the dark and rabbits wearing tiny jackets, sitting in a vegetable garden. I saw giant blue whales that could swallow me whole, no pain, no more misery. The beautiful sleek whale would carry me and the baby across the Atlantic to Jackson. He was waiting for me on the rocky coast of Europe, arms ready to embrace me forever. He would take us home and sit by the fireside reading aloud from a book of Irish poetry, while I rocked our baby daughter.

If I jumped to the whale from the bridge, I might scare it. It would be better to slip into the water, slow and gentle, as it swallowed me. The water may have been cold, it was only April, but to me it felt mellow and intimate. It was like a down feather bed, submissive, yielding to my curves, the caressing embrace holding me with reverence. I waited for the whale. I would be precious cargo in her belly, just like the child I was carrying in mine. Jackson's child. "Hold on Jackson. Wait for me, I'm coming."

CHAPTER TWENTY-SIX

Present
James Island

PENN ARRIVED WITH THE back of her Mercedes station wagon filled with food, casseroles, salads, bags of fruit, and several cases of wine. How long was she staying? I wondered. Then she carried in a few containers that looked like tackle boxes and one giant suitcase. The most unusual aspect was her appearance. She was wearing faded blue jeans and a Carolina t-shirt that was vintage twenty-some years ago.

"Penelope," I exclaimed. "Where is your linen suit?" It came out of my mouth before I could stop myself.

"Bite me," she said, with a wink. I was catching a glimpse of the old Penn. "Em is on her way. She had a meeting at the aquarium but should be here within the hour." Penn opened a bottle of wine and carried two glasses to the deck. "Let's talk," she said.

"I called Ian." I wasn't planning to lead with that but he was on my mind.

"And…how did that go?"

"It was nice, little shaky at first, but we agreed to get together and talk. I told him I missed him."

"That's a great start." She leaned over to give me a quick hug. I refilled our glasses and watched three children play in the surf. The squeals of delight carried on the wind to wrap around us. I didn't feel the same horrible pangs of despair that used to overwhelm me. Now it was just wistful sadness; I could breathe through that.

"I have a lot to explain to him. I don't know if he's going to understand, but I have to be brutally honest if we have a prayer of staying together."

"Your suicide attempt?"

"I will tell him but I need to do it in person. Looking in his eyes will tell me what he's thinking, since he doesn't talk much, it's essential to glean all I can." I turned my chair to face her. "I need to talk to you about something before Em arrives. It's about our last summer here, before senior year."

"Oh, Jade, let's not do this. We were dealing with a lot of shit and none of us handled life very well then."

"I know, but trust me, there's a reason I have to do this. We have to talk about Zeb." Her chair skidded as she jumped out of it.

"Jesus, Zeb? Not this. We do not need to go there." She poured both of us another drink, took a huge sip, and topped hers off again before walking to the deck rail. "I'm sorry I acted like I did then. Time was moving so fast and I didn't know how to handle it."

"That's not why I'm bringing this up. Our attitudes and behaviors that summer were all about growing pains. I'm talking about something different. What do you know about Zeb and Emerson?"

"Zeb and Emerson? There was no Zeb and Emerson." Penn ruffled her brow, as she so often does when wary. "What are you implying?"

I explained my last night at the beach. "After our fight, I walked to the end of the island to cool down. Returning to the empty cottage, I cleaned up and left again, looking for Zeb. Stopping by our sand dune, I saw him, with another woman."

"Damn Jade! What did you do? Why didn't you tell us?" Penn turned her wine glass over as she shifted in her seat. "Goddamnit, I love this shirt." Heading inside for a towel, she told me she would hurry. "I've got to hear everything."

Replaying that night in my head was torturous, all the flashbacks, the naked skin, the betrayal, the blood, but I could finally think of it without feeling sick to my stomach. Penn let the door slam on her way out. "Okay, now, back to it, tell me all about it. What did you do?"

"Nothing good, actually I freaked out and scared myself. The girl ran off and he and I fought. Then I hit him in the head with a piece of driftwood."

"Holy shit!" Penn exclaimed. She had changed into a different shirt. Another vintage Tarheel t-shirt, this one with paint stains on it. What prompted her to wear that shirt? "Did you hurt him? Who was the bitch?" she asked.

"Yeah, I hurt him. He slumped in the sand, bleeding, and I left him there. If I had not run away, I don't know whether I would have helped him or killed him. I was out of my mind. As far as the girl is concerned, that's the big problem. At the time, I thought it was you."

"Me? What the hell? I despised him. Couldn't you get that from my asinine behavior that summer? Why would you ever think I could do that to you?" Her face said everything she just said aloud. I was sorry I had made her feel so bad.

"It was your sweatshirt, the blue one with silver Greek letters. I tripped over it in the sand. So, I thought you were the bitch. That's why I left. I couldn't face any of you or stay on this island one more second."

Penn sat staring at me for a few minutes. I could see visuals from the last days playing behind her eyes. "I lost that sweatshirt or I thought I did. It turns out Em borrowed..." Her voice trailed off and she was quiet. She closed her eyes, resting her head against the chair back. We sat that way for a little while until Penn went inside. She returned with a bottle of bourbon and three shot glasses.

"Emerson should be here soon."

Emerson blew in, a hurricane of bronze skin, healthy blonde hair, and perfect-fitting white jeans paired with a sleeveless turquoise blouse. Her firm arms carried bags of food.

"There's wine in the car," she called out, as she unpacked tubs of ice cream, bags of barbecue Fritos, Cheetos, and a case of Diet Cokes. Emerson was to junk food what Penn was to healthy. "I have Krispy Kreme doughnuts."

The delectable puffs of fried dough are a southern staple, especially at the beach. When their *Hot Doughnuts* sign flashes neon red, customers line up for the fresh ones. Looking beyond the service counter you could see the conveyer belt system carry the pastries forward through the curtain of hot vanilla glaze. Chocolate iced, jam filled, custard and cream, all variations of sprinkled rings, but far and away the most popular was the simple glazed ones hot off the belt. They melted on the tongue and a person would fight a demon from hell for the last one in the box.

"You two started drinking without me," she said. "I can tell by your eyes. Penn, what the hell are you wearing? All your clothes at the cleaners? Excuse me. Penelope."

"Call me Penn."

Emerson and I looked at her, standing barefoot in her faded jeans and t-shirt, her hair in a loose pony tail with sprigs and curls escaping around her face. She looked like Penn, our Penn, but tired, I noticed. Not so much expensive make-up today covering up the fatigue and tiny wrinkles. "Is that an easel by the back door?" Emerson asked.

"It's mine," Penn said. "I thought I would paint a little while I was here. I never get to at home."

That would be fantastic, I told her. "We might unearth you yet."

Dinner was fresh tuna steak salad made by Penn and chips and onion dip with doughnuts for dessert provided by Emerson. For me it was a happy combination, a few moments of pleasure before I had to disrupt the peace. The sun was passing behind the canal. Fiery orange exploded behind the outlines of the graying clouds as the sun set behind them. It looked like someone had set fire to blue cotton candy and it was melting around the edges. I grabbed the second bottle of bourbon and headed outside. The first one was almost gone from Penn and I earlier, and we were going to need more.

I poured three shots. Over dinner, I had updated Emerson about my emotional progress and relayed my conversation with Ian. "I'm so proud of how far you've come," she said, pulling our chairs circular to face each other. "You already look much better than you did two weeks ago." We finished the first shot and I poured a second round. "Are we celebrating?" she asked.

"Emerson, I have to talk about something serious." I took a deep breath. "I've told y'all about my series of miscarriages, and the emotional wreck I became over those years. I finally hit rock bottom last month when I tried to kill myself, but there's more to my story. It begins our last summer here before senior year."

"Oh, let's leave all that stuff alone," Emerson said. "We were all losing it and taking it out on each other."

"Yeah, we were, but I can't leave some of this alone, not if I'm going to recover my life. There are things I cannot get past until they are resolved, and part of that concerns you," I said to her. She was staring at me, eyes wide. "I made decisions that affected my life then, and now, that summer. I made choices I felt were my only solution. Now, I take full responsibility for them. I don't blame anyone, but myself, but I have to get this out and rid myself of the toxins."

Emerson looked at Penn, raised one eyebrow, kicked her sandals off, and poured a third round of bourbon.

"We should buy bourbon by the gallons," she said.

"I know y'all remember Zeb," I said.

"Zeb. God, that's a name from the past. That sexy summer fling of yours. You were crazy for him," she said.

"Yeah, I was. It was a time of big changes for me. For the first time I felt liberated. Making my own choices and doing what I damn well pleased, it was fantastic, until it all crashed on top of me that last night I was here."

"We hated you had to leave so abruptly," Emerson said. "You never did explain that to us. Who was sick?" I just waved my hand as if her questions were unimportant.

"No one was sick, but I had to make an excuse. I could not stay here a minute longer. I was too hurt." I was giving Emerson a chance to say something about the betrayal, but so far she was dancing around the issue.

"Who hurt you? I know you and Penn were throwing boulders at each other. I told you that y'all were crossing lines." I sat for a minute looking out over the ocean, nursing my bourbon. Leaning forward, elbows resting on my legs, I spoke directly to Emerson.

"Emerson, I know." She was quiet, just looking at me. She wasn't going to make this easy. "I know about the two of you. I found out that night." Penn was sitting back, one leg folded in front of her trying not to speak, something really hard for her. I watched her open her mouth, then close it, twice.

"Who? Two of who?" Emerson seemed genuinely confused. Was she going to feign denial. The last chance for our friendship hinged on the next thing she said to me. I had to find resolution from the abortion before I could heal myself. It all started with that.

"I'm over the betrayal. We were all young once, but please be honest with me now. You and Zeb." Emerson just sat there, staring openmouthed, like I had slapped her. "Are you really going to sit there with that blank look? Pretend nothing happened? I know we were young and stupid, but it's been twenty-one years and we're grown women. Can't you be honest with me now?"

"Me and Zeb? There was no me and Zeb!" Emerson pushed her chair back and stalked to the rail. Whirling around, she spoke loudly. "I would never do that to you…how could you say that?" I knew I was right. I had proof. I came to my feet in a retaliatory stance.

"The night I had the horrible fight with Penn, I left and walked to the south end of the island. After I cooled off, I came home but no one was here, so I went looking for Zeb. I climbed over our dune and saw you with him. Naked in the sand." I was agitated and my voice was escalating with blame.

"I was never naked with Zeb! What the hell is wrong with you?" She took a step toward me. "How much have you had to drink? I don't even know what you're talking about." She looked at Penn, "What is this about? Do you know? Besides, I sure as hell didn't need Zeb. I'm pissed you think I would do that to you."

"I found the sweatshirt. Remember the one you borrowed from Penn, the Carolina blue one with silver letters. It was beside his pile of clothes between the dunes. I thought then that it was Penn, until you replaced her shirt at school and apologized for losing it. I knew then it was you."

Emerson jerked her chair back around and sat down, poured another round, drank it quickly then turned to me, her pretty face furrowed and earnest. "Well, it wasn't me. I was wearing the sweatshirt when I left. I got hot and tied it around my waist. I stopped at your dune and found Zeb sitting in the sand drinking beer. Remember, he called and cancelled on you. I told him that if he was screwing around on you, I would cut it off. He offered me a beer and asked me to sit down. I drank the beer and we talked about you for a little while. He knew it would be ending soon. I told him I didn't think you were expecting anything from him, that he was just a summer beach fling. Then I left. I must have left the shirt there. I thought I lost it later at a beach party.

My eyes filled with water and I went back to that night at the dunes. I never gave him a chance to explain who and why. But there's not much explanation needed for naked. Then I thought of Emerson and Penn. If I had just calmed down and talked to them, so much would have been different.

"Jade, I was going to tell you all about it the next day, but you were gone. When we got back to school, you never mentioned him, so I let it go."

The tears spilled over my eyes and ran down my cheeks. I drank another shot and poured another. Penn laid her hand over mine and asked. "What happened to you? Did he hurt you? I know you found him with someone else, but I didn't think he meant so much to you that you're this emotional decades later."

"Emerson, I'm so sorry. I've carried this around for so long. And yes Penn, he hurt me, but not the way you think," I said. "I made some horrible judgments then and made a choice that still haunts me." I reached for Emerson's hand and continued holding Penn's. "I doubted this," I said, squeezing their hands. "I thought you had betrayed me, Em, you with Zeb and Penn you by not supporting me. Everything I did after that night was decided because I thought I was alone."

"What aren't you saying?" Penn asked.

I took a really deep breath, knowing I had to confess my darkest secret to them. "When we got back to school, I discovered I was pregnant."

CHAPTER TWENTY-SEVEN

1945
James Island

Agnes

HANDS WERE PULLING ME, large hands, strong and warm.

"Jackson," I mumbled. "Jackson, I'm here."

"Hush baby. You gonna be alright now." My eyes weren't open but kaleidoscope colors flashed under my lids, scattering as I breathed. I felt like I was sinking into softness. It was warm and comforting, like I was floating in a bowl of chicken soup. My stomach gurgled and lurched, a belly roll of great proportion. I was hungry. I placed my hands on my abdomen to hold it still and felt a tiny protrusion tickle my palm, an alarming action, startling and scary. What was wrong with me? Something was inside of me.

"Child, you awake?" I heard her voice, smooth and silken like buttercream icing. My eyes were stuck, my mouth was stale, and words wouldn't come from my throat. Nodding my head in response made the room eddy and spin, dipping and churning, I tumbled into a vortex of pain that tormented my body. Maybe this whirlpool would wash me clean. The hands from before pulled me to prop against the bed frame, then they gently washed the matted crust from my eyes with a warm cloth. Opening them, I saw her wringing the cloth out in a china basin on the bedside table. She washed my face and put the cloth under my hair on the back of my neck.

"You took quite a swim last night," she chuckled. "It's a good thing I was gathering mussels or you might've been washed out to sea." I knew this woman from the market and had seen her collecting berries and flowers in the woods. She always pulled a red wagon behind her, wearing a large brimmed straw hat with feathers on the sides. She was as black as a raven and looked at me with a kind, wide grin. Her hair was wrapped in a brightly colored cloth, her dress large and baggy.

"Your babe is alright." My baby. The panic hit me between the eyes, matching the rhythm already pounding in my temples. It all came back to me in a frantic rush, the despair, the fear, all the horror of my life. I last remembered being on the bridge watching a blue whale. I wanted to touch it as I made my way down the bank and waded into the swells. She was going to take me to Jackson. Jackson. Jackson was dead.

"Jackson's dead," I said aloud.

"Jackson that baby's daddy?"

"Yeah, but he's gone." I started to cry, not weeping, but sobbing. The kind that starts with the last beat of your heart and rises, boiling and frothing until the anguish overflows.

"I'm Maggie." She said to me as she held me. My life washed from me in torrents. I don't know if it was cleansing me or consuming me, but when it ended, I could hold my head up and look into her eyes. Teeming with compassion, they were the color of black coffee swirled with a bit of sweet cream.

"It's gonna be okay," she said. "I got you. You get it all out and then we'll eat a bite. I sent word round to your mama that you were here. They had called the sheriff when you didn't come home. I said after a rest, we'd be on over. I've got tea brewing and some cornbread just out of the oven. I'll open a jar of jam, blueberry or blackberry?"

"Blackberry."

"Just stay here," Maggie said, as I started to get up. "You need some bed rest. I'll bring it." I watched her move around the room. The bed I was placed in early this morning was in the corner. The rest of the space contained a corner kitchen, a small table, a couch and chair facing a window open to the canal. Her granddaddy owned the house before her, she said proudly. "He was born after the Civil War to new freed slaves. This little house and patch of land is the legacy of my family's worth. Now it's mine."

"It's lovely," I said. There were fresh flowers on every flat surface, bundles of herbs hung from the rafters near the kitchen. It smelled like mild, sweet onions and mint with a breath of floral scent. She popped the lid on the jam and tangy blackberries mingled into the collection of aromas. The heat of the oven warmed the room. I noticed a door ajar, to the side, her bathroom, I guessed. She noticed me looking and said to go use it if I needed. The church men had built it for her last year, she added.

"No more outhouses for me," she laughed. "If you're feeling steady enough, come on over to the table and sit with me. The cornbread's steaming and that butter and jam is gonna drip down your fingers." Maggie smacked her wide mouth and smiled. It was a dazzling face and I felt better by just being near her. She was right about the bread and jam. It was delicious and I realized I was starving.

"I made us a fried apple pie. I dry apples every fall. They keep a good long time that way," she explained. "I make up a little pie-crust and then here's my secret. I soak the apples in some brandy to plump them up. Mix in some cinnamon and sugar, some butter and a pinch of black pepper and then stuff it all in a fold of crust. Then fry it in my skillet." The filling of the crust was hot and a bit spicy. Maggie poured a little honey over hers and handed the jar to me. The golden syrup caught the light coming through the window and illuminated the hexagonal maze of saturated honeycomb. I loved chewing pieces of it. The chewy comb gave way with bursts of sweet nectar.

"This is good," I said. "All of a sudden I'm very hungry."

"The babe is hungry. How far are you, bout six months along?"

"About seven, but we're a little bit small. I saw a doctor a month ago or so, they said we were fine. She's just a little ball of fire," I said, rubbing my belly. She kicked my hands in response.

"A girl huh? That's probably right. You're carrying high. What happen to your man?"

"He's a pilot in the army, or was. They told me a while back that his plane was shot down over Europe. We met last spring. He was at the airbase at the end of the island. We fell in love."

I needed her to know how much I loved him. My parents didn't want to hear anything about Jackson, told me never to speak of him again, I told her. "He was a good man, wanted to marry me, he said, and that was before the baby. We had planned for me to go to Europe to meet him." I picked at the last bites of my pie, twirling the filling around on my fork.

"I don't know if he knew about the baby. I wrote him letters, but I don't know if he ever got any of them. I think he would have been happy about her."

"I'm sure he would have, child," Maggie said. She leaned over and put her large hand over mine. "So what you gonna do?"

"I guess I'm going to do what I'm told. Mama is giving my baby to my sister and her husband. They haven't had any children, and mama said I was too young to raise a baby. She said I would never have a future," I said. "But it seems to me that the baby was my future."

Maggie walked with me most of the way home. I told the family I slipped and fell into the canal. After a week of bed rest, I started spending a lot of time with Maggie. She was the only friend I had, besides Jackson. I wasn't going to school anymore. Mama didn't want anyone to know about my baby, so I was free to wander the island now with Maggie. She showed me how to gather herbs and dry them. We picked berries and planted her spring garden.

Her stories of the spirit world intrigued me and seemed similar to tales my granny told me when I was little. Instead of God, she believed that the Holy Spirit was the God and the Goddess united. The Tidewater Baptist Church would think about burning her at the stake, I thought. The Pentecostal one would build the bonfire. Maggie had odd beliefs about religion, but stirring them up with granny's ideas, they started making sense to me the more she explained. Before the Christian church, people worshipped the earth and the Great Spirit that created it. Fire, water, earth, and air made up the four directions of the world, she said. Sometimes, she prayed to them and lit candles to honor them.

"Where did you learn all this," I asked her one day. "From my granny, she was a wise woman, a healer. Folks came all the time to ask her about stuff and get the mixtures and medicines she made."

I knew about the goddess and the full moon but Maggie knew and understood so much more than me. She taught me why she believed and how this had changed her life for the better. She explained about the power of the moon and how she has three faces. I knew the moon and women had a powerful connection but there was so much more to this beautiful belief.

Maggie taught me how to pray to the Goddess and how to perform rituals. She prayed to her at different times of the year, about her plants, her home, health, and all kinds of things. I was never one for religion and church, stuffy and uncomfortable, with men in charge. Except for singing, it seemed the only thing women did was cook for everyone. Like Maggie says, mother earth gives birth to all things through the goddess. I liked that. It made me feel special because I was a woman. Energy was like faith. It was in every one of us, she said. "It's what guides us to make changes in our life and do good things for the world."

We talked to the goddess together about blessing me and the baby and guiding me through this hard time. Maggie explained that when powerful blessings were needed, prayers weren't enough, rituals were needed too. Those involved lighting candles of specific colors and collecting objects that related to what powers were needed. She had a collection of these rituals written in a book with a leather cover. She let me read it when I came to see her.

I told her about the bones and the spell my granny showed me long time ago for protection. "Do you understand what you were doing?" she asked. "Cause spells and prayers are serious business. People that don't know what they're doing can cause problems. This is strong work." She promised to help me. After that, we spent more and more time together.

"There's balance to all life," Maggie said one day when we were out by the water below her house. "There's light and dark, good and evil, we carry both within us. It's the choices we make and the actions we take that separate grace and wickedness." She spread her broad apron over her legs and leaned toward me. "No one's only virtuous. There's sin in all of us."

CHAPTER TWENTY-EIGHT

Present
James Island

"CHRIST JADE!" PENN EXCLAIMED. "Pregnant?"

Emerson was quiet for a moment then gave me a hug. When she sat back there were tears in her eyes. "You couldn't count on us," she said. "I'm so sorry." Now I was crying.

"This is not about you not being there for me," I said, wiping tears from her face. "I made my choice and I've had to live with it. Almost died because of it."

"I knew something was wrong, but I was so consumed with my own life," Penn said.

"Em, I'm relieved that you weren't with Zeb. But truthfully, I think I made the best decision for that girl then, it's just the grown woman in me who has to rectify what I did. I never knew that was my only chance to be a mom." With those last words, I let my tears flow. Unashamed and unreserved, I sat in my chair letting the ocean breeze dry them, salty and stiff on my skin.

"So when did you know? Was it when you left the beach or later?" Penn asked.

"I left the beach because of Zeb and the girl whom I believed to be Penn," I explained. "It wasn't until I got back to school that I realized about the pregnancy. By then I thought it was Emerson. Everything was so strained between all of us the last weeks of summer, then Zeb and that girl."

"Penn you hated him. You always warned me to stay away and I couldn't bear having you tell me how right you were. It wasn't about either one of you, I knew I couldn't have it, but my decision was based on emotions. I never had a logical, intellectual conversation with anyone including myself."

"We were lost in our lives then," Emerson said. But we should have been better."

"Penn was getting ready for her art show and everything after that was a chain reaction. I didn't get to Penn's show because I had the abortion that weekend. Then I was a complete wreck. I really felt alone after that, so I withdrew even more. Y'all probably sensed me pulling away and you did the same."

"I was so angry and let down when you didn't come to my exhibit," Penn said. "Of course, I wasn't thinking beyond myself."

"That's the point I'm making. We made the choices we did as young women, barely more than girls. What did we know of the future? To us, the future was the next weekend. I've forgiven both of you. It wasn't your problem to solve."

I went inside, grabbed a few throws off the sofa. I kept one for myself and tossed the other one to them to share. "I've met this older woman here named Agnes. She's like a fairy, a sprite with cotton top curls. She has helped me with my perspective."

"Why do you get that one?" Emerson asked, trying to lighten the tone.

"Because I went and got them," I said. "Here, I'll pour you another shot to keep you warm." I wanted to tell them more about Agnes, but I thought it best to wait a while. I had been forced to review so much of my history lately, it was making it easier to talk about though. My past was no longer the demonic force clutching my heart in its wicked grip. It had been downgraded to the slightly, frightening monster under the bed.

My eyes were puffy the next morning. I wondered what Penn was going to force us to eat for breakfast. She seemed a little different thank goodness. Her clothes were definitely not her style of late, more reminiscent of our college days. Maybe we were getting to her. I hoped so. I really missed her. I pulled a wrap on around my long tee-shirt and headed toward the kitchen. The coffee pot was on but there were no tofu granola bars or cottage cheese parfaits. After grabbing a Diet Coke from the fridge, I walked to the door. The beach in the morning was great. Black skimmers, shore birds with bright orange legs and beaks, were flying inches above the water searching for food. They had white fluff around their head and belly, but the rest was black. They made a sleek profile skimming above the waves.

I could watch children play in the sand now. Several weeks ago that made me nauseous. Talking to Ian helped me more than I realized. I felt like he was my secret. He was the delectable, private treat I was eager to savor in the quiet moments before I fell asleep. I hoped I wasn't getting ahead of myself. There were some harsh and bitter days between us. I had shut down, repressed all my feelings, ultimately, I bankrupted our relationship.

I thought we still had a chance though, I could hear it in his voice. He still loved me but could he live with me? Was I enough for him anymore? There were still secrets I had to tell him, but I could only do it face to face.

I picked up a chocolate-iced, crème filled doughnut, my favorite deadly combination of fat and sugar, and stepped onto the porch. Surprised, I found Penn there, easel facing the beach, a tackle box open, and paint tubes of every color scattered on the table. Penn, the absentminded artist, was studying her canvas, a paintbrush in one hand and two stuck in her hair. "Where's Penelope?" I asked. She whirled around, deep in concentration. She had been oblivious to my approach.

"What do you mean?" she questioned.

"It's just nice to see you painting in casual clothes, not making us eat pretend food like that hellish bacon."

"It wasn't that bad." She added two shades of blue to her palette and a touch of yellow, leaving a streak of color on her chin as she swatted a gnat.

"Yes it was," Emerson confirmed, joining us. She popped the top of her soda can and pulled a chair close enough to the rail so she could rest her tanned, perfectly-proportioned legs. "How are you this morning, Jade?" She ruffled my hair as she passed by me. "I had a hard time sleeping last night. All I could think of was you alone and pregnant, God, I let you down. We were all too young to make those adult decisions then."

I wanted to ask her what she was referring to, what decisions had she made. The tone in her voice insinuated there was more to the story than just my issues. Her senior year was peculiar. So distant the fall semester, then she left abruptly after Christmas break for an internship. She didn't tell anyone she was leaving, just didn't come back in January. She sent us a letter explaining the opportunity to go aboard a research ship in the Caribbean.

Penn continued painting most of the morning and I pretended to read a beach novel I took from the den shelf. At least it provided my cover, they were hesitant to disturb me and I didn't have to talk anymore. Eventually, the boredom overwhelmed Emerson and she took a walk heading south along the beach.

CHAPTER TWENTY-NINE

1945
James Island

Agnes

MAGGIE WAS RIGHT. I was feeling wicked. I didn't want anyone to have my baby, not my sister, nor my mother. She belonged to me and Jackson. Without him, she was the only living, breathing remains of my beautiful man. Who were they to take her from me?

Priscilla and Henry came to lunch Sunday. I was told to be there, dressed appropriately. After lunch, my sister announced she had told all her friends about the adoption and they were giving her a baby shower in two weeks. She and mama spent the rest of the afternoon discussing who to invite and what they might get for presents. I told her my baby was going to be a girl. It was not going to be my baby much longer, Priscilla reminded me. I wasn't invited to the party either.

"You're pregnant," she said. "People can't see you like that. We haven't told anyone about you or where the baby is coming from. It's just a private adoption as far as our friends are concerned. My baby will not be part of some sordid family scandal." Her words cut through my skin, piercing my heart.

"Maybe I'll just keep her, raise her myself," I said to the table of stunned faces.

"You don't have any money, a place to live and most important you don't have a husband," Priscilla said. My parents echoed her summation.

"Jackson said he was going to marry me and that wasn't because of the baby. That was because we loved each other and wanted to be together."

"And that's worked out for you, huh? He left you here and ran off, abandoning you both," she said. "You believed him and see what happened. You can't be trusted with a baby."

"I believed him because it was true. He never abandoned us either. He was a pilot. He had to go fight in Europe. He was going to send for me and we were going to live in Paris as a family." We were shouting across the dinner table at each other.

"You're so stupid Agnes. Paris has been blown apart by German bombs. You're not going there. Besides he's dead." Priscilla was so cruel. Couldn't she see my agony and how much I loved Jackson? I carried the proof with me cradled in my body. She didn't care how much she hurt me. She never cared about me or bothered to understand me. I was five years younger and we were never friends. We were never anything to each other. I was just a nuisance that kept her from being a spoiled only child.

After the fight, I was forced to sit in the formal living room in my uncomfortable, binding dress while they planned my baby's future. It pulled across my stomach and breasts. I only had two good maternity dresses and they were both smaller than me. I started to cry. I tried to hold the tears back, push the sadness and heartache into that deranged pit where my heart used to be. It was a cavity turbulent with loneliness and grief, the mixture of emotions taunted and terrorized me, my vulnerability, anger, and betrayal. My sorrow shrouded me like a death veil.

"Jackson could be lost, surviving somewhere, a prisoner of war, trying to get back to me. We can live in the fishing cabin out by the canal."

As my sister and I got louder, my father interrupted, putting an end to our argument. "Agnes, he's gone and he's not coming back," he said. I was told not to discuss Jackson ever again. The arrangement has been settled, he added. He had spoken with the base commander who confirmed Jackson's death. "Your sister and Henry will do a fine job raising the baby. This discussion is over," he concluded.

I excused myself, changed my dress to the baggy everyday one, and left to find Maggie. Let Priscilla have her party, collect diapers and crocheted booties, bottles and blankets. I was done with them. I had a plan and Maggie agreed. Friday was a full moon. It was time to seek the Goddess. This was the time to work powerful magic. Full moons inspire a flow of emotions, bring positive energy and clear out the negative. It was a time to begin. Like me, the moon was pregnant with potent energy. Representing the divine Goddess in the motherhood phase of womanhood, the full moon symbolized the feminine connection. I was the Goddess and she dwelled in me.

Awareness, Maggie had told me. Awareness is everything. The full light of the moon illuminates our awareness, revealing ignorance and guilt, as well as clarity and grace. The full moon in June was called the Strawberry Moon to mark the beginning of berry season. The strawberries were ripening, and so was I. It was time to invoke a blessing, beseech the Goddess to honor my request, and forgive my actions.

I waited for the house to quiet late Friday night then tiptoed down the stairs. The third step creaked and so did the seventh. If I timed it with the chimes of the grandfather clock, I shouldn't be discovered. It was easier when my body wasn't lopsided, off balance, with more weight in front. I had to use the railings more than I liked when sneaking out but I didn't forget my bag. I had so much trouble remembering things lately.

Crossing the bridge, I reached the island but I didn't stop to look at the dark water tonight. That wasn't the right way for this to end. Walking around our island along the shore, I made my way to the secluded side where the ocean waves broke in swirls of sterling across my bare feet. The moon was expectant, fertile with spirit and strength. I would need her to share her abundance with me tonight. Foamy, salty droplets sprayed over my nakedness. A few more steps, the breakers behind me, the ocean took me in, kneading my aching muscles and lifting my anxiety. I stretched out on the water, my worry and fear drifting out with the current.

Cleanse me, restore me, and forgive me, I asked of the water. My tender breasts and round abdomen rose above the surface of the swells. I touched them with my slender hands. I was soft around the edges, barely recognizable. It wasn't going to be long. The delivery was imminent, judging from the ripeness of my body. This was the cycle of life, creation would never be denied. It was the force of nature, the energy of the Universe. I was carrying the greatest offering I could make to mother earth. I wasn't just in nature, I was nature itself. To all things there is a balance, in life there is also death.

It was a sinister world I was living in, a grim place for a new life, uncertainty and fear, war and tragedy. I could feel the earth weaken, drowning in the blood of boys too young for the brutality of combat. The air was thin and suffocating from intolerance and fanaticism. Even if the world survived, it would never be the same. Residents on the island were required to use blackout curtains. If I believed the gossip, German subs lurked off the coast. It sickened me to think of our waters being infected with bigotry and hate. I was afraid it was true; I had to trust my instincts. Awareness is everything. I could feel the heinous darkness seeping like used oil around me, permeating and sticky, constipating the balance of the natural world and mine. I was losing my footing and falling into a world I didn't recognize.

As I walked from the ocean, my skin dripped, shedding water droplets while I pushed through the deep sand and beach grass. I crested the ridge and picked up my pouch. Heading into the forest, the blackness pressed in on every part of me. I felt its weight thrust against my legs slowing my stride. It was heavy and dragging, desperate to keep me from going forward with my plan. But I was not afraid. I was the darkness. I was the light. This was my refuge, my sanctuary from humanity. This clearing was my holy place.

Naked and smooth as a baby, I knelt before the stone altar and laid the contents of my bag on the sleek stone. I sprinkled sea salt around my space and took a birch wand, slender and strong, and drew a circle in the sand with my altar in the center. Beginning by facing east, I called the first of four elements, air for intellect, communication, and decision-making. I must be sure I was doing the right thing here tonight. Turning to the south, I called fire, for strength and passion to give me the will and focus to follow through with my actions. I turned west and called for water to bring balance to my emotions, to find trust, and harmony. Finally I faced north and knelt before the altar. I asked mother earth, the manifest body, for nurturing stability.

The moon slid through the branches and radiated white heat around me. I inhaled and exhaled, taking in the joy, blowing out the misery, fighting my body for control. I slowed my heartbeat and asked the Goddess to cradle me with gentle hands. The small dagger was shrewd and sharp, cold to the touch. Lifting it straight above my heart, I closed my eyes and took one last, deep, cleansing breath.

It was time to draw down the moon.

PART III

CHAPTER THIRTY

Present

James Island

EMERSON OFFERED TO MAKE lunch while Penn cleaned her brushes. "Doughnuts and Cheetos?" I joked.

"I'm capable of more than that," she countered. "I'll add some Hershey's kisses." I sat on the deck watching the sun dip in and out of the slight cloud cover, like someone shading me with a giant umbrella at irregular intervals. Penn washed up but missed a smudge of lavender paint on her forehead.

"It's so good to see you like this," I said, reaching to wipe off the paint. "You said you didn't paint at home, why not?"

"I stay so busy with the kids and taking care of Brian."

"Who's taking care of you?"

Penn was quiet for a minute, pretending to be busy cleaning her palette. "I'm fine. I'm good with my life. I do what needs to be done and that's a win for me."

"Who are you trying to convince, me or you?" I asked.

"I'm going to help Emerson with lunch." Penn left the porch, but I knew I had annoyed her. Her life might be pretend-perfect, but Penn wasn't happy. She was not a woman to be content behind the scenes. It would catch up with her and it would hit hard when she realized the returns from her sacrifice.

Penn and Emerson returned with lunch. Crab salad on a bed of soft, buttery, bibb lettuce, a tray of pickled dill carrots and cucumbers, some fresh berries, and Hershey's kisses for garnish. The salad was delicate, sweet and creamy and the vegetables, crunchy and tangy. "Where did you learn to make this salad?" I asked.

"It's my grandmother's recipe," Emerson said. She rarely mentioned her childhood. She was raised by her grandparents after her mother took off. She left Emerson the first time when she was a toddler, but came in and out of her life until her early teen years, when she disappeared completely. Emerson never told us much about her relatives. She changed the subject most times. We learned during our college years not to ask. Everyone wanted to know why she started school late. She was twenty-one years old and just starting her first year. She never explained it, only gave crazy answers each time she was asked. For all we knew, some of them may have been true. Who knew?

She said she was excavating gravesites in Egypt, painting murals in Spain, weaving sweetgrass baskets in Charleston, dancing professionally in Paris, tending bar in London. Her stories got wilder with each explanation. Eventually, we asked her just to be entertained by her answers.

After lunch, we agreed to some quiet time. Emerson had grant writing to do. Penn wanted to finish her painting then check in with her kids at camp. I wanted to talk to Ian. How could I call him again without seeming needy? I wanted to know he missed me enough to call me but that seemed childish and petty like we were keeping score. This was so hard, not trusting myself to claim what I wanted, and making assumptions about Ian. Maybe he was working, out of town, mowing the grass, moving on. After that exhausting dialogue with myself, I decided to take a nap.

Ian and I were on a picnic. It was a lovely summer day. We shared a bottle of wine. We talked and laughed. He touched my hand and I rubbed his arm. He leaned in and nuzzled my neck and I stroked the weekend fuzz on his face. We looked at each other and he kissed me, his soft lips salty and sweet from lunch and the wine. It was a gentle kiss. A kiss that said we belong together. Uncomplicated and effortless, a kiss that makes you feel loved. In a quick movement, Ian shifted to lie on his back and pulled me against his chest. I propped on one elbow and stroked the hair curling behind his ear. I leaned in for a kiss, this one deeper, more intimate. I savored the taste of him, lost in him, in the delicious connection we made. His lips lingered on my mouth and then trailed south along my bare collarbone, my loose shirt falling away at the neckline.

"Did you wear this shirt for me?" he asked. "Cause I'm loving the view." He laughed, a sexy, satisfied sound. His admiration was appreciative and smoldering. I loved the look in his eyes when he was looking at me. Ian wrapped his fingers in my long hair and pulled it around to tickle my shoulder then he gently tugged me toward him. I obliged and met his mouth, passion igniting. His hands moved to my hips, long fingers pulling my body to his to feel the length of him stretching under me. I trailed my mouth down his neck knowing that was an especially sensitive spot that would make him shiver in the sunlight.

"You do that on purpose," he murmured. "You know what's going to happen when you start that."

"It's intentional," I whispered in his ear, my breath tickling his delicate skin. That got the expected shiver and he countered by un-buttoning the top two buttons of my already revealing shirt, trailing his lips down to the lace at the top of my bra. Taking the edge, he tugged it playfully with his teeth.

"Darling, we're getting ready to make a spectacle of ourselves. Much more of this and I'm going to take you right here."

"Well, don't stop now," I said, looking right into his eyes as I issued my challenge. He laughed his beautiful laugh and rolled me in for a giant bear hug. I laid my head on his chest and let out a happy sigh. Then I saw the baby, a tiny precious thing on the edge of the blanket.

"Ian. Ian." I pushed off him, reaching for the child. Just as my fingertips brushed the silken wisps of dark hair, the infant was snatched by a giant bird, the wing span longer than Ian's height. I screamed at the creature, its blood red talons sunk into the tender flesh. It elevated, screeching at me, its black feathers ruffling on the updraft.

"Ian! Ian! Help me!"

"Jade, Jade? Wake up. You're having a dream." I heard Penn's voice in the distance. She would help me, but the bird had disappeared into a black sky and Ian was gone too. Sobs exploded from my throat and I waved my arms searching for the baby, my baby.

"Jade! Jade!" Someone was wrapping me in a blanket and a light appeared at the side of my head. Slowly, I gave up the pursuit, and stopped waving my arms at the beast. I heard Penn and Emerson talking before I opened my eyes.

"Should we do anything?" Emerson asked.

"No, let's just keep her calm and she'll either go back to sleep or wake up. Lay down on that far side so she won't thrash herself to the floor." I kept my eyes closed, replaying the dream, such wonderful tenderness with Ian. The tension, not overtly sexual, but certainly passionate, was still clinging to my skin when the horrible nightmare blindsided me. The baby was helpless and frail. I couldn't reach it. I couldn't save it.

My tears came faster and I heaved with their discharge. On either side of me, I felt the warm bodies of my people, my tribe, my sisters. Decades between us crowded with secrets and misconceptions, nonetheless, they held me through the darkness. They didn't let go, didn't let me fall into the void. I was still trembling and afraid, but for now their support was enough. I was going to lay here and slow my heartbeat, let the terror of the giant bird glide away. The pleasure of Ian's touch, I would focus on that, be grateful for it and hope I would feel his skin against mine again.

I didn't know how long the three of us lay in the bed. When I finally felt strong enough to open my eyes, the darkening twilight had replaced the sun ribbons flowing through the blinds.

"Are you alright?" Penn asked. She rubbed the hair back from my face where it was stuck in the residue of my tears.

"I think I will be," I said, thoughtfully. I didn't want to tell them what happened. I was still raw and ragged around the edges of my heart.

"Hell of nightmare," Emerson offered.

"Yes, it was, but it didn't start out that way," I answered. Pushing up from the bed, my temples throbbed and my head felt heavy with grief and resolution. I felt inside that it was truly over. I wasn't ever going to have a baby, but I could have Ian. The comprehension penetrated to my core. Consumed with creating a family, I had thrown away the one right before me. I needed to find it again and hope it was still within reach.

"You know what I need," I said to them. Anxious and motherly, they looked from me over my head to each other, like two parents worried about a sick child.

"I need potato chips, dip, chocolate, and wine." Emerson laughed, and Penn let out a gigantic sigh of relief.

"We can handle that," Em said. "Let's eat."

CHAPTER THIRTY-ONE

Present

James Island

I WAS ALL OUT of nightmares after yesterday afternoon's ordeal, so I woke up refreshed and slightly optimistic about my future. The three of us were walking on the beach or at least two of us were. Emerson might as well have been crawling for all the time she spent bent over or on her knees examining shells and patterns in the sand.

Penn was talking about a neighbor of hers from home that was harboring some secret. "The problem is I think she was lying to me," she said. I didn't know what she was talking about only that someone in her world wasn't being honest. No one said anything for a while. I was thinking of reasons why we would lie to one another. I had done it for years, not so much lied as just non-disclosure. A woman could collect a lot of secrets in twenty years.

Emerson stopped to explain different kinds of whelks to us. Penn and I nodded and smiled. Obviously, this was her passion and I was so happy she had found that part of her life. I did wonder about the men, the very few that she mentioned, but especially the ones she didn't talk about. She was exhilarated by her work with the sea turtles, but I couldn't help feeling she was lonely, something about her seemed unsettled. It was early for me and her to be moving around. Penn was our early bird, even in college. Emerson had a conference call early this morning that got her out of bed and because she couldn't talk quietly, I was awake. Now we were walking.

The beach was nearly deserted. Even the kids were still sleeping or watching cartoons and eating dry cereal while their parents slept in. The fishermen were out. Emerson switched her focus from shells to fish, peering into each bucket and lifting cooler lids. Mostly older men out this early, they were delighted to have a gorgeous blond admire their catch. Finally, after stopping to wait on her every ten yards, Penn and I just kept walking. She could talk as long as she wanted. Looking ahead, I saw a pixie in a blue windbreaker, cut off shorts, bare tanned legs and a mop of white curls blowing in the wind. Agnes.

It's going to get interesting now, I thought. Approaching the woman, I nudged Penn and told her I knew this woman. She's the one I've told you about, the one helping me. She's quite a character, I said. Agnes saw us about the same time, threw her hand up in greeting then placed her long fishing rod in a PVC pipe stuck at an angle in the sand.

"Morning Agnes," I said. "Anything biting? This is my friend Penn, uh Penelope." I looked at Penn, needing clarification about her name.

"Penn," she said to Agnes. "So you and Jade are friends. How do you know each other?"

"Oh, we met one morning on the beach," Agnes said, with a quick wink at me.

"It's okay. I told them about that night," I said. "Agnes found me the morning after my suicide attempt, shared her breakfast and some words of wisdom."

"What are you catching?" Emerson asked, approaching the bucket.

"Blues are running. I was hoping for some Spanish mackerel or red drum but I can still fry these."

"I'm Emerson. The guys back there have some good sized flounder, but I thought it was too early for those right now." She opened Agnes' cooler to get a look. "What are you using for bait?"

"Bloodworms. You a fisherman?" Agnes asked. Emerson laughed, and explained she was a marine biologist.

"My focus is sea turtles, specifically loggerheads," she said. Agnes studied Emerson with her intense blue stare she had focused on me so many times before, tilting her head slightly to one side.

Emerson picked up the coffee can beside the cooler and took off the lid. Plump, pink bloodworms climbed over each other in a tangle.

"I fished with my grandfather when I was young," Emerson said. "We would leave just before dawn and go to the pier. After we got the first poles in the water, he would get us a country ham biscuit and a cold bottle of Coke. I still remember those stubby green-tinted bottles. It was such a treat. Grandma would have never let me have one for breakfast. It was our secret."

"That sounds like quite a special time," Agnes said.

"Yeah, it was. I really miss him. He passed away eight years ago. He knew a lot about fish and fishing. He fished with bloodworms too, occasionally shrimp, but mostly these fat, red worms he let me cut in half with his pocket knife." I looked at Penn, silently asking if she knew about Em's grandfather. "They really are full of blood," she said, looking at us. "When you cut them, it drips in the water attracting fish."

"No, I didn't know he died," Penn whispered when Emerson turned back to Agnes. We knew they were incredibly close, but she never told us he was gone. After a moment, I realized I had not properly introduced Agnes.

"Sorry Em, I was telling Penn that Agnes is my new friend. She found me the morning after my suicide attempt and has been a real guiding force in my recovery. That's kind of an understatement as to what she's done for me."

"Oh, I just helped you find your feet." Agnes glanced at me, but returned her ice blue look to Emerson. She opened her mouth to speak, but just then Penn began to point and screech.

"Fish! Fish! Agnes your pole!"

Agnes turned and grabbed the flexible rod that was straining toward the surf. The line was unwinding from the reel as something took the bait out to sea. She pulled hard, planting her feet in the sand, toes curled. The muscles of her forearms and hands flexed as she played the line, reeled in, dipped the rod and pulled back, reeling in the line a few spins each time. She continued this process until we saw breaks in the surf, splashes cresting above the waves and swirling disruption in the water. Whatever was on that hook was putting up a hell of a fight. I had ideas that it was still no match for Agnes.

Stubborn and gritty, Agnes continued, walking slowly toward the water, reeling hard with each step. Finally, she stood on her tiptoes, shouting for one of us to bring the pole that was beside her bucket. It was a six-foot pole with a hook on one end. Whatever she had, was close and big. Agnes danced in the foam. Her spry, little legs kicking like Irish jig steps. Emerson waded out into the water with her, about as excited, and very curious.

"Catch the jaw with that hook," Agnes called. "That fish hook will tear him, got to keep him from pulling." Agnes continued to call directions to Em while Penn and I waited to see the prize they were so excited to land. "Come here girls," Agnes called to us. As we approached, I saw the source of their excitement, a four-foot shark thrashing, lunging, fighting, the line tight in its mouth. "We got to get it ashore and free that hook," Agnes yelled over the splashing.

"Work fast," Emerson yelled. "It can't be out of the water." Agnes took a pair of well-used pliers from her pocket and reached into the edge of the shark's mouth. Emerson placed her sandaled foot on the body, right behind the dorsal fin, hoping to still it briefly. In one practiced motion, Agnes snagged the hook and yelled at Emerson to back around behind her. With one last tail flip, the shark disappeared quickly into the waves.

Both women were soaking wet and laughing. "That was great," Emerson said. "That was a beautiful black tip shark."

"Sure was," Agnes agreed. "You were a great help. I don't like catching those, especially by myself. I'm always afraid I'll hurt such a magnificent fish. It galls me that people hunt them for sport. As usual, people feel so threatened by things they don't understand."

"Absolutely," Emerson said. "I saw an article the other day highlighting that the Carolinas are fourth in the country for shark attacks. That stirs everyone into a frenzy to kill sharks. There is a greater risk of being in a car wreck than being bitten by a shark."

"Just for curiosity's sake, what kind of sharks do we have around here?" Penn asked. Emerson rolled her eyes.

"Not you too," she said. "They're not going to hurt you. Just don't swim near the piers or swim during feeding time at dusk and dawn. They just want to coexist. As for types, off the southeast coast it varies greatly, bull, tiger, and black tips are the most common but there are hammerheads and even great whites."

"Okay science lesson is over," Penn said. "But since y'all have so much to talk about, Agnes, you should come to dinner." We agreed on a time and left her to her fishing.

"Such a cool woman," Emerson said, turning for home.

Later that morning, Penn and I lounged on the beach, planning the menu for dinner. "Want me to shift the umbrella?" Emerson asked, dropping her bag in the sand beside my beach chair.

"I'm good, but you can bring me a rum and Diet Coke," I said, without opening my eyes.

"I'm not your waitress," she said, unfolding her chair and slinging sand in my direction.

"There are water bottles in the cooler," Penn suggested.

"I don't want water and besides, Em, haven't I had a really hard month?" She bent and kissed me on the cheek.

"Yes, you have Jade and you can walk your lazy ass inside and get your own drink." She laughed as she plopped down into her chair, scattering more sand. "Exercise is good for the soul."

Penn reminded us it wasn't even lunch. We had been up since dawn and in waking hours, it felt more like late afternoon, I explained. "We're having a liquid lunch," I said. "You can drink before five if your feet are touching sand. It's a rule." I got up, reluctantly, kicking sand over Emerson's feet. I had walked about ten steps when she called over her shoulder. "Hey, Jade, bring me one too."

"Bitch."

I returned with three drinks, handing one to each of them. "I can't drink this early," Penn said. "Besides, someone has to drive to the market. Agnes is coming for dinner and I'm making shrimp and grits."

"We can bike to the market," I said.

"You want the three of us to bike, intoxicated, to town, in a hundred degree heat. Then bike back with shrimp spoiling in the sun. No thanks."

Fine, I'll have yours too I told her and poured the contents into my tumbler. For a few hours we enjoyed a beautiful beach afternoon, sparkling water and just the right amount of heat, with surprisingly low humidity for the Carolinas in the summer. It was a rare treat.

Later, Penn and Emerson headed to the fish market and the specialty store in their quest for tasso ham. Penn insisted she have the gourmet ham to make brown gravy for her shrimp dish. That should take them a while to find, I thought. I decided to use my great buzz and alone time to call Ian. Sunday afternoon, wonder what Ian was doing at home alone. My god, I thought, what if he's not alone? Should I call? All this indecision lately was torture. I needed to start making definitive decisions about my life. Inaction, hesitation, I needed to go after what I wanted. However, first I should decide what I wanted. I wanted Ian, but did he want me. I had to stop doubting myself. "It ends now," I said aloud.

Ian answered after nine rings. I was ready to leave a message when he picked up.

"Hi. I was going to leave a message."

"I turned the answering machine off. People are leaving messages for you and I don't know what to do with that."

"I'm so sorry. You must hate me. I never thought... I didn't think... oh hell, Ian, I screwed up. I fell apart and didn't know how to tell you. I was scared and just lost it, an honest to god breakdown. Like the ones that send you to the hospital and get you fitted for a straitjacket." I said all this without taking a breath or giving him a chance to respond. I was terrible at communicating. For days I wouldn't talk to him then I assault him with revelations and confessions.

"What are you talking about?"

"Ian I gave up. I gave up on us and I gave up on me." The more I drink the more I talk, I thought, no filter, no restraint, no secrets. I say it aloud as soon as it comes to mind.

"You needed a break. I get that now," Ian said. "I don't appreciate how you handled it but I can see why you needed to get away."

"No Ian. I didn't just need a break. I was done. I quit. I gave up on everything, especially me." I should probably drink some coffee before I told him too much.

"I know, you're taking a break. Is it helping?"

He still didn't understand my level of desperation. Suddenly, I needed him to know how far down the rabbit hole I went.

"I went all the way Ian. I went completely down the rabbit hole, all the way to the dark, ugly place no one believes they have. But I have it. I have a hideous crater and I've been lost in that goddamn blackness for a long time."

"Have you been drinking?"

"Just a little, a few rum and cokes before lunch, or rather, instead of lunch and then two more for dessert." Lying on the bed, I rode the room spin like a Tilt-A-Whirl. It was better with my eyes closed.

"Where are the others? Weren't you having some kind of re-union? By the way, you picked a hell of a time to throw a party. Meanwhile, life here goes on."

"No Ian, there's no party. I need you to listen to me."

"Then make some sense." Ian's voice was elevated and irritated. Maybe I should just hang up. I considered it, but I was already hip deep in this grave, I might as well dig the rest of it.

"I tried to kill myself." I only said the one sentence. I didn't have any more words. I wanted this to be the only thing he heard me say. It needed to sink in and get his attention.

"What the hell? What do you mean? When?" His voice trailed off and I waited until he was quiet.

"I'm not doing this like I wanted to. I wanted to tell you face to face, not over the phone. The day I left Charlotte, you were in Chicago. I drove to the island and walked into the ocean. I tried to drown myself."

"That was weeks ago and you're just telling me this?" I could hear his breathing, uneven and frayed, like worn cloth. He had heard me this time.

His comments struck me wrong. They sounded selfish and needy. "Of course Ian, this is all about you. That was my first thought, how do I tell Ian what I did?"

"Okay, let me say this differently. You're my wife. Didn't you want me to know or didn't you think I would care?" His voice was pleading and desperate.

"At the time, I wasn't thinking about anything. Just release. Release from the pain and despair suffocating me. For one thing, I was much sicker than anyone thought, including me. I just wanted it all to stop, the failure and guilt, inadequacy and anger."

"What failure? Inadequacy? I don't understand."

It was so hard to explain this to him. "The miscarriages, motherhood, a family, I couldn't survive knowing how much I had let us both down."

"Jade, those miscarriages weren't your fault. It's just circumstances. It's unexplainable. Honey, please tell me. You thought this was your fault and that I wouldn't want you. I've always wanted you. I didn't think you wanted me."

"I couldn't look in the mirror anymore. I hated the sight of myself. You don't think I sensed your distance, even when you sat beside me or lay in bed next to me. You stopped looking at me. You stopped touching me."

"You didn't want me to touch you," he said. His voice cracked. "It was like you never wanted me again."

I listened quietly, replaying so many scenes in my mind, taking my dinner into the den, instead of sitting at the table with him, cutting short phone calls, and turning away from him in bed. Maybe it wasn't failure I had seen in his eyes, but sadness. "I think we both had some distorted vision. That's why I wanted to talk to you in person. I wanted to see your eyes. I wanted to see what you're feeling."

"Right now, I'm feeling horrible. My wife tried to kill herself and I was too wrapped up in my life to help her. I've really let you down."

"How about we stop blaming each other?" I offered. From my window, I saw Penn and Em in the driveway. "The girls are back from the market."

"Your mother is expecting me for dinner. God, your mother? Does she know any of this?"

I snorted a stupid sound. "No, and I would like to keep it that way. Telling you and them has been all I could handle." He was quiet, not a sound from the receiver. "Ian?"

Finally, he spoke in a very soft voice. "How long have they known?"

Tears pooled in my eyes. Any minute they would spill over, probably about the time Penn and Emerson came inside. "It's a long story. They came for that twenty year reunion I had completely forgotten about. It had been only a few days since my swim. I was a train wreck."

I heard the back door slam as they came in with groceries. "We all got into a big fight and I finally realized one of my fatal flaws. I need help and I'm too stubborn to ask for it. I broke down and asked them for help. That's why they're still here."

"Obviously you didn't succeed in your attempt. And I'm glad, so this may sound strange, what happened? Were you rescued? Change your mind?"

"I walked into the ocean, relaxed my body, and planned to drift away. But then I heard voices telling me to save myself. I'm sure that sounds crazy, but I really heard them." He was quiet, probably wondering how nutty I really was. "I realized, I wasn't ready to let go. It was almost too late, but I found hope. Then I felt a primal need to survive."

Penn called to me as she knocked on my door. "Jade, we're back."

"Do you still want me to come this Friday?" Ian asked.

I opened the door and motioned Penn away. "Yeah, I do, it's time." I held the phone next to my face long after he hung up. Like it was a giant whelk, and I could hear my future instead of the ocean. I hoped it was my future and not some giant void absorbing my destiny. My rum buzz had faded while I exposed myself to Ian. I needed a little more liquid courage to talk this through with Penn and Em. God, I hated being vulnerable, losing control, asking for help. What did they know anyway? Penn let her husband treat her like chattel and Em's love life was like hurricane season, her relationships last for a few volatile months, then blow out. Who were they to talk to me about my marriage?

Belligerence wasn't an attractive quality. Neither was projecting my frustration on to the few friends I had in this world. Maybe I would keep this one conversation to myself for now.

CHAPTER THIRTY-TWO

Present
James Island

"EM, GET JADE IN the shower please. Maybe it will sober her up a little before dinner. Then maybe one of you can make a salad, but don't give Jade a knife, it'll be a damn bloodbath in here."

I was not drunk. However, I was drinking and doing a damn fine job of it. Penn was performing some weird ballet dance in the kitchen to the *80s Rock The Music* show on the radio. She stirred gravy, washed lettuce, checked the grits, and stuck her finger in the custard pie. I applauded as she pirouetted around the kitchen. I sang along loudly to the words to show her support and channel positive energy for the meal she was cooking, but she didn't seem to appreciate it. She had already kicked me out of the kitchen for playing with the food. She has no sense of humor anymore, I thought. Playing with the shrimp, I put them on a wooden skewer and had them performing a Rockettes' dance number.

I guess I could channel positive energy from the den. So I collected shells from the glass jar, arranged them in a circle on the coffee table and sat cross-legged inside it with a lit candle from the dinner table. They didn't know about the elements like I did. Penn was fire, passionate and opinionated, crazy creative and artistic and annoying. She used to burn like a blue flame. But she barely had a pilot light anymore. Em was water, fluid and graceful, but ever-changing and elusive.

"Hell fire, Emerson, do something with her before she burns down the house."

"I don't need help taking a shower," I insisted, as Em pushed me into the bathroom.

"You smell like a pirate," she said. "Rum, sweat and seawater. We're having a guest for dinner. At least you can smell clean, even if you do swear like a sailor."

"Oh, hell, Agnes doesn't care what I smell like. She and I've shared some crazy moments." I pushed her out of the bathroom, shutting the door behind her. "She's even seen me naked," I yelled just before it closed. Leaning my head against the cool tile helped. After a lengthy shower, I wrapped a towel around me and walked to my room. Before I crossed the threshold, Em shouted from the kitchen.

"What did you say about being naked?"

"What? Naked? Yes, I was nude in the shower. That's generally how it's done. You don't get your clothes wet that way."

"Woman! You know what the hell I'm talking about," she continued, moving toward me. "You said Agnes had seen you naked. That's weird, even for you."

"I said what? How much have you had to drink? I'm going to get dressed now before she arrives and does see me naked." Oh, that had been close, and stupid, I thought. I did not need to be quite so open with them. It had been a long time since we all lived together. Who knows what prejudice they had developed. Besides what a disservice to Agnes, they were her secrets, not mine.

Agnes apparently owned some shorts that weren't cutoffs. She looked pretty in a yellow top with tiny embroidered flowers on the collar and navy shorts with a cuff. She carried a basket, bringing us goodies. It was rare that she didn't give me something when I saw her. This time it was like Christmas, a plastic bag of mussels, a bouquet of wild flowers, and two jars. She took the jars from her basket and sat them on the counter. One was small and held herbs and spices.

"This is my seasoning blend. I use it on everything," she said. "Put it in boiling water to cook shellfish, or dust vegetables then roast them. I sprinkle it on grilled fish." She grinned proudly, her smile impish, blue eyes radiant. "I grow all the herbs myself, but I do buy the salt," she said, with a wink. The other jar was larger and contained a translucent liquid with cherries floating in it. "And this here is my home brew. I make it too."

"Home brew. Like moonshine?" Penn sputtered.

"Yep, my friend, Maggie, and I make it. There's a good market for it."

"You mean you sell moonshine?" Penn said in disbelief. I just laughed. Nothing about Agnes surprised me.

"That's about the coolest thing I've ever heard," Emerson said. "Let's crack it open." I took four shot glasses from the cabinet over the stove and set them out for Agnes to pour.

"Before dinner?" Penn whined. "We're almost ready to eat."

"Lighten up Penn. It'll enhance the flavor," I said.

We held our glasses and touched them together. "To friends," Emerson toasted.

"Damn," I said. "It's got a kick, but smoother than I expected."

"Another round," said Em, pouring. Penn started to protest, again. "Why don't you loosen up and live a little, Penelope. You might be able to get that pole out of your ass."

Penn's dinner was really good. The cheese grits creamy, the shrimp were fat and tender and swimming in rich, spicy, tasso gravy. Em's homemade ceasar dressing was tangy and garlicky over the crisp mixed greens, bitter and buttery, finished with salty, shaved parmesan, not the powdered stuff in the can. She was helping me with the dishes until her sea turtle conversation with Agnes took her completely from the kitchen. Perched on the arm of the sofa, she was totally absorbed in Agnes' description of the island's turtle activity over the decades.

We took the custard pie to the porch. The sun was in the last stages of setting and the sky was a collection of colors. It looked like someone had spilled condiments and the contents of the refriger-ator shelf onto the sky, ketchup red, honey mustard yellow, apricot jam orange, with stains of pink grapefruit juice.

Penn opened a bottle of dessert wine and spooned the home-made butterscotch and walnut sauce over the chilled slices. When Emerson brought out the shot glasses and moonshine jar, Penn reached for the fourth glass and turned it upside down before Em could fill it again. "No offense Agnes, but I can't handle any more home brew."

Agnes just laughed and threw her shot back, draining it in one swallow. Then she reached for her pie. The frozen custard was pale yellow, fluffy and light, with a hint of Meyer lemon. The sweet, buttery sauce dripped down the sides and pooled in luscious little puddles on the plate. I swiped my finger in one of them, getting a little custard too. It was so good I went all the way around my plate repeating the action.

"Are you too drunk to use a spoon?" Penn seemed slightly irritat-ed at Emerson and I. We were relaxed and having fun. God knows I needed to have a good time.

"Yes, I can use a spoon and point my pinky finger too, if that suits you." I picked up my spoon and pointed it at her. "Besides, what's your problem?" I stopped and took a deep breath. "Penn, I really appreciate your help through my crisis but sometimes you seem so different I just don't know how to react."

"You haven't changed at all in twenty years?" Penn snorted. "You're not exactly young and carefree. We're not kids anymore. I have responsibilities, obligations. My life is about my family. I can't be frivolous."

"Penelope is back. She's not one for fun. Why is that?" Emerson asked. "I didn't realize enjoying life had age limits. Does having a family require you to suck all the pleasure out of life?" Penn began gathering the dessert dishes then stopped abruptly, letting the forks clatter to the table.

"No, Emerson, I don't get to do what I want like you do, sailing around the world, chasing turtles. My life is about deadlines and meetings, school conferences and carpool, cooking meals, cleaning up from meals. It's not enjoyable. It's not fun. It's not any of those things your sarcastic tongue can't shut up about."

"Well, Penelope, that should tell you everything," Em said. "Where does it say to have a family you must completely sacrifice you. I know I don't have one, but even I know this is not the way it's supposed to be. You are choosing to be miserable."

I noticed that through the entire exchange, Agnes remained silent. She was listening intently. Her blue eyes alert, the slight tilt of her chin, she missed nothing, not even the nuance of slight body shifts.

"Penn, did you ever consider that being the best version of yourself, being your authentic self, would give your family a tremendous gift," Agnes said. Surprised, we all turned to look at her. "Giving away all of yourself is unhealthy, eventually you become resentful. When the last bit of you disappears, and in anger, you finally draw a line in the sand, the guilt will devour you."

Penn looked at Agnes like she had been slapped across the face. I couldn't tell if she was angry at the intrusion or stunned at the revelation.

She excused herself and went into the kitchen. She never responded to Agnes. We heard her banging pots and dishes, slamming cabinet doors. Then all was quiet. Emerson eventually went inside to check on her, after she and Agnes discussed the mating habits of loggerheads.

"Never dull around here, fights and turtle sex, fascinating," I said to Agnes. "Sorry about Penn. I don't know what's wrong with her. She behaves like her life is so perfect, then she exposes herself by revealing how unhappy she is." I explained Penn's erratic behavior and the extreme personality changes we had seen.

"She seems a little lost," Agnes said. "Stretched too thin, sometimes we snap. But she's got to want help before she'll accept it." Agnes poured us another shot, emptying the jar of her home brew. "Let's talk about you. How are you really doing?"

"I'm making progress." I didn't know what else to say. So many thoughts were careening off one another inside my mind, the suicide attempt, waking up to Agnes on the beach, standing naked in the clearing, crying on Agnes' shoulder, on Penn's shoulder, on Em's. It seemed like I had done a lot of crying, purging, Agnes called it, releasing the toxins.

"As long as you're moving forward." Agnes stood to leave, thanked me for dinner and threw back the last dregs of her moonshine. She put the empty jar in her basket. "I might refill it for you." She laughed as she went down the steps. "Jade, right now, breathing is progress. Just keep doing that."

I watched her head north and wondered where she lived. She kept her boat at the edge of the canal but there wasn't a house nearby. She never talked about her life, past history, or family, full of wisdom, she was short on personal details.

The sky was dark, only a sliver of moon, like a slice of honeydew melon, was visible. I sat in the darkness and thought about the last month of my life or maybe I should call it the first month of my new life. Over time, Agnes had explained about the moon phases. The time between the new moon and the full moon was the waxing period. It was a great time to begin a new endeavor, she said. Conversely, after a full moon was the waning time, the time to let go and move on. I had been letting go, recognizing there was another life for me besides the one I had assigned myself. We can make choices, Agnes said, even though the universe had a plan for me before the stars were born, she said. It's up to you to recognize what's healthy and right for you, and to decide what must be discarded and left behind.

The more I thought about the last several weeks, I realized I did die. I drowned that feeble, dispirited, miserable version of myself and emerged from my watery birth a cleansed woman. I had the power to make myself whole, fill in the gaps lost to miscarriages and pity, anger and surrender. Not only was it my choice to take control, it was my responsibility. As the prayer reads, *serenity to accept the things I cannot change, courage to change the things I can, and wisdom to know the difference.* I was gaining wisdom, thanks to Agnes, and my courage was emerging. I felt its advance, a gradual but intentional procession, like the slow march of a parade band. Courage was the prerequisite to my transformation. With enough courage, I could let go of my fear, and gather enough grace to make peace with my past.

CHAPTER THIRTY-THREE

Present
James Island

A LATE NIGHT AND Agnes' moonshine made for a lethal combination. It was after lunch before any of us staggered out of bed into the blinding sunlight. Penn was only slightly less hung-over than Em and I. Of course she always was a little smarter, and proved it last night by curtailing her consumption of moonshine. However, she was not brilliant since she topped it off with a bottle of sweet, dessert wine. Em's eyes sagged low and heavy, like she had been on a Vegas bender. I didn't look in the mirror. I didn't want to see my post-inebriated face, sallow skin, and bloodshot eyes. God, we smelled worse. Moonshine sweating from our aging pores was funky and foul.

Diet Cokes for all, paired with melted cheddar on sourdough toast. "The same truck that hit me, hit both of you," I said. "Then I think it backed up and ran over you again, Emmie."

"You look like hell too," she growled. Finding the bottle of Tylenol in a kitchen drawer, she took two pills then passed around the bottle.

"We are too old for this shit," Penn said.

I put my hands on both corners of the table, hoping to keep the room from rotating. "Agnes has got to be over eighty. Are you going to let her drink you under the table, Penn?"

"Yes." Penn whispered at me from the sofa. "Each and every time."

"Okay ladies, I think it is naptime," Emerson said. She was squinting at her wrist like she was looking at her watch.

"You're trying to tell time with a bracelet," I said. Just then, she jumped up, one hand on her head to hold it in place, and began flipping through her journal.

"Damn, damn, damn," she muttered. "It's Monday. You two are really screwing with my schedule. You know I'm still supposed to be working while you two are on vacation." She grabbed her folders, a pack of saltine crackers and another Diet Coke and headed off to her room. "I got a deadline," she called, before her door closed.

"Flip you for the shower," Penn said. I told her she could have it as I headed to the sofa. I was probably asleep before she turned on the water.

I woke to a firm tapping on the glass door. Prying open my dehydrated eyelids, I peered over the sofa and immediately thought, I'm going to need a drink. Ian was leaning into the darkened glass, his hands shielding his eyes from the sun. What the hell was he doing here? Our plan was Friday. He saw me sit up, tapped again, then tentatively opened the door.

"I'm a little early. Can I come in?"

I fumbled over my words and invited him in, appalled and apologizing for my appearance. I know I appeared shell-shocked, but he was showing up four days before expected. Four days that I had to prepare myself, put myself together, discuss strategy with Penn and Em. I had not even told them about my phone call with him yesterday, and that I admitted my suicide attempt. I wasn't prepared to confess my sins nor my confusion. I had worked so hard to make sense of my behavior so I could present a healthier version of myself and here I was, hung over, tongue tied, and reeking of moonshine.

I jumped off the sofa, my head tilting with the room's rotation, and motioned him inside. It occurred to me how long it had been since my legs were shaved. Why did that matter? We weren't hopping into bed, or could we? Oh shit, I was in trouble. Discombobulated was the word that came to mind, not that it was a word I used frequently. Rattled, flustered, befuddled, embarrassed, the entire thesaurus ricocheted like marbles in a pinball machine. I felt like an animated cartoon with speech bubbles exploding around my head. They all labeled me mental, nutcase, fruitcake.

Ian's arms felt awkward and familiar. I desperately wanted to melt into him, seep into the soft, safe place we found in the dark, a rare and out of reach place as of late, but a promised land for which I longed.

"I'm sorry I just showed up but I needed to see you." He stepped back, his hands resting lightly on my shoulders as if examining me. Did I look different now that he knew how desperately dark I could descend? Now that he knew I was breathing, was he planning to go on with his life? What did he want?

"I need a shower," I blurted. That was painfully obvious but I didn't need to highlight it.

"Should I leave?" He looked confused, and tiny lines of hurt creased his forehead.

"No, no. I didn't mean that. I'm just surprised to see you and this is not exactly how I wanted to present myself." I could tell he was worried and if the situation had been reversed I would have come to him just the same. How could I expect nothing less? It also meant I still mattered to him. He took my hand and led me to the sofa.

"I haven't stopped thinking about our conversation yesterday. I was shocked at your admission but I should have seen it coming. I should have known you were on the edge. I'm angry too, at both of us. Why couldn't we handle this better? I'm angry you left me, almost forever. Then I feel guilty for this being about me when you're the one in so much pain." I watched his jaw tighten and knew this was about as emotional as I had ever seen him.

"Ian, I am so sorry. I couldn't see a way out or forward and I couldn't feel anything anymore. I wasn't thinking about you or even me. I wasn't thinking. I was reacting to decades of despair and circumstances. Finally I imploded."

His touch was tender and gentle as he wiped the tear from my cheek. I wanted to close my eyes and evaporate into his touch, dissolve into this mist of affection around us. It had been so long since I felt warmth between us. I moved a tentative hand toward him and grazed his face and chest, letting it casually fall to his thigh. He shifted slightly and I wondered if I had mistaken the moment. Maybe he just felt pity for me.

The cloth of his khaki shorts was brushed cotton and worn from repeated washing. There was a hint of fraying at the edges, but I knew they were his weekend shorts. He was wearing a collared golf shirt though instead of a t-shirt. That was a tell that he was making an effort and had thought about his appearance. I was absent mindedly twirling my finger in the curls of his leg hair when I had a flash of sensation of how that warm fuzz felt rubbing against the smoothness of my own legs. But my legs weren't smooth and there was probably a layer of gunk on my teeth. Oh hell, was Penn out of the shower?

"Do you want something to drink, a beer, soft drink, but we only have diet? Penn made some sweet tea."

"A beer? It's just mid-afternoon. Oh hell, I guess it doesn't matter. What's time when you're at the beach?" I opened the bottle and handed him the cold beer. He looked at the label, nodding his approval at the small craft brewery. "Sparing no expense, I see."

"They're Em's. I guess when you're single, you can splurge on the small things." I walked to the door where he stood looking out at the ocean.

"I forgot how beautiful it was here, so peaceful, never crowded with hordes of people like Myrtle Beach and Charlotte," he said.

"Are you good for a little while? I need to get a shower. I think Penn went to her room when she saw you were here and Em is working or sleeping. There are snacks and leftovers in the fridge."

"I'm good," he said, giving me a sweet grin.

I was getting undressed when Penn and Em blew into my room. No knock or anything. It's good we are as close as sisters because I was finding myself naked with a lot of women these days.

"Did you ask him to come?"

"When did he get here?"

"How do you feel?"

"He looks great."

They were talking over each other, asking questions, not waiting for responses. "You two have to shut up if you want me to answer." I slipped into my robe and we piled onto my bed together.

"Between dinner with Agnes and the moonshine, I never got a chance to tell you I called him yesterday when you two were shopping. Didn't you ever hear that friends don't let friends dial drunk?"

"Ooh, was it a booty call?" Em rubbed her hands together, a dumb smile splitting her face.

"No, it was not. But he does look damn good. He's gotten some sun. His muscles are tight and he's lost those few extra pounds a desk job brings. He told me he had been doing a lot of yard work."

"What did y'all talk about when you called him?" Penn asked.

"Well, at first it was our usual tip-toe-eggshell-dance around each other then we touched on the obvious topics. Then the morning of rum on the beach caught up with my mouth and I blurted out that I tried to kill myself. After that it was a blur of questions, apologies, accusatory displays of misplaced anger, and a little tenderness. I told y'all he was coming down Friday."

"Yeah, we were planning to clear out Friday morning," Penn said. "I'm going home to check on the house and make Brian some more frozen meals. Em, did you decide if you're coming to my house or going back to Charleston?"

Emerson explained that she had a full schedule including a grant meeting and a lecture over the weekend. "How long do I need to be gone?" she asked, then they both looked at me.

"I don't know. We didn't get that far. The last thing we talked about was his weekend visit. I was shocked to see him today. He's either really worried or feeling really sorry for me."

Emerson snorted, and slapped my arm. "The look he gave you didn't say pity."

"Em's right for a change. He looked like a man who was worried about his wife and he's here four days early. What does that say to you?"

"Were you watching us?" I tucked my robe around me as if that made a difference.

"No, not much, but it's not a big house and even trying not to eavesdrop, I could still hear you talking and I saw him when I came out of the bathroom. I closed my door." Penn said the last sentence like closing her door made all the difference. "Oh quit giving us that look, you were going to tell us everything anyway."

"Okay, nevermind. How did he look at me?" That was the most important question of the hour.

"Like a man who still loves his wife," Emerson said.

"You didn't see him, Penn did."

"Well, that is what he looked like," Penn confirmed.

I leaned back against the headboard absorbing their statements. They waited anxiously while I twisted my fingers in my hair, opened my mouth to speak a couple of times, but never said anything. Then

I finally got up and walked to the window. After a few minutes, I turned to face them. "Okay, what now?"

"That's what we're waiting for you to tell us," Emerson said.

"This is your story to write," Penn added. "What's the next chapter?"

It seems more like a sequel, I told them. "My new start is bigger than a chapter."

"So, are you looking for a leading man or going solo? You've told us your marriage was pretty far gone. Is it redeemable?" Emerson asked.

"That was going to be my topic for discussion this week, before Ian came on Friday. I was going to pick that apart like a knot of Christmas lights. Now I've got to wing it and I'm already flying without a net. You two can be my buffer." I smirked slightly.

"Hell no, Ace. We're leaving," Emerson said, looking at Penn for confirmation. "I'm not having a foursome with y'all no matter how close we are."

"Nope, and you don't need an audience either," Penn said. "I can have my clothes ready in less than an hour, Em. And speaking of clothes, you might want to take a shower, put some on, and get out there. We've been in here for an hour."

At that, I started throwing things from my drawer. I didn't have anything nice to put on. Jesus, I didn't pack a bag to come here and drown myself. All I had bought were beach shorts and tourist t-shirts.

"Well, you're tan looks fabulous," Penn said. "I've always hated that olive skin of yours and your black hair, sleek and shiny as usual. Do you color it? Nevermind." Penn started digging through the clothes piled on my bed. "Where are you white shorts? Emerson get that turquoise top of yours, the low-cut one." As usual, Penn was taking charge.

"It's not going to make a damn bit of difference until she takes a weed-eater to that jungle on her legs," Em said. "When is the last time you shaved?"

I flipped her off and dug out my bra and panties, not Victoria Secret, more like Wal-Mart cheap, but it was all that I had. "Okay, please Emerson, may I borrow your top? Pretty please?"

"That is some granny underwear," she said. "You'd be better off going commando."

"Jesus, Emerson, she's wearing white shorts. Everybody move. Jade, I've got a new bra with the tag still on it, got to be better than that. As far as the granny drawers, you're on your own, but if you get naked, you should ditch those before Ian sees them."

"Somebody get him another beer," I yelled, as they went into action. Later, I emerged, shaven, smelling like Em's coconut shampoo and Penn's wild orchid body wash. I hope the combination worked and I didn't smell like a whorehouse. The three of them were on the porch at the table. Penn, the consummate Martha Stewart, had thrown together some snacks and a pitcher of sweet tea, lemon slices floated in the sienna liquid. I needed something a little stronger, but no rum, and definitely no moonshine, so, bourbon on ice with a splash of ginger ale. I drank a large shot, refilled, added the ginger ale, then headed outside.

Emerson and Penn carried the conversation for a little while then excused themselves to prepare dinner and pack.

"I didn't mean to push them out," Ian said, when they were inside. "They can stay."

"Actually, they would probably like a break. They've been taking care of me for weeks." A grimace flashed briefly over Ian's face, but he quickly replaced it with a blank expression. He gazed toward the water. It was the end of the day. The time after the sun worshippers vanish, when families are having dinner, but before the sun completely set. It was my favorite time of a beach day. Not yet evening or dark, but the sun had slipped past the shoreline, resting beyond the canal before the exertion of dropping behind the horizon. The ocean was a different shade of blue, dark navy with gray swirls in the surf.

"Let's walk," he said. He kicked off his shoes and held out his hand to me, then closed it and shoved his hands in his pockets. It was clear neither of us knew what to do. Agnes' voice in my head was telling me to be patient. *Your life didn't get this way overnight and it won't be resolved this week.* I could hear her. *Move forward, that's progress.*

We walked in silence, wary of the friction between us, anxiety and a dose of attraction, agitation and allure, like a mixed cocktail affecting our behavior. Part of me wanted to run from him with my secrets still undisclosed. The other part, deep inside, wanted to fall across him in the sand and feel his lips on mine. I wanted him. I really wanted him. I hadn't wanted him in a long time. Unaccustomed to feeling desire, I didn't know what to do with it. Unable to contend with my emotions, I had labeled them and tucked them into the apothecary chest of my heart for years, compartmentalizing my desires and needs, acknowledging only those that screamed the loudest. Pity. Despair. Pain. Fear.

The need of him, my craving of him, hung around me like a cargo net, catching my lust and hunger. Unfortunately, my courage fell through the voids and washed out with the waves. I wanted to be bold. I wanted to be strong. I wanted to be loved. I guess for now I could find satisfaction in that I had opened the drawer and unboxed any positive emotion.

We walked toward the pier, neither of us aware of direction or distance. Ian stooped to pick up an ebony, black triangle in the sand. He swished it in the water and held it out to me, a shark's tooth. I loved collecting them but had the hardest time actually finding any. Their shiny blackness was different from shells but somehow

I could step right over one while Ian saw it clearly. I had a cut glass jar at home I put them in after every trip to the island.

"Thanks." I smiled at him. My hand lingered in his, nerves tingled from my fingertips up my forearm. I felt a shiver, even though it was humid and warm. "We should head back. Penn is cooking."

He turned and we started down the beach. I noticed his fingers twitching at his side as he fiddled with his thumb and ring finger, his gold band rotating. At least he's still wearing it, I thought. That was a good sign. He talked about work and the projects he had completed around the house and filled me in on the extended family's activities. My mother was planning a charity event.

He never asked about my confession to him or any of the details regarding my last several weeks. It was like roommates conversing or neighbors catching up. The conversation was strained and unnatural one minute, and affirming and calm the next. Our emotions were all over the place, reverberating like popcorn kernels in a copper kettle. I did feel alive though, my awareness sharp, my body animated. I had been robotic and distant for such a long time, I probably seemed neurotic to Ian. He seemed content though, not rushed, not nervously walking ahead of me like he usually did. I had not seen him this composed in years, he was almost peaceful.

Should I bring up the topic we were avoiding or let it go for now? The house was just ahead and once that box was open, there would be no closing the lid. I'm sure dinner was ready. It was. Penn had set the table and chilled white wine to go with the fish. She had prepared stuffed flounder fillets with crabmeat. Herbs and paprika steeped in the basted butter and the house smelled savory and peppery. A dish of shredded purple and green cabbage slaw, with tart granny smith apples and tangy vinaigrette, sat beside Penn's special honey-roasted carrots which smelled like cinnamon and honey with the spicy bite of grated nutmeg. A loaf of multigrain bread rested on the wooden board and a dish of softened herbed butter glistened under the light.

Ian was salivating and exclaiming how great dinner looked before excusing himself to wash his hands. He had barely closed the bathroom door before they both unleashed their questions. We just walked, I told them. Penn seemed placated but Emerson raised an eyebrow at me and asked where he was sleeping. Damn, I hadn't thought about that. Not only was that an awkward idea, but my sheets were filthy, sandy and sweaty. I closed my mouth, my bewilderment showing in my expression.

"I changed your sheets," Emerson said, winking at me. We sat down for dinner and Ian ate with gusto like he was starving. I knew his culinary ability was fairly limited to breakfast food, grilling meat and opening cans, so that was something else to feel guilty about. I hadn't stopped to think how lonely and hard my absence had been on him. We weren't communicating or sharing much together before, but at least I kept the house in order and cooked dinner. Of course he was defensive and angry. Why not? I abandoned him. The realization slammed into me like a runaway train and I dropped my fork. It clattered to the plate, bounced on the table and fell to the floor. Embarrassed, I jumped up and nearly turned over my chair in the rush.

"Just a little clumsy," I exclaimed. I walked into the kitchen for a new fork and a second bottle of wine. Noticing Ian's plate was almost empty, I carried the fish platter to the table. It's a good thing Penn always brings extra food, I thought. Dinner conversation was weird, as everyone pretended it was a casual, weeknight dinner. Emerson talked about her grant and turtle research. Ian asked polite questions. Penn talked about her boys.

Then it was over and I busied myself cleaning. Ian carried dishes to the counter and praised the two for the fabulous dinner. Penn pulled me aside to tell me she and Emerson were leaving the next morning. She gave me a big hug and whispered to me, "You can do this. You have to believe in both of you. You made the choice to live for a reason. Embrace this chance. No fear." With a last squeeze for emphasis, she turned, said goodnight to Ian and went to her room.

I filled our wine glasses and we went into the den. Handing him one, I sat down in the chair facing him.

"You still okay that I came," he said. "You seemed a little nervous at dinner."

"I am glad you came. Dinner wasn't about me being nervous. I just had some thoughts that bothered me." This was going to be hard and I didn't want to start it tonight. "I realized as we ate dinner that you've been alone for a long time, no one in the house, no one to cook for you. It was really sad for me to comprehend how my actions hurt you. I abandoned you and didn't even tell you why."

I knew I was going to cry. I didn't want to do this now with Emerson and Penn a wall away. "Let's go outside," Ian said, as if reading my mind. The chairs faced the ocean and we propped our feet on the rails. The breeze blew from the side, going down the beach, blowing my hair across my face. "Yes, I've been lonely," he said. "But I was lonely before you left. Your absence in the house didn't change much. When I realized that, I understood we had reached the bottom. Then the house really felt empty. I've been too hurt and angry to reach out. I didn't consider how depressed you were, only how isolated I felt."

I sat quietly, letting his words soak into me. "We screwed it up good, didn't we?" I squeezed his hand lying next to me on the wooden armrest and left it there covering his. He didn't move it away. Twenty-four hours ago, I was sitting in this very seat talking to Agnes about progress. It seemed I had traveled miles since then. Sometimes, it could be as easy as stepping forward.

I needed to think less and act more. Thinking made me hesitant and unsure. I questioned my instincts and motives, anticipated responses, and postured counter moves. By the time I had analyzed all that, I would have missed the moment. I walked through the forest and despite the trees in front of me, I was running to the next forest in search of a tree. I wanted everything to slow down. I wanted to move deliberately, with purpose and design. I wanted to feel solid and safe instead of being in the constant freefall that I had experienced the last decade, and have a soft place to land whenever I crawled out of my comfort zone. Take risks, luxuriate in life, I wanted to be real with myself and Ian.

I wasn't searching for a clichéd version of second chances; I wanted genuine and real. I had chosen to live beyond the suffering of that lost girl and desperate woman. It was on me that their pain not be in vain, that my lessons were learned and accepted with grace and humility. "I wanted to make this work," I said. "When I was drowning, I saved myself when I realized I would never feel your touch again."

With those words, I felt an overwhelming rush of grace, like a celestial intervention blessing me. I could open my heart. I could be authentic. I could be vulnerable and my world wouldn't implode. I felt strong.

Ian squeezed my hand and turned into the wind, a single tear rolling down his cheek. It was late when he finally spoke, his voice hoarse and husky.

"Is it okay if I stay here?" I hesitated just a second too long. "On the couch." With relief on my face and disappointment in my core, I told him I would bring his linens.

CHAPTER THIRTY-FOUR

Present
James Island

EMERSON AND PENN WERE gone when I got up. It was late morning but I was still exhausted from the last few days. It was almost dawn before I went to sleep. Torrents of thoughts, possibilities and ideas rushed through my head all night, cutting into the sediment that blocked my path. I needed change. I needed to change. I wanted to feel positive energy flow from my center, surge through my limbs. Confident that I could bring change to my life, I visualized energy, like Agnes had taught me, until I finally drifted off in the soft hours before dawn.

Ian was sitting on the porch in swim trunks, a towel around his shoulders, his brown curls dripping with seawater.

"Morning," I called out to him. "Breakfast?"

"Are you asking if I want something or if I've had some?"

"Either."

"I had coffee with Penn but no breakfast. I took a swim and thought I'd give you another fifteen minutes before I ate without you." I offered to make scrambled eggs with ham and cheese. I knew that was one of his favorites. I found some cinnamon raisin bread, a little stale, but it would toast fine then sliced some orange wedges, silently thanking Penn for her abundance of groceries. Now, that was a pretty plate, I thought. Pushing the door open with my foot, I carried two plates on one arm and the coffee pot in the other hand, fingers intertwined with two mug handles.

"I was coming in to help, just needed to dry a little more," he said. "Throwback to your waitress days?" His grin still lit up his face, accented his dimples and made his eyes twinkle. And my body still reacted to it with a tightening low in my center. I made a quick little noise that sounded like a chirp. Ian laughed at me and took the coffee pot from my hand. He took my breath away. It was good to know that some things are just action and reaction. We still had a powerful connection if we could get out of our way and let it happen.

Ian told me about the stepping stones project he completed. The pride showed on his face and the physical labor showed in his muscle tone. Both were amazing. I had been after him for five years to lay that walkway. I guess I just had to leave to get it done. Who knew? Finally, the small talk dwindled as our plates emptied. I couldn't stand it anymore.

"Why did you come yesterday?"

He didn't answer me right away, just set sipping his coffee. "I was worried. After you told me about your suicide attempt, I couldn't think or work. I knew I had to see you before Friday."

"I know I scared you. I didn't mean to blurt it out like that. I planned to tell you this weekend, face to face preferably, after we had re-connected a little."

He stacked our plates and fiddled with his napkin. "I wish you had felt you could tell me sooner or even better, before you tried it." He held his hands up as if to say *wait*. "I didn't mean to approach it this way," he said. "I want to be sensitive and understanding. Give you space to tell me at your own pace." I stared at this man before me, my husband, a stranger. When had he become so perceptive? Not so long ago, I annoyed him. My inability to adapt to our circumstances made him angry and resentful. Mostly, he just avoided me. Now, he sounded patient and sincere. It went well with the calm aura I felt from him last night.

"I appreciate that. It was never my intention to hurt you even though that was a consequence. I was a lot sicker than we knew." I looked away from him. The tide was coming in, encroaching on forgotten towels and pulling sand toys into the water. Children shouted and laughed, dodging and dancing in the incoming surf, mimicking the large gulls darting through the wet sand searching for crabs. A woman's hat blew off and she slapped her sleeping companion on the arm to chase it. I doubted she was going to see that hat again. Teenage boys played football in the waist-deep swells. I wanted to look anywhere but at him.

I felt his hand on mine, stretched across the table, the calloused scrape of his palm on the back of my fist. Slowly, I unclenched it and twined my fingers with his. It was warm and familiar. Then I cried. Vulnerability be damned. My life wasn't about hiding anymore. Don't think. Just feel. I repeated my mantra in my mind until the chant was echoing in the background, waiting for me to reach out, give in, feel my feelings. If my life was ever going to be authentic, I had to be honest right now in these moments. There was nowhere to hide.

Ian came around the table, never letting go of my hand, and pulled me to him. He held me, wrapped his arms around me, cradling my head against his shoulder, one hand smoothing the back of my hair. He let me cry, didn't try to stop me. I wasn't making him nervous and uncomfortable. He didn't rush me. He felt strong and safe and I felt the pulse of tenderness from his chest to mine. When had he become so attentive? Quit thinking, and accept what's offered.

He led me inside and sat me on the sofa his arm around me, cradled against his chest. When there were no more tears, we just sat together, quietly, no need for words or movement. Eventually, I got up and splashed cold water on my splotched and swollen face. I looked like hell, eyes with tiny red threads crisscrossing the white, little pockets of dark flesh under my lower lashes, puffy and tender. I brushed my teeth and hair, twice for good measure, and ran black eyeliner along the edges of my lashes hoping some definition would help.

When I returned, Ian was cleaning the kitchen, another new behavior. I watched him load the dishwasher and dump the coffee grounds in the trash. It was damn sexy. "You're different. In a good way," I added quickly. "You're thoughtful and helpful and I must say I'm slightly surprised at your calm demeanor. It's nice. Thank you. I was so worried about seeing you."

"Have I made you that miserable?" he asked. "For how long?"

"No, Ian. It wasn't about you. It was the toxicity of my depression." Before I could say more, he interrupted to tell me this wasn't about me but about us.

"That's at the center of this whole crisis," he said. "We made it about ourselves instead of it being about us, together, as a couple." I touched his face, so earnest, so receptive. He was really trying. "That's what my therapist said, and I agree."

"Your therapist?" I echoed. "When did you start seeing a therapist?"

"About a month before you left, I should have told you. It might have made a difference." I was speechless, no words, so many words, but I didn't know which ones to use. Hell yes, it would have made a difference, to know he was trying, to know he wanted a better life, to know we mattered, that I mattered. I had been sure he didn't care anymore. Maybe I was too far gone by then and he was just trying to save himself. The critical point was that the past only mattered in so far as we learned from our mistakes. Destined to repeat...you know.

"I don't know if it would have mattered then, but it certainly does now." I put my arms around his neck and kissed his lips lightly, gently. I was so overwhelmed by the emotion between us that I just reacted, no hesitation, just a physical expression of my love, yes love. I loved him and his response suggested he loved me. I backed up a step and looked into his eyes, bits of blue, streaks of green, flecks of whiskey gold. He took a breath and cupped both hands around my face. Lips no longer tame, taking and tasting, quenching the thirst of an arid existence in a multiple-year drought.

My hands wrapped around his shoulders, pulling myself closer so my breasts pushed into the tight muscles of his chest. A tiny groan from Ian then he slipped a hand under my hair at the back of my neck. The other trailed to the small of my back. When we connected like this nothing else exists.

Our first kiss was like that, magic from the first contact. We were dancing, slow, really just good friends, until the kiss. From the first touch, his lips owned mine, insistent and possessing, the taste of him exquisite, satisfying a hunger I didn't know I had, creating another only he could satiate. I forgot where I was, never remembered the song that was playing, or the couples around us. Time stopped and the earth fell away from my feet. The kiss now in the beach house kitchen rivaled that one from twenty years ago. The one that made me vow to follow him anywhere. We definitely still had magic, a combustible sexual connection.

"Wow," I breathed into him. "Damn, I've missed this." Ian wasn't smiling now. He was serious. Things were about to get intense and my body was electrified in anticipation. I put my hands under his shirt feeling the curly chest hair and muscles under my fingers.

"Lift your arms," Ian commanded. I did, straight over my head. With one swift movement, Ian tugged my shirt over my head and tossed it behind me. His mouth was on my neck, lips nibbling along my collarbone. I shivered with delight, my cells exploding with desire.

"Shirt," I said, tugging on the fabric. He obliged then slid my bra strap off my shoulder, my hands deftly handling the button and zipper of his shorts. With a practiced move, he flicked the hooks around my back and my bra fell to the growing pile of clothes littering the kitchen floor. A breast in each hand his tongue swirled around mine teasing and taunting, as his thumbs rubbed the tips of my nipples. My belly contracted, the sensation erotic and salacious.

"Ian." I moaned his name as his mouth closed over my breast, his tongue tracing a circle in the center. I grasped his hips for support, my knees weak with desire and pulled him against me grinding into his hip bone.

"No," he said, gruffly, grabbing my hands. I froze, disoriented and breathless. I wanted to scream.

"What? Why not?" The lust in my voice made it raspy and low. Then he saw the shocked look on my face.

"No baby, I didn't mean no to this. Hell no, I just meant not here." I exhaled with relief and slapped his hard butt. With a quick kiss of reassurance, he led me to the bedroom, tugging off my shorts and wriggling out of his as we hit the bed in a tangle of limbs and lips. Our joining was savage and frantic, consummating a primal need hard to describe with words. It was all about sensations and lust. Later, I lay across his chest, my breathing shallow, matching his.

"Why did we ever stop doing this?" I asked. He wound his fingers in my hair pulling gently to lift my face to his.

"Give me half an hour and we can do it again."

I expected it to be awkward between us after our complicated past. Sex had ceased to be about desire and all about forced reproductive efforts, clinical and stale, based on thermometers and charts. It was predictable and depressing. Neither of us enjoyed those infrequent unions, like two mannequins, stiff and tedious, devoid of passion and expectation. This was like movie sex, fiery and intense. Animals full of need and deprived of touch unleashed on each other to satisfy a primal appetite. My body wouldn't have survived another second without feeling him inside me, moving urgently and visceral. It was glorious.

CHAPTER THIRTY-FIVE

Present
James Island

Ian

DAMN, JADE WAS INCREDIBLE, sexy, vibrant, ravenous. That woman disappeared a decade ago from my bed and my life. She left the outside shell of my wife behind, but like a dried exoskeleton, there wasn't much underneath that wasn't depressed and angry. I missed her so much, so much that it hurt physically. I had headaches, my chest hurt and my balls crawled inward, cowardly and sore.

In those early years, we had everything, a stable marriage, great sex, and dreams. Jade wanted three, maybe four kids, and I wanted whatever made her happy. I worked hard at my job. She loved teaching. She had the most creative ways of keeping her students attention. I helped her make a large cardboard boat for the kids to sit in while they did a lesson on sharks and ocean creatures. They sat in their pretend craft on the high seas and studied hammerheads, tiger and sand sharks and great whites, giant stingrays, giant squids, and jellyfish while traveling from the Indian to the Atlantic.

Jade was amazing like that. She loved to learn, constantly reading books and immersing herself in every subject that interested her. That's why the pregnancies and miscarriages consumed her. She couldn't learn enough to fix the problem. In the beginning, we delayed having a family for several years because she loved teaching and we wanted to have enough money in savings so that she could stay home after their births.

The night she told me she was pregnant, I had never seen her more beautiful. She was wearing a print sundress with shades of blue that enhanced her sparkling eyes, with tiny shoulder straps that I wanted to slide down her arms. Her legs were smooth and tan and her feet were bare, her toenails painted dark red, a nod to her inner wild child. She joked about being barefoot and pregnant and waited for me to get the joke. I kissed her hard and swung her around the patio knocking over a chair. Our gourmet dinner waiting, candles lit, she had planned to tell me over the entrée, but she blew out the candles and led me to the bedroom for one of the most memorable nights we've ever had. Dinner was completely forgotten.

When we lost the pregnancy, I never saw her so despondent, except when she lost the second one. I think she thought it was her fault, something she did or didn't do. She read every book, article, journal she could find or anyone recommended. By the second pregnancy, she took all my briefs away and bought me loose underwear. We drank green shakes that tasted like artificial turf and ate shit like bean sprouts and tofu. I hated it, but Jade thought it would make a difference and that was enough motivation for me.

I wanted to make her better. I wanted to fix everything. I would have shaved my head and chanted naked on a street corner if we could have delivered a healthy baby. The second miscarriage destroyed part of her and damn near took our marriage. She turned away from me, never wanted me, and never touched me anymore.

I tried to share her pain. I wanted to bring her into my arms and hold her until she no longer cried in the darkness. Flinching, when I touched her progressed to avoiding me. Staying up late instead of coming to bed or going to bed early and pretending she was asleep. She turned down every chance to go out except the smallest family gatherings that missing would have raised an alarm. Finally, I didn't know what to do and like a coward I gave up. I couldn't bear to be around her. I couldn't stand her so miserable and I was exhausted with guilt and frustration. I worked and worked and then worked more, taking any traveling assignments and all the complicated accounts no one wanted. My resume got management's attention and I rose upward with promotion after promotion. Then I was so busy, I couldn't focus on her, life at home, or our marriage.

The third pregnancy was a complete surprise to us, conceived essentially from a one-night stand. I never tried to touch her anymore because the rejection hurt. It made me question myself on levels too deep for me to explore, from my manhood to my faith. Heartbreak, failure, frustration, even resentment, haunted me, followed by the guilt I felt for resenting my wife. Short-tempered and horny is a lousy combination and too many times I snapped at her or more often walked away, disengaging, because everything I did was wrong. I didn't want to think about it or analyze it. I wanted to be better so she would love me again and forgive me for whatever I had done, or not done, that made the crisis worse.

She was right that I didn't notice she was gone. I was on a business trip and we rarely communicated. I told her where I was going and an anticipated return date but not much else. She had taken a leave of absence from work after the holidays. She stayed in bed long after I left most mornings, then sat in the sunroom staring at the backyard bird feeders wearing her pajamas and ratty, nubbed, cardigan sweater that hung to her thighs. I thought about buying her a dog to give her some companionship and force her to get outside to walk it but I was afraid she wouldn't take care of it and that would be another source of conflict between us. The therapist I started seeing in April thought the pet was a good idea, but said Jade needed to make some positive progress first. I was told she was clinically depressed and maybe I should consider committing her. If I did that, I really would be a failure. What kind of husband can't take care of his wife? What kind of man can't love his wife enough to heal her? She would think I abandoned her, was throwing her away because of the miscarriages. Hospitalization was a desperate act from which we would never recover.

I called her mother when I couldn't reach her from Chicago. Didn't she tell you she was going to the beach house, she said? Surely, she left a note.

No, she didn't leave a note. She didn't care enough about me to include my feelings in her plans. Maybe she needed a break. Maybe she was leaving me. Fine, she could be bitter and withdrawn and it would be a hell of a lot more pleasant around here without her grief and misery hanging in the air. As soon as I entered the house each night, I inhaled its noxious decay. It poisoned me from the inside out, rotting any joy I salvaged, smothering all the satisfaction I found at work, generally permeating our marriage with toxicity. Let her stay in that damn beach house.

Then worry and pity overtook my outrage and I called to check on her. She was as cold and distant as an arctic iceberg and felt no need to explain her disappearance. I tried to watch television, sports, ballgames, sitcom reruns. The remote was mine to control but that soon lost its appeal and I felt tired and bloated from fast-food every night, or beer and pretzels for dinner. I left the office and went home early one day and my neighbor asked to borrow my tent. After digging in the garage for two hours, I started sorting and throwing away and organizing. Three days later, I had put keepsakes in labeled storage bins, built shelves, hung the ladders on the wall, and arranged tools, the holiday decorations, and everything else I kept, into designated sections. Looking at the completed project gave me a sense of satisfaction I had not felt in years. It was something that I had started and completed. I had finished a project and that felt great. From then on, I discovered I could put my house in order if not my relationship. I painted the front porch railings, laid a stepping stone walkway, replaced a couple of broken window screens, and trimmed all the shrubbery. I planted a hydrangea bush I accidently mowed over three years ago, that made Jade yell at me. I changed light bulbs, cleaned the gutters, put new batteries in the smoke alarms. I hit every to-do list Jade had ever made. When summer arrived, the Carolina weather turned hot and humid and I turned my efforts inside. I painted door facings, baseboards, and patched a few sheetrock holes in the downstairs stairwell.

I didn't miss Jade. I worked all day at the office and nights and weekends on the house. I felt productive and content, not happy, but not suffocating in misery either. My brief telephone conversations with Jade had been a nightmare. On different planets we were so far apart. I needed a human. I needed a woman. She was hosting college sorority reunions, hanging out at the beach and I was taking care of myself and my house. I was lonely but I knew I still loved my wife no matter how hurt and angry I felt. The key was to stay busy and I was great at that. Three days ago, I was between projects, sleeping in the recliner to the background noise of a baseball game, when Jade called. She sounded remorseful and buzzed.

She was talking nonsense and apologizing and I was disoriented from my nap. Clumsy and hyper she started sentences without finishing others and I could barely understand her. Yes, I acknowledged she needed a break. Mine had helped me, changed my perspective and made me feel better about myself, that is, until her confession.

I tried to kill myself, she said. And then all the satisfaction in which I wallowed detonated, blasting me into pieces of terror, panic, shame, and regret. My world had just blown apart. Why hadn't I realized she was so sick? I was a disgrace, painting baseboards, and watching baseball while my wife determined her life was not worth living another day. So withdrawn and indifferent, I ignored her pain and let her think no one, including me, loved her enough to save her.

Even though we had agreed to see each other next weekend, I had to see her, look in her eyes, see her alive and alert, know that she was breathing. I had to tell her I was sorry and let go of the exasperation I felt that she didn't tell me sooner. I didn't know what shape I would find her in when I got to the beach. At least she had turned to Penn and Emerson. They had been with her long before me.

Peeking in the door, I saw her sleeping on the sofa. Tanned, healthy, her hair shiny and black, those gorgeous, long legs bent slightly. She looked peaceful. I hadn't seen her sleep like that in years, so deep and tranquil. I knocked lightly and she jumped up, startled and a tad dazed. She looked stunned to see me. Maybe this was a mistake. No, I had ignored her for too long and it had almost cost me her very existence. This was something I had to do. My heart thudded loudly and rapidly. What if I lost her? What if I never got to run my fingers through her silky hair or hear her laugh or feel her body move with mine. Damn, I've been so stupid and selfish.

She let me in, her hair ruffled, her eyes heavy. It reminded me of how she looked after a night of sex, disheveled and seductive. God, I had to touch her. After a hug, I led her to the sofa then blurted out my apology. She talked to me, rational and intelligent. No more of the sluggish, drugged demeanor I had come to expect. She was clear and bright and looked fresh. She smelled a little like strong liquor, but I could overlook that.

She touched my leg. Electricity shot straight to my crotch. She was twirling the hair on my thigh and it felt fantastic. How long since she had touched me voluntarily? We talked. We apologized.

We said meaningful words to each other and she looked at me with those vibrant eyes the color of deep ocean water. I sat sipping my beer while she showered, imagining her body wet and soapy…

"Ian, glad you've come," Penn said. Startled from my fantasy, I dropped the beer bottle, fumbling to stand. Like a teenage boy caught looking at a dirty magazine, I felt embarrassed and my face flushed, hot and red.

Penn and Emerson looked stunned to see me. "Jade went to take a shower," I said.

"Good. She smelled like moonshine," Emerson said.

"So that's what it was," I said. "Where did y'all get moonshine?"

"Long story," she said, with a wink.

"Weren't you coming Friday?" Penn asked. "Not that it's not nice to see you, it's just unexpected."

"I needed to check on Jade after our conversation yesterday. She told me about the suicide attempt."

"I didn't know she called you," Penn said. "Em?"

"Nope, I didn't either but she was weird as shit when we got home from the market. Remember, she had a lot of drinks at lunch."

"It was her lunch," Penn added.

Emerson handed me another beer and they sat down in the den with me. "She called me while you two were at the market. How is she really?"

"Improving." Penn opened a bottle of wine and began fixing a tray of snacks. "I'm sorry about the last miscarriage. We didn't know how bad it had gotten or we would have helped you with her." I told them I appreciated it but both of us had made a real mess of things. It's been going on longer than the last miscarriage, I said.

"I'll buy you some more," I said, tipping my bottle at Emerson.

"You're good, no worries." She retrieved one for herself and then we heard loud noises coming from Jade's room. They bolted from the den. Even though I was hurt Jade didn't turn to me at least she had those two. I knew they loved her. They had rearranged their summer schedules to take care of her.

Jade emerged a little later looking smoking hot, wearing a low cut shirt showing tan cleavage and just a hint of lighter skin. I knew what was under there and it excited me so much that my body parts were reacting in appreciation. She was so vibrant. Maybe a near-death experience woke her up. She said on the phone she found hope, that she wanted to live. She looked more alive than I had seen her in several years.

Dinner was great. I had really missed good food. I had eaten so many fried eggs over the last weeks that I could start laying them. Jade seemed nervous but I did surprise her.

Walking on the beach reminded me of our early married days. We didn't have any money for vacations. Jade's parents would lend us the beach house. Everything slowed down for us here. It was uncomplicated, just me and her, having sex in the afternoon, catching fresh seafood for dinner, walking on the beach and kissing in the moonlight. Our lives were in front of us then, all the possibilities that have fallen away over the years. I wish we could go back. Talking before bed, Jade actually apologized to me. Then she started to cry and let me hold her. I was comforting her and she was responding. I wanted her. I wanted to feel her skin under my hands, kiss her mouth that I had seen smiling for a change.

I offered to sleep on the couch but I wanted to be in her bed. I didn't want to push her and truthfully, we weren't ready for that yet.

Waking to the smell of fresh coffee was a luxury. Penn offered to cook my breakfast but I wanted to swim before it got too warm on the beach. Since I had started working around the house, I had more energy and felt like moving my body more, so I took a morning dip in the ocean. Jade emerged and offered to cook my favorite breakfast. I felt really close to her. Our connection was coming back or starting anew. It had been so incredibly long since I didn't feel sad for both of us. She started talking about her depression. She seemed so vulnerable and open. When the tears came, I wanted to absorb her pain and take it from her. Pulling her to me, she let me hold her. No words, nothing needed but human contact. She seemed to feel my emotional support and it flowed between us.

Living alone had clued me in to how much work Jade did around the house that I never knew or appreciated. When she excused herself for the bathroom, I took that opportunity to clean the breakfast dishes. Damn, was that ever a smart move.

She unleashed the dogs when she kissed me in the kitchen. I couldn't stop myself. I ceased thinking and took what I wanted. She wanted me too. Thrusting her tits in my chest and grinding against my hip. She tugged on my clothes and unzipped my shorts. Aggressive and hungry, she was the Jade I assumed was never coming back. We left a trail of clothes from the kitchen to the bedroom, but all I could think about was her skin under my hands. Her mouth sweet and yielding, moaning my name as I teased her nipples. I was rock hard by the second kiss and couldn't wait to fill her with me, hard and quick, feeling her arch under me to take me deeper. I thought we could melt fire between us. She wanted me just as much. Holy hell, it was great. I could screw her for a month. Her legs wrapped around my waist, her tits bouncing to our rhythm. I exploded as she tightened around me, shuddering and moaning my name and then she cried out and lightly bit my shoulder. The waves of pleasure billowed around us holding us in some kind of orgasmic time warp suspension. Christ, I couldn't believe how fantastic that was.

CHAPTER THIRTY-SIX

Present
James Island

I EXCUSED MYSELF TO shower and think about the astonishing encounter with Ian. What next? Where do we go from here? I let myself abandon all control, but Ian seemed to like it and was sleeping quietly with a smile on his face when I left the bed. Leaning against the door frame, I watched him, naked, barely covered with a sheet. He made a soft funny snort when he turned over. I wish every day could be like this.

An hour later I was clean, the clothes from the kitchen collected, and I had perused the fridge for lunch and dinner menus. God bless Penn. I found fresh shrimp, crisp greens, sourdough bread, thick-cut applewood bacon. I had things to work with for both meals. I peeked in on Ian, he was still out cold. Wonder how long it had been since he slept that soundly? Deciding to make a market run, I left him a note and made a list. First stop, the women's boutique for some stylish clothes, sexier underwear and maybe a piece of lingerie, since I was feeling flirty.

At the market, I bought beer for Ian and Emerson, snacks for Ian, cinnamon rolls for breakfast, a pound of tavern ham, and sliced, baby swiss cheese, the ingredients for Charleston red beans and rice, then I stopped at the morning farmer's market for summer squash and some plump red tomatoes. After paying for the veges, I noticed Maggie in the corner with her fresh flowers. Agnes was in the adjacent folding chair and they talked intensely, heads together.

"What are you talking about?" I called out. Agnes seemed startled. That was unusual. They quickly separated and turned their full attention to me.

"We heard you had a house guest," Agnes said.

"Wow, word travels fast in a small town," I said. "Who told you?"

"Maybe two early birds out buying fish to take home."

In other words, Penn and Emerson stopped by to gossip about me and Ian this morning, I said. Agnes tilted her chin to the side and gave me that sheepish grin, paired with a raised eyebrow. It was a funny expression and made me laugh.

"I see you're in a happy mood," she said. "What a difference a good lay can make."

"Agnes!" I exclaimed, but my blush gave me away. "Why do you say that?"

"Cause sugar, there's only one thing that puts that smile in a woman's eyes. I remember the feeling." Maggie laughed loud and hearty at my embarrassment.

"Don't be shy, child," Maggie said. "Be glad you the one getting some."

A good lay can do wonders, I thought. Maggie made two bouquets for me, one for the table and one for my bedroom. Ian met me at the door and carried my groceries.

"How about BLTs?" I already knew the answer. That was his favorite sandwich. My version had thick bacon, leafy butter lettuce, tomatoes, but I also added Swiss cheese and ham. It was more like a club sandwich, but I knew he really liked it. Add cold beer, some kettle chips and crab dip and we would have a feast. Ian sat the groceries on the counter and brought me to him for a bear hug. He nuzzled my neck and made his way to my chin. By then, I had found his mouth and was saying my own greeting. Kissing him had become my new favorite activity. Finally, we pulled apart and looked at each other. It was intense holding his gaze then we both blinked and looked away. He knew I was replaying our morning romp and my face was getting flushed. I finally found my wits and remembered I was trying to make lunch.

"Lunch was great," he said finishing his second sandwich. "How about I take you to dinner tonight, like a date?"

The idea of a date night with Ian was thrilling. We had long ago given up on dates or much of anything that nurtured our relationship. "I love the idea but can we go tomorrow night? I'm planning a special dinner for you and have ingredients that won't keep. Is that okay?" He came around the table, took my face in his hands and brushed my lips.

"Darling, whatever you want, I'll do." Then he cleared the lunch dishes. I was falling hard and fast for this new improved Ian. He was a keeper.

I left the windows open when we went to bed. The soft breeze played through the screens causing the blinds to tap gently against the sill. Like perusing a rare bottle of wine, I could smell the sweetness of the summer night, honeysuckle and night jasmine, the ripeness from the canal, pungent and salty. When I opened myself to nature, it seems to wrap me in ecstasy, a euphoric rapture. My skin drank in the awareness and it spread like warm maple syrup around my heart.

Easing into bed next to Ian was strange and provocative. We had enjoyed a delicious dinner and an evening walk on the beach. I felt good about the progress we had made. Not aggressive or bitter, just small simple steps toward each other. I wanted tonight to be about Ian, cooking his favorite coastal meal and dessert. Shrimp scampi with garlic sauce over red beans and rice, a green salad, and French rolls with whipped butter was the main course, followed by banana pudding for dessert. It was a southern classic with layers of rich custard, banana slices, and vanilla wafer cookies then topped with fresh whipped cream. He thanked me repeatedly and seemed so grateful for my effort. I wanted the night to be low-key, even though I knew there were issues we had to address.

My crisis still existed, the sharp angles of depression hovered on the edge of my sanity. But tonight, I just wanted to spend a normal night with my husband. I was finally learning to separate my pain, thanks to Agnes. I wanted Ian to see I had changed. I asked him to sleep in my room. By the time I was ready for bed, he was laying on his back, his curls like a halo on the pillow around his head, snoring slightly, his chest rising and falling. I wanted to touch him, anticipating the soft t-shirt covering his chest. I didn't want to push reconciliation. We needed to get to know each other again, discover who we really were as individuals. Neither of us had slept well for a long time.

The sex this morning was unexpected and maybe rushed in the scheme of our relationship issues, we just couldn't contain ourselves. It was one of the most intense passionate connections I had ever experienced. We didn't talk about it the rest of the day, maybe a little embarrassed and unsure, we avoided our sexual intensity.

Ian didn't move when I adjusted the feather duvet at the end of the bed and pulled the light cotton blanket over my arms. I tried to still my mind, practicing the breathing and grounding techniques I learned from Agnes. My toes wiggled in imaginary dirt, rooting me to mother earth. The energy rose through my feet to my calves, thighs, hips, and breasts then my arms and face, as if I were standing next to a blazing fire. The heat flame-kissed my body and burned away my fear and apprehension. I knew I loved Ian. It was liberating to hear my brain say those words even if they were only to me right now. I had something to live for, not for Ian, but for me, and what I could share with him.

Sighing with contentment, I turned on my side and faced the window and fresh breeze. Instinctively, Ian turned too, resting his hand along my bare hip where my nightshirt rose up above my skimpy underwear. Who was I kidding? How carefully had I picked out that barely there wisp of lace? I fully expected Ian to see it, even if I was too anxious to admit it.

His hand was smoldering against my skin. Just this simple reflex brought tears to my eyes. So much had passed between us, so much pain unshared and unspoken, and just like that he could curl his long fingers along my hip and melt away my hesitation. The moscato wine was still sweet on his breath, my ear tickled as he exhaled behind me. A fat round tear rolled slowly down my cheekbone and dripped onto the pillowcase under my head. How had I ever thought I could leave him? This man, who just wanted to love me and make a life together, he wasn't thinking of how I had let him down, that I was a failure as a woman because I was unable to carry his baby.

He still loved me and wanted me. The proof was his unconscious action in this antique bed we had shared many times, without ever considering what that really meant. Not realizing that sharing a bed and reaching for one another in the dark was as intimate as two people could be.

Pushing myself back, I nestled against his chest, my legs curling to match his. I wanted to touch him, reach out to him. I needed him like my next breath. I laid my hand on top of his then slid it behind me to smooth the soft fuzz of his thigh muscle below his boxers. He sighed quietly in his sleep. Feeling his skin sent tiny electrical impulses through my fingertips, erotic and provocative, eager and urgent. I wanted more.

I held my breath with anticipation, and slipped my tingling fingers under the fabric, taking him in my hand. That got his attention.

"I want you." I breathed into his mouth, arching my hips into his, angling my torso so I could meet his mouth with mine. His eyes were drowsy, but his body was waking at an accelerated speed. I smiled at him, my eyes aglow with desire. "I want to feel you, every inch of you, on me, in me."

Ian opened his eyes wide as I acrobatically rotated from facing away to sitting astride him. I removed my nightshirt and let him look at me, all of me. I held his gaze, refusing to break eye contact. That might have been the hardest thing I had done all week. It felt glorious. Tentatively, he touched my face and pulled me to his mouth for a long, deep kiss that told me all I needed to know.

"It's always been you, Jade. Through everything. Whatever's happened, I've always loved you."

A single tear escaped, dripping from my chin to Ian's lower lip. He tasted the salty drop then leaned up to flit gentle, butterfly kisses across my eyelids. Of course his tenderness created more tears. All the while, his hands touched my body and mine touched his. Never did we break contact. The intimacy of our exchange was so powerful it made my chest hurt with its intensity. I inhaled sharply and Ian hesitated, until he saw me smile. I took his hands in mine, kissed his knuckles then I placed his broad palms on my breasts.

Oceans of words came to mind but they washed away, dissolving into the sand. Apologies, declarations, I wanted to tell him never again could we do this to each other. I watched his eyes drift over my body and back, to gaze into mine. I knew our touch and rhythm, our love was moving us forward, a rising tide bringing deliverance and redemption. We could be clean and free, liberated from a life of pain, lost dreams, and wasted moments.

"I love you Ian." I leaned down to kiss his sensuous mouth. Deep, probing, uninhibited, unguarded, I opened all of me to him. I heard him repeat my words back to me as I slipped him inside. We were one with each other and the universe, giving, trusting, sharing.

The cool gray fog sifted through the windows, settling around the bed like an ephemeral nest. Husband and wife, linked together, my head on his chest, his arm behind my back, we breathed in unison.

CHAPTER THIRTY-SEVEN

Present
James Island

THE REST OF THE week was a vacation for us, cooking seafood, walking on the beach, lots of sex. During the hot afternoon, Ian worked, setting his laptop on the table and sorting through files.

"Hey, look at you working at the beach," I said. "Does your boss know where you are?"

"Actually, I've been working from home a few days a week. Because I always take the most complicated files, it requires more computer work and a lot less customer interaction. Another guy in the firm set up a home office. Management loves it because it frees up an office in the building. It's a trend they've been looking into recently for our division."

"How do you feel about that?" I know how excited it made me, but I wasn't sure how Ian would adapt. He was very traditional in certain ways.

"I'm going to say this because I promised I would be honest with you," Ian said. Apprehensive, I sat down at the table bracing for what was coming. "I haven't wanted to spend an increased amount of time at home over the last years. I know that's on us both." He hesitated, waiting to see if I would break down. I realized just how precarious we had lived for so long.

"Ian, I don't blame you for not wanting to be at home. Why would you? Do you feel differently now with our changes, our potential?" I didn't know how to phrase what I wanted to say. I was too afraid to ask if he felt different about us. It might be too soon for that, but maybe we had a chance.

"Darling, I feel great about a lot of things, especially what we did yesterday, last night, and again this morning before breakfast." I blushed and smiled wide.

"Yeah, you've been on fire lately," I said.

"If I'm on fire, it's because you're lighting the flame."

"Okay, we sound really hokey, like a cheap romantic comedy."

"As long as the sex is like this, bring on the romantic and sappy." Ian closed his laptop and looked out beyond the surf. He sat there quietly and I knew he was thinking hard about something. It was his pensive calculating, problem-solving expression. Abruptly, he jumped up, gathering his work.

"Let's go play in the ocean," he said.

"Okay, give me a minute to change clothes."

"No," he said, grabbing my hand. Laughing, he tugged me off the porch and pulled me toward the waves. He was whooping like a little kid. He towed me into the surf, kicking up water and foam, soaking us both. My shorts, my shirt, dripping, my hair and face showered from the spray. Ian was delighted, his boyish charm lighting his face, eyes sparkling with pleasure.

"I can see through your shirt," he teased then grabbed me in a bear hug and kissed me loudly and thoroughly in the middle of the public beach. We looked crazy dancing in the water, splashing each other and shrieking like children. Spotting an abandoned plastic pail and shovel, Ian grabbed it.

"Ah, sandcastle time," he said.

"You have lost it," I said. But I flopped in the sand beside him, and started digging. Eventually, we created a very haphazard castle. Looking around the beach, I saw it was mostly bare. It was that in-between dinner hour. Covered in sand, we sat down together in front of our creation, looking like we had been rolled in brown sugar. It was blissful. There can be happiness after misery.

I took Ian's hand. "Thank you. Thank you for showing me we can have fun. Life can be like this, if we just let it happen. It really can be this simple."

"Your happiness is what I've always wanted. I just forgot to make it a priority."

"How about you introduce me?" Agnes' perky voice interrupted from behind.

Startled, I turned around, spraying sand as I rotated. "Agnes." My cotton top friend was smirking at me like we were teenagers caught making out in the backseat. "Uh, this is Ian, my husband." I looked at him as I said those last words and couldn't help a silly grin. It felt good, solid and sweet, to say that aloud. "This is Agnes, my good friend."

Ian crawled out of the sand to stand and greet the older woman, always the respectful southern gentleman.

"You're a handsome devil," she said, winking at me. "Jade didn't tell me about that mop of curls on your head and that sexy smile."

Ian was completely flustered. He had never met anyone like Agnes and had no idea what to say in response. He sputtered thank you and turned a beautiful shade of dark rose.

"Where did you meet?" he asked, regaining his composure.

I looked at Agnes and took a deep breath. We had not talked through all the details, but sometimes you just have to dive in. "The morning after my suicide attempt, I woke up at daybreak lying near the sand dunes, Agnes was sitting beside me. She offered me breakfast but most important, she has shared her wisdom of survival." I hugged her tightly and wiped a tear from my eye. Why did I cry so much now? "She checked on me all summer, counseled me, fed me, and encouraged me."

"Can I hug you?" Ian asked.

"Absolutely, big boy." Agnes patted Ian on the shoulder as they embraced. "She's an exceptional woman, she just needs to accept it, and live it."

"Agnes, would you like to come to dinner tonight?" Ian asked.

She perused the sky, squinting and searching. "Thanks, but there's a storm coming and you two look like you're doing just fine alone."

"I don't see storm clouds," Ian said, but I knew there was no reason to question Agnes.

"Maybe some other time then," I suggested. She nodded and headed north up the beach.

"Wow, she's a force of nature," Ian said.

"You have no idea," I laughed. "Race you to the shower."

The outside shower was under the house, where the stilts elevated the house fifteen feet off the ground. I reached it first, closed the door and removed my sand-covered clothes. Then Ian knocked on the door.

"Let me in," he said.

"No fair, I got here first."

"Well, I guess you don't want the towels I have." It occurred to me as the water showered over me and my clothes lying at my feet, that I had nothing to put on or wrap around me.

"Oh shit," I exclaimed.

"I tell you what. You let me in and I'll give you a towel." I opened the door a little, so Ian could squeeze in.

"You're a smart man. Where did you find towels out here?"

"I may have left a tiny trail of sand through the house." He grinned. "But I needed a bargaining chip."

I leaned toward him and nibbled his jaw until he shivered, while my hands worked the buttons and zipper of his shorts.

"You seem to have a clothing advantage," I said.

"We need to fix that."

Soon, we were standing in a pile of water-soaked, sand-covered clothes. Our naked flesh pressed against each other. I let my hands start at his shoulders, soaping his muscles as they slid toward his hips. His mouth was on mine, teasing and tasting then he nibbled along my collar bone. His hands stretched out behind me fumbling with something. I flicked my tongue across his chest while kneading the tight skin of his hips.

That's when I felt his hands in my hair, gently massaging shampoo into my scalp.

"Oh my god," I exclaimed. "Ian." It was the most luxurious feeling. He turned me around and leaned me against him, his chest hair tickling my shoulder blades, I closed my eyes. His fingertips made small circles on my head, relaxing and romantic, he lowered his mouth kissing the skin just below my hairline.

"Don't. Ever. Stop." I whispered.

"But if I don't stop, how can I do this?" Just like that, I forgot all about my hair.

Much later, we wrapped towels around us and streaked to the door. We were getting dressed when I first heard the thunder.

"Damn, she's always right," I said under my breath. Ian asked what I was saying. Just a commentary on Agnes, I told him.

"So she found you that next morning? We haven't talked much about that."

"I know and I was planning to, but things just took a more intimate turn than I expected this week. This reconnection felt great." I walked toward him and took his hand. He raised it to his lips.

"I aim to please," he smiled smugly. "You felt pretty great too."
I laughed at his goofy face.

"That's not what I meant, but I guess that's exactly what happened." I opened a beer for us both and got out the rest of the crab dip and chips. It's starting to rain, I told him.

"How did Agnes know about the storm?" I ate a chip and took a long swig of beer thinking about his question and how much I should tell him, how to phrase it.

"Agnes is very unique," I started. "She has a distinctive connection to nature and is instinctual about anticipating its fluctuations."

"You make it sound like she's some kind of a witch," he joked. I was quiet and took another sip of beer. "Jade?"

"Well, I think she might be something like that. It's not weird or scary. It seems very natural. I also think she is the most grounded, wisest woman I've ever known." It was Ian's turn to drink most of his beer.

"So does she put spells on people?"

"She helped me get you into bed." He hesitated half a second then playfully hit me with the pillow. "No, that's not what it's like. She has a relationship with the earth. She honors it and reveres it, draws strength from it, like energy." I wasn't sure how Ian would react. He could be judgmental, so I didn't mention the naked chanting.

"She's really helped you, huh?" He swallowed the last of his beer and went to get a second one. "You?" he asked raising the empty bottle.

"Sure, why not? I'll get Em some more." I thanked him and wondered if I should keep talking about Agnes and her methods. "Agnes helped me understand that being a mother or not, didn't define me. I've struggled a lot, with finding my purpose and identity. You know I always thought I would have a big family. Being unable to do that made me question my existence, which is one reason I didn't want to continue my existence."

"Jade, that's not how I see you." I interrupted him to explain it wasn't about how he defined me. It was how I did.

"It's about my perception, about believing that I planned to be a mom and every miscarriage screamed failure to me."

"But you didn't cause the miscarriages. It's just biology." I put my beer down and turned to him.

"That's just it. I think maybe I did cause them." I didn't want to tell him this way or at all, but I had to if I was ever going to be free. My last remaining secret was bad, maybe unforgivable. What if it destroyed what we had just discovered?

"What are you talking about? You're not making sense."

"You said you love me," I said. "Please remember that, because I love you more now than ever before. I feel like we have a chance for a new start, one that's just about us, without expectations and fantasies, a life here in the moment." Ian didn't move, just looked at me, waiting for the ball to drop. God, I hated having to do this. I had no idea how he would react. He might consider it something from my past or a horrendous betrayal. How would I feel if he had kept a monstrous secret that affected our life? This could be a disaster.

"We both have a past, right, relationships that happened before us. There's something that happened in college that I never told you. I didn't think it involved you until now." Ian shifted in his seat but didn't speak. He just looked at me, expectant and wary. His silence was making me more anxious. Telling him was a bad idea but it was my last walk through fire. When this was out, I would be free, good or bad, married or not, at least I wouldn't drag this with me anymore.

"Everything began the summer before my senior year. I know we dated in the spring a few times but we weren't serious or exclusive. We discussed it. I was coming to the beach and you were doing that internship in Charlotte." I swallowed hard and drank a long pull of my beer.

"Jade, what are you trying to tell me?" His voice was impatient and made me doubt the necessity of this whole conversation. Maybe I didn't need to tell him anything.

"I met someone. Someone that became special to me. I was involved with him all summer."

"Did you sleep with him?"

"Yes."

"Were you still sleeping with him in the fall when we got together?" Ian had not moved his body, only talked. His stillness was unnerving.

"No, it ended before I left the beach."

"Then how does this matter?" He stood, walked to look out the door, his back to me. I guess it was easier to listen to me if he wasn't looking at me.

"It was a bad break-up and I never wanted to talk about it. A few weeks later, when I returned for fall semester, I discovered I was pregnant." There, I had said it. My confession was ironically like giving birth, a huge build-up and once it's out, you can't put it back in.

"Pregnant!" Ian whirled to face me, his eyes wide and scary.

"Yes, I was pregnant. He was a summer fling. I did like him but it was never going to be anything other than what it was. I couldn't have a baby then, especially his." I sat on the edge of the sofa, my legs taut, like a rabbit ready to flee at the first sign of danger, my tense feet bouncing on the floor. "So, I had an abortion. I never told you. I never told anyone. Not even Penn or Emerson until a few weeks ago."

"How could you keep that from me?" He was very angry, his arms braced against the door facing. "I get you not telling me early in the relationship but somewhere over our eighteen-year-marriage you couldn't mention this to me?"

"I told myself it didn't matter. Truly, I was afraid of your judgment, of hurting you, of a total misunderstanding. It was the past.

You were my future." He poured bourbon into a glass and sat down on the sofa. He didn't offer me one, nor would he look at me.

"I've felt so guilty over the years as we had trouble conceiving, then the miscarriages. I believed it was my fault, some cosmic punishment for aborting the pregnancy. The doctors found no evidence of uterine damage, but I knew it was my fault."

"You were damn right to feel guilty, all those years of crying to me about how you couldn't have a baby. I walked on eggshells around you. I tried not to upset you. I went to the doctor, got poked and molested, had my sperm counted, and you tell me you were pregnant. I guess you could have a baby, just not my baby."

He could have kicked me in the gut, ripped my beating heart out of my chest, drug me across broken glass with my hair, and none of those things would have hurt like his words.

"Ian! Ian!" He walked through the door and out into the dark rain. I didn't follow him. He looked confused and hurt. It would have been easier if he were angry. I didn't know what to do with hurt. I picked up his bourbon glass from where he had left it, drained it and poured more. Then I cleaned up the kitchen just to stay busy. When that was finished, I did the bathrooms, dusted the furniture, and swept the floors. He was still gone. I wondered if I should look for him.

Why now? We were doing so great. I was so sick, my stomach heaving and rolling. After having so much fun this week, his reaction was brutal. Enduring his pain was agony. I was used to my pain but Ian suffering because of my actions, was breaking my heart.

Walking out on the porch, I felt the rain. Not as hard as before, but still steady. I couldn't see far in either direction and he wasn't visible. I sat down in the chair and looked out at the waves. They weren't visible either, but I could hear them battering the shore, a monotonous barrage of loud and soft as the waves hit, then slid into the sand. The rain soaked through my clothes and the wind chilled my skin. I refused to go inside. If Ian was out in the storm, then I was too, like some warped idea of penance. I hoped it washed away my sins.

"What the hell are you doing?" Ian shouted over the wind and rain. I had not heard him approach, until he was standing on the porch yelling at me. With very little composure, I told him I was waiting for him. "Why are you sitting in the goddamned rain?" I started toward him then stopped when I saw the wild look in his eyes. I knew he wasn't going to hurt me but he looked lethal.

Returning inside, I grabbed two towels and returned to the den. He was dripping water on the rug by the door when I tossed him a towel. He pulled off his wet shirt and dropped it by the door. Hours ago, I would have touched him, licked the rain off his neck, stripped down and known he would have taken me to bed. I had ruined everything, me and my secrets.

"Ian, I fucked up and I know you're hurt. I've hated myself and blamed myself for so long but I can't do it anymore. Agnes helped me put it in perspective."

"Well, maybe she should be married to you." I stepped toward him.

"Please don't do this," I said. He held out his hands, palms toward me, halting my approach. "We've found something special this week. Please don't…"

"I'm not doing anything," he said. "You started all of this."

Not knowing what to do or say, I took my wet shirt off and dried my arms and chest. My new lacy bra was soaked. I swiped at my hair dripping water on the floor I had swept earlier. That had been a waste.

"I had an abortion. Before us. It wasn't yours. We weren't a couple. I expected it to be a shock, but your extreme behavior is bewildering. Why did you walk out?"

"Me? I'm just following your lead. I thought you would understand that kind of reaction." Now he was just being cruel.

"Really? You're going there," I said. Ironically, my instinct was screaming for me to walk out. But I was different now and he wasn't going to rattle me. "We've talked about abortion. You know I'm pro-choice."

"Yes." Ian said, slamming his wet towel on the floor. "Yes, we have many times and you never once mentioned your own abortion. Couldn't tell me then? None of those times felt right?" His tone was sarcastic and taunting. He was baiting me for an argument.

"You know, you're acting like an ass," I said, walking to my bedroom then I slammed the door. I was shaking, from the chill and fear. I had gotten the most glorious taste of what our marriage could be this week. If I lost it now, it would be devastating.

CHAPTER THIRTY-EIGHT

Present
James Island

STRIPES OF WHITE LIGHT pouring through the blinds, woke me around nine. My head hurt with a dull ache situated right behind my eyes. My hair was stiff and tacky. It took me a moment to recall the fight with Ian. I went to bed wet, and angry, a bad combination. I repositioned the pillows and laid on my back staring at the rotating ceiling fan. That's how I felt, like I was spinning fast, going nowhere, seeing the same scenery.

I was doing much better lately, had made significant progress in facing my demons and fighting back. Then this blindside. I knew this discussion would be difficult, but Ian was vicious. I wonder if all this was about the abortion or if there was more to it? His anger couldn't just be about me making that choice in college. Then again, I had decades to get used to the idea and Ian only minutes, when he reacted. Still, what a jerk, we needed to talk this out or it would fester like an infected wound.

Having slept in my wet underwear, I changed quickly and went to find him. He wasn't on the sofa or the porch. He could have slept in one of the other rooms or he could be walking. I made coffee and baked the cinnamon rolls. I put away clean dishes and tidied our wet mess from last night. I wasn't quiet. He had to be awake. I checked the bedrooms. Emerson's room was empty. Penn's room was empty. I looked in the driveway and felt the lurch in my stomach.

Gone. Searching the house, I saw only his wet shirt I had hung out earlier and the boxers in my room from night before last. His shoes, clothes, laptop, briefcase, shaving kit from the bathroom, all of it was gone. Now who had run away?

I ate the whole damn pan of rolls, warm from the oven, went for a walk, washed the sheets, made the bed then took a shower. All the while I was in an emotional cyclone. Whirls of anger and sadness, love and loss, I cried when remembering something funny from the week, I laughed, then cried a little more. Later, I found a note from Ian on the floor near the coffee table. The ceiling fan must have blown it. *Need some time, going back home, Ian.*

Not one word about the week we enjoyed, the great conversations, the sex. He didn't even sign the note *love, Ian.* This was excruciating. I laid myself open before him and he slammed the door on me. Determined to hold it together, I needed to stay busy. There wasn't anything else to clean.

My journal. I sat on the porch in the shade of the eaves and wrote the latest chapter of my life, *How to Make Up and Break Up With Your Husband in Three Days.* Writing made my brain hurt and exhausted my body. It was too hot to stay outside, an air-conditioned nap was calling.

The children sat with me in a circle. Using my handmade props, I described how the loggerheads came ashore, dug their nests, laid dozens of eggs, covered it up and swam away.

"Why doesn't the mother turtle sit on her eggs like a chicken?"
"How do the babies breathe?"
"How do they know when it's time to come out of the sand?"

Maybe this was the wrong lesson. I had planned this talk and thought I executed it perfectly. I just misjudged my audience. When did six year olds turn into tiny little monsters? I don't know why mama turtles don't sit on their nest or why they lay the eggs and leave? How do they know if their babies hatched and made it safely to the sea? I would never leave my babies. I closed my eyes for just a minute to formulate my answers. I counted to ten and tried to ground myself. When I opened my eyes, the scene was horrible. We had been transported to the beach and the children were tiny little creatures standing around the turtle nest. As a baby turtle hatched and began its trek toward the water, a miniature child climbed on its back and floated out into the ocean.

When I looked out over the horizon, the children were being carried way beyond the breakers. I would never recover them all. I was frantic. Where do I start? How do I get them? I needed help. "Emerson! Agnes! The turtles! The babies! Help me, help me now!" I screamed.

The surf was deafening. The waves towered and toppled and slammed into the sand. The children and the turtles were going to die in the savage water. It was louder, the noise, distraught and hysterical, I tried to chase them, they were too fast and there were too many. I couldn't make a difference. It was futile and the pounding, so loud.

"Jade! Jade!"

I rolled off the sofa and hit the floor hard enough to wake me from my nightmare. The banging was still there. How loud were the waves?

"Jade! Jade! Open up!" Finally, I saw the mop of white curls waving in the wind. Her small hands beating on my door. Agnes. I waved, a halted motion meaning I'm trying to get there. "Are you okay?" Agnes was breathing loud. I had never seen her flustered.

"Yes, yes, I was dreaming. Come in." She stepped across the threshold, a bucket of mussels in her hand.

"Some dream, huh?" she said. I stood looking at her, as I scratched the top of my head. My sensations were strange and frenetic. The dream was coming back to me in snatches of visions. "I was calmly teaching children. Then they were riding baby loggerheads into the ocean and I couldn't save them."

"That's a powerful dream," she said. "Turtles in dreams have very significant meanings, especially for you right now." She handed me a bucket. "Put these mussels in a bag then put them in your fridge. I brought them for your man."

"Well, my man left," I said, taking the shellfish.

"What for? Business?"

I finished in the kitchen, put the bucket outside and poured us both some bourbon. "We had a fight. I don't know when he left. Late last night? Early this morning? I told him about the suicide attempt last week on the phone, not my finest moment, which is why he came down Monday instead of Friday as we had planned." Agnes sipped her drink and sat quietly, letting me talk. "So, last night, I told him about the abortion." I slumped back into the sofa cushions and propped my bare feet on the coffee table, scattering magazines to the floor.

"We had such a good week, laughing, talking and the sex, sweet Jesus, the sex was unbelievable. We were having the best time with each other. I cooked. We played cards. We swam in the ocean, and played in the sand. He worked in the afternoons on his laptop. At night, we talked and kissed, lying entwined in bed. I didn't want any more secrets between us. I was purging the toxins, like you said. We got into a horrible fight. I never thought he would ever react that fiercely." Agnes got the bottle and poured us another.

"Let's talk about your dream."

"My dream, did you hear what I said about Ian? That's kind of the pressing topic right now." I would never understand this woman. She confused me always with her trail of logic, but eventually we got there, and she was always right.

"What about my dream?"

"Do you know much about totem animals or dream symbology?" I drank a sip of bourbon and curled my legs underneath me on the sofa.

"Just the obvious, that animals have significant meanings."

"In dreams, loggerhead turtles are earth symbols, of being grounded and patient. They encourage the dreamer to slow down, look for long-lasting solutions and choose their path with wisdom, determination, and serenity. Besides wisdom and patience, sea turtles can indicate you are sheltering yourself from the real issues of your life. You're keeping a protective shell around your emotions and not letting people in. That makes you feel withdrawn and distant. Does any of this sound familiar?"

She leaned back on the sofa, propping her bare feet on the coffee table. She sat patiently, waiting, like a freaking turtle, while I absorbed the information.

"Well, damn." I replayed snippets of conversations with Ian and thought about how I handled the abortion conversation. "Okay, I wasn't very patient with him. He just heard about the abortion and I've had over two decades to process it."

Shivering slightly, I pulled the throw over my legs, holding the other half out to Agnes. "I've come so far, made incredible progress. It was like I didn't get an acknowledgment of that. He just went off on the abortion issue."

"Why do you need Ian's approval? You just told me about your incredible progress. Wasn't that for you? Saving your life? Did you save it for Ian or for you? You have to be able to answer those questions." She poured us both another shot. "While you're sitting there defensive and shutting down, remember the turtle and its protective shell. You had a lot of fun this week letting Ian into your life. Do you want to withdraw? Or seek a long-term solution that's better for you?" She drank her bourbon, and came around behind me, kissed my cheek like a doting grandmother, picked up her bucket and left. As usual, she never looked back. As usual, she left her wisdom behind.

Why did I save my life? A hundred thoughts rotated in my brain. Like a slot machine, I waited for them to match up and make sense. There were reasons for saving my life but at the critical moment, an instant from surrender, I hesitated, thinking there was something more for me, more for me to experience, challenge, embrace, just more for me. That wasn't about Ian or my friends. Their images flitted through my consciousness but in the juncture between life and death, I thought only of me, that I wasn't finished with this life.

Why do I need Ian's acknowledgement that I've made progress? I wanted Ian to see that I had changed, I was embracing the positive and letting go of the negative. I didn't want to indulge in the misery of the past. I was moving forward, trying to find the authentic me. No more sorting through identities like I was trying on thrift store clothes.

I needed him to love me, the real me, Jade the woman. Show him the woman I was becoming and not a fantasy, delusion, or a fabrication, of either of our imaginations. I was excavating myself, unearthing a treasure to be proud of. Agnes was right, always right. I had to do this for me. It was very simple. Be the woman I know I am and let Ian make his choice. In the end, I could only control my own life.

I needed to forgive that young woman for her decisions those years ago. She made the best with what she knew and I would advise her to do the same if I were her advisor. It might not be what I would do again, if I could go back in time, but that woman didn't have the luxury of the knowledge and maturity that I had now. It was time to make peace with young Jade. I didn't need Ian's permission, acceptance or forgiveness. I owned my actions. I had an abortion because I felt it was my only solution. I never told Ian because by the time I thought it was relevant to our relationship I was terrified of his reaction. I had to accept that withholding a secret hurt him, and give him time to process his feelings. He deserved that consideration from me.

He needed to sort through his feelings. I didn't want to rush him or make him feel like I was issuing ultimatums. I would be patient and gentle with him, turn my energy forward. Like the turtle shell symbol, I often protected myself. I wasn't comfortable showing vulnerability. But I had learned that wasn't going to work for me anymore.

I picked up my journal and went out on the porch. I would write down my dreams as a way to remember my objectives, so that the paranoia wouldn't take over my life ever again. Too obsessed to see my irrational behavior, I became a victim of my own creation. I undermined our marriage and characterized Ian as callous and selfish. I presumed the worst in him.

The trauma and anguish of the miscarriages destroyed me, years of depression, weekends I spent sleeping, the leave from work. I sat staring at the television or the wall. I was like a hologram, a thin wispy version of myself that vibrated in and out of sight, then faded away. I've spent years wanting Ian to walk in my shoes, feel the cold sterile removal of our happiness and hate himself for his inabilities. What kind of monster was I? I had been a horrible wife and partner.

Only days after confessing my attempted suicide, essentially saying I would choose death over my current status as his wife, I told him a horrific secret that contributed to my breakdown. I gave him no time to get used to the changes I had made, I lulled him into feeling I was stable and confused him with my tangled circumstances.

What if this was his breaking point? What if he couldn't go forward with me? I represented a destructive force in his life.

Call him or let him have his space? Go home, but something about that churned like a bad meal in my gut. It was a brick and mortar reminder of my shattered expectations and fractured identity. The house used to be about how we would arrange the nursery, where in the yard we would put the playset, and decorating for wide-eyed children at Christmas. The house was designed for a family with lots of bedrooms, big open spaces for Hot Wheels tracks and Little Tikes kitchens. The location was chosen for the school system and the neighborhood park. It wasn't a house for a childless couple.

I couldn't walk back in that house knowing that I had built my reality on a foundation of fantasy. What was real, what never was? How could I tell Ian our home made me sad, so sad I wanted to leave him and this earth? How would I move forward if I had to go back there? What did this mean for my marriage?

CHAPTER THIRTY-NINE

Present
James Island

SLEEP WAS HARD TO find between my racing mind and the snippets of nightmares. I woke exhausted and lonely. Ian sleeping in my bed had been phenomenal. We could be great together. But we had to base it on reality. No more fairy tales and presumptions.

I ate two pieces of peanut butter toast and went for a walk. The island was experiencing the late summer rush before school started in August. Couples with children were as prevalent as ants at a picnic. They darted to and fro leaving a trail of debris and disruption. I loved the beach when it was desolate, wild with abandon, the primal connection to nature heightened by awareness and proximity. The wind whispered its wisdom to me, the tides washed my worries out to sea, the sun infused me with warmth and the shore grounded my anxiety. This world felt like my home now. I was happy here. I had discovered where I belonged.

I washed my feet in the outdoor shower and sat on the porch to dry them in the sun. I laid my head back and closed my eyes to the bright sky then the telephone rang. Maybe it was Ian. Breathless, I answered the phone.

"Hi Jade. It's Penelope, Penn. Am I interrupting your love nest?"

"Ian left yesterday." I didn't offer any explanation. What was I to say? I told him my secrets, gave him my body a few times, and he walked out.

"How did it go? I thought he was staying through the weekend." My initial reaction was to tell her it was a good visit. We reconnected a little and leave it at that but I had learned I could ask for help, that I must ask for help. It was not a weakness to need people. I took a deep breath and started my story. When I finished Penn said she would be back by bedtime. Emerson can return when her work was over, she added. "Honey, I'm so sorry. Maybe he just needs some time to process. You've hit him with a lot of information in a very short time."

"We were good and I just didn't want any more secrets."

I had the afternoon to myself before they arrived. I wondered where Agnes was hiding. I didn't know where she lived. She walked everywhere so it must be close to the pier. Pulling the bicycle from the storage closet, I swore to trash the rusted beach chairs, once again, or I was going to need a tetanus shot. Taking the main road north to the intersection, I cut through two parking lots and arrived at the fish market. Sure enough, Agnes and Maggie were sitting at a table.

"Want a tomato sandwich?" asked Agnes. "We can make you one." My toast was long gone and a juicy tomato sandwich sounded great.

"Sure, but I'll make it. You eat."

"There's mayo in the cooler." The traditional southern staple was two slices of soft, white bread, slathered with Duke's mayonnaise, thick slabs of ripe, juicy, red tomatoes and lots of black pepper. A perfect tomato sandwich was appreciated more than the best steak dinner in the Carolinas in the summer. The bread melted on my tongue and the juice dripped down my chin.

"I put sour cream and onion potato chips on mine but Maggie says barbecue chips are the best. What do you think?"

"Chips on a tomato sandwich?" I had never seen anyone debase the culinary classic.

"Just try it," she urged. "Have I ever given you bad advice?" I cut my sandwich in half, minus the missing bite and put Agnes' chips on one side and Maggie's on the other. Biting through the bread and crunching the chips with the juicy tomato was even better and the flavors were so intense, they erupted in my mouth, spicy and savory.

"I will never eat another tomato sandwich without chips, but I might try jalapeno kettle chips." Agnes took a quart jar from her cooler bag and set it on the table. "I cannot do moonshine again. Besides, it's only midday, woman."

"It's lemonade." Agnes raised one eyebrow and pushed the Mason jar toward me. "Besides we don't start the moonshine for another hour." She winked.

"You're so easy," Maggie said. "And you're fun." I smiled at her, she was so likeable. She and Agnes made a unique pair.

"Agnes, after lunch can we talk a bit?" The easy friendship between Maggie and Agnes was tactile. I could feel their humor, devotion, and unconditional support around us like the comfort of a cardigan sweater. It was clear they had known each other for decades, one of those woman to woman relationships that lifted you up and brought you back to reality when necessary. I believed it was our primitive link stretching through time, when women lived in communal tribes for survival. We had our own homes now, but the longing to gather, persevered.

Maggie stood to leave, speaking to Agnes, "Want to come early tomorrow? We can fry some fish, make some Johnny cakes."

"I think I can do that." They walked to Maggie's wagon and Agnes leaned in to whisper in her ear. Maggie looked at me, grinned widely and nodded to Agnes. "Jade, you want to eat supper with us tomorrow night and do a little soul searching?"

"I would but Penn and Emerson are coming back today."

"Even better," she said. "Bring them with you. It's a party." The two shared a look then Maggie left, pulling her empty flower wagon behind her. "You want to sit here or walk on the beach?"

"It's too hot to walk. Let's stay in the shade," I said.

Agnes took a swig of her lemonade. "You young people are so delicate." She laughed, but reached out to pat my hand. "What's going on with you, dear?"

I sipped the lemonade and told her I had a dilemma.

"You always do," she laughed again.

"Yeah, you're not kidding. This time it's about Ian. I've been thinking a lot about what you said, how I withdraw and protect myself. I may have pushed him too far. My insecurity crippled me again. I wasn't strong enough to let him feel his feelings. I hit him with a damaging secret and expected he could just absorb it instantly and move forward. Where is my compassion? Am I incapable of love?"

Agnes dumped some chips out on a napkin and crunched a few before she answered me. "You didn't seem incapable of loving all that sex y'all were having," she smirked at me, but continued. "It's a good thing you can see all this now. I know you're scared, but a man, no matter how enlightened or educated, needs to protect his woman. It's not about dominating her. It's about needing to feel needed. It's how he measures his self-worth. When you are hurting and miserable, he feels it too, but usually don't know how to express it, especially if you don't turn to him for support or trust him. You've undermined his manhood."

I wiped the sweat from my eyes with my sleeve and stretched my arms over my head. "So now what?"

"You want another sandwich? How about a half of one?" I nodded and she pulled the sandwich stuff out of the cooler.

"The first thing you do is work on yourself, which you're doing. Then you need to empathize with him. Feel his pain. You've wanted him to feel yours. That's not what a relationship is about, it's merging your strengths, united, harmonious. When you let a crisis separate you, it's like letting a stranger into your house. Can you stand together and defend what's yours or do you let it destroy your security and take all your belongings? Divide and conquer. You ever heard that? It works in war and it works in a marriage." She stopped making the sandwich and pointed the butter knife at me. "This is trench warfare, my dear. You got to dig deep, plant your feet, and not let anything move you."

We ate our sandwiches without talking. I was mulling over her advice and Agnes was content with the silence. The food was just as good the second time.

"Thanks," I said, popping my last luscious bite in my mouth. "Do I call him, go to him? Agnes, I can't stay in that house. Living there will pull me under for good."

"So make changes. This is your life. The only one you get. You can waste it or live it fully. Ask for what you want. Do you want to include your man? If this is all about you, then take what you want and move on." Agnes always simplified the issue.

"Were you ever married?" She got that faraway look every time I asked her about her past.

"I was in a relationship long time ago but that's a story for another time." Then she steered the conversation back to me and her life was a closed topic again.

"Thank you for finding me and being my friend," I said.

"Well, you're quite welcome but what brought that on?"

"I've just been thinking about women, and friends, and what we mean to each other. As women we need to do a better job honoring our female relationships. They make us better versions of ourselves." I drank the last of my lemonade and walked to my bike. Turning back to her, I asked, "Can we bring some things tomorrow night? Where are we going?"

Agnes rubbed her chin. "Cole slaw, marinated or mayo, home-made dessert, and anything you want to drink besides moonshine. I got a new batch you're going to want to taste," she said with a wink.

I asked her where to meet and she told me to be in the parking lot of the hardware and tackle shop about half past eight. "Is it a special occasion?"

"You'll see." I walked my bike to the road edge watching for traffic. As I pushed off, I heard her call, "Clothing optional." Then she cackled loudly as I swerved in response.

CHAPTER FORTY

Present
James Island

I BARELY HAD TIME to take a shower and tidy the house before Penn arrived laden with food, bags of fruit, and white dishes wrapped in foil.

"Lasagna or chicken enchiladas for dinner?" she asked.

"Enchiladas. What can I do?" Penn started dinner while I brought in her luggage.

"Em is picking up some beer and wine. The house looks nice." I retrieved her suitcases, garment bag, and a few extra bags, placing them in her room. Then I dug through the vegetables.

"Did you bring some cabbage?"

"I have napa cabbage. Will that work?" I found the oblong sheath with light green leaves, a carrot and some green onions. I can do something with this, I thought.

"We have a dinner invitation tomorrow night and I offered to bring marinated slaw and dessert." I explained that Maggie and Agnes were cooking fish for a special occasion and had included us. After putting apple cider vinegar on to boil, I washed the cabbage, shredded it, then washed and diced the onions and carrots. I sprinkled a spoonful of sugar over my bowl of veges, added some celery seed and black pepper. After the vinegar boiled, I added a little balsamic vinegar, poured it all over the cabbage then put it in the fridge. By tomorrow, it would be spicy and tangy, marinated with a bare hint of sweetness. I cleaned up my mess just as Emerson burst through the door with the inventory of a small liquor store.

"Think that should last us a few days," I said.

"This is just mine. Get your own." She leaned in and kissed my cheek. "I missed you. Now help me with this. There's more in the car."

I brought in the alcohol and wine and the death by chocolate three layer cake. "We can take this for dessert tomorrow night," I said.

"Whoa, whoa girl. Where are you taking my cake?" As I explained the dinner invitation, Emerson looked wistfully at her cake decorated with thick dark chocolate buttercream icing and thin chocolate curls.

"I'll make a blueberry and peach crisp," Penn offered.

"Which wine goes with enchiladas?" Emerson asked.

"Wet," I said, taking three wine glasses from the cabinet.

"You're getting as sarcastic as Emerson. Too much time together. And a blush will be just fine."

They updated me about the events of their week, Em's grant project and Penn's fall charity planning. Then we made small talk until dinner was over. Emerson piled the dishes in the sink, opened a second bottle of wine and brought the cake to the table.

"Alright Jade, it's time. Tell us what happened," Emerson said. "I want all the details, especially the sex ones."

Penn slapped Emerson on the arm and made a face at her like she was a disobedient child. I laughed at her weird, quirky expression. "Sex? They're barely talking. Is that all you think about Em?"

"All the wicked details," I smirked. Starting at the beginning, I told them everything. Even the sex details and how erotic and hot it was connecting like that with Ian "It was mindblowing sex but it was so much more, not desperate, like trying to hang on to something past or making an effort because you're supposed to consummate on command. I wasn't thinking about having sex when we were in the kitchen. Okay, I was thinking about it, but we had stuff to discuss. I wasn't planning on the physical need that came over me, but we couldn't stop ourselves."

"Did you have sex in the kitchen?" Penn's face was pinched with dismay. "I just cooked dinner in there."

"I bet she wiped off the counter," Emerson said, laughing so hard she snorted wine that dribbled down her chin. We could've been twenty again. Some things never change.

Penn was dumbfounded and had no reply. "Relax Penn, all we did was kiss in the kitchen, and we may have lost some clothing. Oh, well, you get the idea. Leave her alone Em," I said. "You know Penelope can only take so much. Now Penn, she's a different story. Do you remember the time she had sex behind the couch in that frat house on the corner? Seriously though, our time together was a great blend of intimacy, talking and playing. We built a sandcastle. I cooked dinner and he worked remotely from the porch with his laptop. We talked about how things went wrong."

"So what happened?" Emerson refilled the wine glasses and our cake plates. "Why did he leave?"

"I won't say I got too comfortable because that's wrong, but I felt we were making real progress. I just couldn't keep the abortion a secret anymore. I needed a clean slate. I think it's kind of like admitting an affair. You do it for yourself to release the burden of guilt and shame, but you don't think how devastated your partner will be. I severely underestimated his reaction. It was so long ago I didn't think he would feel betrayed. I was wrong."

"Are you sorry you told him?" Penn asked.

"No, I had to tell him. I wish I had years ago, but I was afraid of how he would react. What I didn't handle well, was his response. I got defensive and angry and couldn't see it from his point of view. I've wanted everyone, especially Ian, to feel my pain and I've been blind to his. When I think of how I've hurt him I... I..." My words stuck in my throat and I was unable to continue.

Immediately they flanked both sides of me, arms around me, one of them stroking my hair. It's okay. All this is good they told me. It's progress. Penn brought a cold cloth for my forehead, "I love you women," I said. "You've known me from the beginning and never given up on me. I asked for help and you came without hesitation."

We hugged each other and for a minute it was twenty-three years ago and we were newly initiated sisters pledging our loyalty and support. Of course we couldn't understand the magnitude of those vows then. "I'm overwhelmed the universe brought us together."

"Can I get some advice?" I asked. "We don't have to hash this out tonight. It's late and we should sleep but maybe you can give it some thought."

"Let's hear it," Emerson said.

"What's my next step? Do I give Ian space to process all this or call him and tell him my new revelations? I should talk to him in person but I have a real problem returning home."

"What's wrong with home? I thought you loved that house?" Penn questioned.

Explaining how it reminded me of a make-believe family I'll never have, took another hour. "I don't think I can live there again. And that's another major issue to throw at Ian."

"You could move to Asheville," Penn suggested. "We could be neighbors."

"I'm not sure I'd be right for Penelope's neighborhood."

"What kind of crack is that?" Penn's hurt showed on her face.

"I'm sorry Penn. It was a bad joke. I'm really tired and my brain is like a sieve, things are leaking out everywhere. Let's get some sleep." I hugged them both and began turning out the lights. "Thanks for coming back. Aside from my suicide attempt and imploding marriage, I'm having a lot of fun with y'all."

Waking up rested and hopeful was rare for me. No dreadful nightmares of lost babies or cryptic messages. I felt strong. I haven't felt like that since my twenties. I thought of calling Ian but talked myself out of it. I wanted to play in the sand with him and go to the market and pick out seafood for dinner. It felt a little like calling to see if he could come out and play which seemed a little childish, but I was giddy and exuberant. Could this be happiness?

This was one of those times I needed to consider how Ian felt. I was enthusiastic but he was confused at best and enraged at worst. He didn't want to play in the sand. Whatever he wanted, I hoped it included me.

Penn was painting on the porch, the morning sun providing just the right amount of light on her canvas. After eating peanut butter toast and opening a Diet Coke, I went for a walk. Ian and I started that last week. It gave me time to clear my head and focus on the day. When I returned, Em was on the porch drinking a protein shake.

"I've given your dilemma some thought," she said. "It's been three days. Call him and see how he's doing. Just play it real. Tell him you didn't handle the conversation well and you want to apologize. Then see where it goes. That's what I would do."

"I'm not sure," Penn said. "Is bothering him a good idea?"

"How would she bother him by checking on him?" Emerson asked.

Penn wiped the paint off her brush and stuck it in her ponytail. Wearing paint-stained faded overalls rolled up to her knees and a white tank underneath she looked so much like our Penn of college days. What had the years done to her? Maybe her marriage wasn't as picturesque as she insisted.

"Men need their space," Penn said. "Sometimes, women demand too much. Men have so much pressure on them to perform at work, make money, and manage their family."

Em and I exchanged looks. She raised one eyebrow and I acknowledged with a nod. This woman looked like Penn but I bet her real name was Penelope. "I would wait until he's ready to talk to you," she said.

I went into the bedroom to call Ian. Taking a deep breath, I dialed the number, no rehearsing, no preparation. I wanted this to be natural and authentic. The phone rang until the machine picked up. He had changed the message to a generic, "Leave a message at the beep."

"Ian. It's me. I wanted to apologize for the way I handled our discussion Friday night. I didn't take your feelings into consideration and I was wrong. If you want to talk, call me. I loved our time together. I love you." All things considered, it was a good message. I didn't stutter over my words. I apologized. I took ownership for my behavior and expressed my love. It felt good.

"You called him, didn't you?" Emerson asked.

"I did, left a message. A good message, I think. Let's play cards, best out of five. Penn?" Emerson and I played rummy inside while Penn painted outside on the porch. "How did Penn behave at home?" I asked.

"Jesus, it was crazy weird. She was like that Stepford wife robot we saw at the beginning of the summer. She dotes on Brian. And he orders her around like the hired help. I would never have believed the change to her demeanor when he was home, but I witnessed it, in a brutal exhibition."

"I knew her home life wasn't as ideal as she pretends."

"Brian has no respect for her or women really," Emerson said. "He barely acknowledged me, acted like I feed fish for a living. What does she see in him?"

"That's a topic for another day. Rummy. That's three out of five," I said. "You get to clean the bathroom this week." She glared at me as she got up from the table, citing the need to work on her project.

"Make sure you pee on the seat for me and shed your long black hair in the shower. Get your money's worth." It was a good thing we loved each other, I thought. Penn closed up her paint and came inside.

"Making a salad for lunch," she said. "Want one?"

"Sure, do you need help?" She nodded no, so I stayed at the table playing a game of Solitaire. "Penn, are you okay?"

"A little flushed from the sun. I don't think I'm drinking enough water either."

"I mean things at home." She stopped chopping for a moment, like she might speak, but changed her mind.

"Of course, at least I think so. I've hardly been there this summer," she laughed.

"Are you happy?"

"What's with all the questions?" She divided the chopped veges into two large salad bowls and sat them on the table with Em's dressing.

"Thanks." I nodded at the salad. "I was just getting a vibe."

"What kind of vibe, an Emerson-induced vibe?" Penn ate large bites of her salad, stuffing green leaves into her mouth with gusto. After a few minutes of silent eating, she asked, "What did she tell you?"

I was afraid I had set her off. I chewed my salad, hearing the click my jaw makes as I crunched a carrot. "Em mentioned a little tension, but in all fairness, I asked about things. We're just a little concerned. You seem so different. We're too old to try on different personas. One of these is really you. You're either pretending at home or here with us, and we've known you a long time."

Penn picked up her salad, mostly uneaten, and sat it in the kitchen. "You know, Emerson spent a day and a half in my home and frankly she doesn't have the experience to gage whether my marriage is good or not. Not everything is perfect, surely you can understand that. That don't mean it's all bad either. Relationships aren't either this or that. They are a living, changing organism. Marriage is organic."

As she shut the porch door, she called over her shoulder that she was going for a walk. Penn was right. Marriage was a living organism, between humans who were exposed to emotions and outside influences. Those pieces adapted and transformed and re-arranged themselves again and again, like a perpetual jigsaw puzzle, creating an ever-changing image. Emerson probably wasn't the best judge of Penn's relationship with Brian. I cleaned up the kitchen but still couldn't shake the feeling something wasn't right with her. It was too hot outside for me. I went to my room to read until time to meet Agnes for dinner.

CHAPTER FORTY-ONE

Present

James Island

THE SMELL OF BAKING fruit led me from my room. Tart blue-berries and sweet peaches, brown sugar and butter, just removed from the oven, it was still bubbling around the edges of the oatmeal crumble on top.

"Jesus, Penn, this smells incredible. Let's cut it now. No one will miss a little spoonful." She swatted me with the oven mitt, shooing me away from the kitchen. "But we need to see if it's any good," I whined.

"I can assure you it's delicious. Stay out of it," she warned. "I need a shower."

"What's that smell?" Emerson emerged from the bedroom. "Can we have some?" she asked, walking toward the kitchen.

"Only if you want to challenge Penn, it looks great but I don't think I'm going to risk it until we get to Maggie's. We need to leave in less than an hour." I went to the porch to watch the late after-noon sun slide toward sunset, such an easy time of day when the world slowed down, except for the blazing ball dropping into the chameleon horizon.

We met Agnes in the gravel lot of the closed hardware store. I had only seen Agnes on foot or in her boat but tonight she was driving an ancient pick-up. The truck was rusty orange and it was hard to tell where the color stopped and the oxidation began. The windows were down. Agnes' arm was propped on the edge. "Come on," she said. "Get in with me."

There was no way we would all fit, Penn said, but Agnes insisted, we could sit close together. So we put the cooler in the back and gathered our dishes, scooting over until we filled up the seat. Agnes laughed her cackled hoot, "This is gonna get fun, ladies."

She backed out of the lot, tossing gravel with her tires, and drove across the bridge to the mainland. We only went a short distance before she turned right into a drive that I would have never seen. Rambling around the thickets and low hanging branches, we came to a small clearing. Agnes pressed the brakes, worked the clutch, shifted the old gear column, and with a slight shudder, we stopped. I didn't see a house or a structure of any kind. Agnes stepped into the dense hedge of flowers and pulled out a rusted wheelbarrow. She loaded her cooler and ours.

"Let's go ladies. We walk from here." Agnes smiled her sly grin and winked at us. So we grabbed the other stuff and followed. We wound through a narrow path in semi-darkness. Occasionally, I heard the lap of water against the shore and the thickets on either side of us vibrated with the intermittent sounds of katydids and cicadas. Tree frogs were abundant and sang their offsetting call from tenor to bass. Finally, the trail opened into a clearing with a cottage. All around the dark air sparkled with the quick gold flashes of lightning bugs, like a nature walk.

"Who knows why those bugs glow?" Agnes voice startled me.

"Ooh, I know," said Emerson. I could practically see her sitting in junior high science class, her arm waving wildly in the air. "They are bioluminescent. When they inhale, oxygen rushes into their abdomen and causes a chemical reaction that makes them glow. The wavelength of light is…" She didn't get the rest out because Agnes interrupted.

"Now I know why you're single," Agnes joked. "They glow to attract a mate. To signal they are ready and willing. I always thought it would be easier if humans glowed. I just can't decide which parts should light up."

We stopped, looking at each other as Agnes trudged off toward the cottage. It too looked incandescent, luminous with blues, greens and ambers. As we got closer, we saw wine and beer bottle lamps hanging from the low-hanging live oaks branches. Inside each was a tiny flaming candle. We walked past the house looking for Agnes. The clearing opened into a wide expanse of shoreline. Maggie and Agnes stood together near a wooden table. I put my marinated slaw down beside a large bowl of sliced cantaloupe and watermelon. Black-eyed peas, thick slices of red tomatoes, a tray of corn on the cob, roasted with butter and herbs, and a large metal pan covered with a plaid dish cloth, all set on a nearby table. I peeked under the towel and inhaled a hot breath of cornmeal with onions and fresh dill. Hushpuppies.

"Welcome, welcome, come on around here." Maggie motioned to us. Emerson placed her cooler under the food table and we greeted our hostess. "I'm so glad y'all came. Hang on. I got to check this fish."

Maggie opened the lid to a homemade deep fryer and pulled up a basket using a curved wooden handle. She propped it on the side to drain then turned out the golden fish fillets onto a tray layered with paper towels. Beside the fish was a pile of browned slices, crispy and crunchy. Fried green tomatoes, I thought, and snagged one to dip in the remoulade.

We shared an extraordinary feast. The food was crazy. The blend of soul food and southern food was so flavorful and comforting. Maggie and Agnes brought out their home brewed peach moonshine, but we all drank sweet tea with fresh mint from Maggie's garden. After dinner we started on the moonshine.

"So where's the still?" Emerson asked. "I think it's too cool that y'all make this." She poured two shots from the Mason jar and set one in front of me.

"No, I swore off this stuff. I told you drinking this makes me see dancing tigers and pink dolphins. And that's the best part. Waking up is when the regret truly starts." They all laughed at me as Maggie slapped the table.

"Well, let's try the peach and see what color those dolphins are tonight," Emerson coaxed. "Come on Penn, you too. I dare you." Em's chiding hadn't gotten her desired response until she dared Penn. That was Penn's strength and weakness, she couldn't back down from a challenge.

"Pass me a shot." Penn slammed it down and held her glass out for another. So we had another round and another and Agnes got a second jar and then we finished off the hushpuppies and collectively smelled like fermented peaches and fresh dill.

"So when do we get to see the still?" Emerson asked.

"Not this time, maybe one day," Agnes said. "We've got other plans tonight. Very special plans." Knowing what I did about Agnes' special plans, I was thinking we might need more moonshine. At least it was warm if we ended up naked. Emerson could roll with it but Penn might run screaming into the night. We followed Agnes to the water's edge. Geographically, Maggie's clearing must be on the canal side of the mainland, but it was very remote and appeared to be part of a marshland peninsula, like a thumb protruding from a palm.

The coast curved around to the left and I could see narrow pieces of land jutting like arthritic fingers into the water, the waves rippled at the edges like the hand was waving a greeting. A grove of live oaks and cedar pines separated a tiny clearing from Maggie's main yard. Hidden behind the trees was a circle of stones inlaid in the sand with a fire pit made of old brown brick nestled in the center. Between the outside edge of the stones and the fire pit was a ring of wooden seats. The whole area was like three concentric circles with a fire in the middle that must have been smoldering for hours. Maggie took split logs from a nearby wheelbarrow and laid them in the glowing blood orange embers. Sparks spit and crackled and shot skyward into the dark.

The wind rippled through the trees and tinkling sounds reverberated from different directions. Looking around, I spied wind chimes hanging from the gnarled branches all around the clearing, intermittent with more wine bottle lanterns. Small pieces of polished glass and broken pottery hung intermingled with slender wooden rods.

Penn grabbed my elbow. "Those are bones," she hissed.

"What?"

"Bones! The wind chimes. Bones hanging from the damned trees. What the hell?"

I had to admit that was a little odd. "I'm sure they're just squirrels or something."

"They're too big to be squirrels or any other rodents. They could be human."

"They are not human. You're crazy," I said. "How much moonshine did you have?" I took one last glance at the bones and walked to the fire pit.

Agnes had her leather pouch slung around her shoulder. She was placing four candles at quadrant intervals on the fire pit wall. Using a thin, lit taper, she was pouring melted wax on the brick wall, setting each candle in it as a base. I had seen her do this on her altar. Apparently it was a common practice in this clearing too, based on the multi-colored wax drippings. She motioned for us to take a seat. So far all this seemed fairly normal, like a circle of women gathering around a fire pit. I wondered what was coming next, Agnes conjuring unicorns from the wisps of smoke rising into the navy blue night. I doubted we were making s'mores.

The large quadrant candles remained unlit as Agnes snuffed the taper and turned to face us. I watched the moonlight ripple in the water while I waited. The moon was full, radiant, resplendent, even whimsical, dancing and skipping among the waves.

"Maggie and I invited y'all to share our full moon ceremony. I glanced at Penn and Em. They were looking at Agnes, intrigued, I hoped.

"We're going to do things a little different tonight since y'all are new at this. We'll even keep our clothes on." That last statement caused Penn and Emerson to look at me with such intensity I could telepathically hear their comments, *What have you gotten us into? Naked? What the hell?* They just kept bombarding my senses as Agnes continued.

"Tonight is about power and perspective. Women have a tremendous connection to the moon. For those of us who believe, the phases of the moon and her influence can bring momentous changes and success to our lives. All three of you are in need of change and the first step is acknowledging your own power. Tonight, Maggie and I will show you how to seek help from the Goddess to light your path," Agnes said.

Em and Penn were still, very still, like statues of lawn adornments. I couldn't tell if they were paralyzed with apprehension or rapt with curiosity. Agnes walked to one of the quarter candles, lit it and held her arms over her head, forming a giant Y with her body.

"Element of Air, we ask you to lend your wisdom to our circle." She worked her way around the circle, calling for Fire to lend passion, Water to lend emotion, Earth, stability. She returned to the front of our group and turned to the three of us.

"Don't be scared," she said. "Be open-minded. This isn't dark or evil. It's a beautiful ceremony of prayer to ask the Divine to share her positive energy and infuse us with the power to face our struggles." Agnes motioned for us to stand. Penn and Emerson finally moved from their frozen positions. It was hard to read any expression. They just looked earnest. Agnes put her hand into her bag and pulled out a small dagger. Penn shifted her eyes to me, they were wide and anxious. Then she looked at Emerson whose eyes had never left Agnes.

Agnes asked us to lift our arms to the sky and cup our hands together. "Form a chalice. Allow the moonlight to pool in your hands. Slowly, lower your arms and pour it over you. The silver blue energy of the moon is flowing into you, through you. Visualize it purifying your body, then your mind, and finally your spirit. Inhale the positive, expel the negative." She pointed her dagger to the full moon poised over our clearing. She mumbled a few words incoherent to us and then with a sudden burst of force, plunged the knife into the ground by her feet. Cupping her hands together over her head, she spoke.

"I draw down the moon, beseeching the Divine Light of the Goddess to surge within us, empower and heal us. Teach us to release the doubt and fear and increase our faith and courage. Hold each of us in the sanctuary of your arms as we seek clarity for our lives. Bless us as women in your image and surround us with the White Light of your love."

Then she asked us to meditate on her words and our thoughts and when we were finished, open our hands and release the moon energy into the air. I had been with Agnes before as she said prayers and asked for blessings of strength but never had I participated. I ceased to care how the others responded. As I poured the moon's light over me, I felt coolness, not chilly or cold, rapturous. Magical and wild, the air around was charged with exhilaration. I inhaled its frosty crispness. It tasted like winter, the air clean and fresh as a solitary walk. Like moments from childhood of being outside, early in the morning, when the snow is falling softly and the quiet drifts through the trees, a secluded instance in which I alone exist in a crystal universe.

Exhaling, I blew out my fear and anxiety, pushing away my uncertainty and reluctance. I really wanted to move forward, accept the grace that swirled around me, lifting me, liberating me. The moon goddess moved through me intensifying the connection we made years ago. I felt ethereal, ascending within her. *Let go of your anger and dread. Give up your guilt. Embrace forgiveness and compassion. Find mercy, your purpose, your love. Your life awaits you.*

I dropped to my knees, as if my breath was knocked from my lungs. My chest heaved and the tears gushed in torrents of sweet, decadent release. "I am alive," I screamed. The women rushed to me and I collapsed under them. They thought I was upset but I tried to tell them it was just the opposite. I pushed through their concern. "I feel healed. Blissful. Restored. I'm going to live."

Penn and Em sat back for a moment listening to me then they wrapped their arms around me. We sat in the sand rocking together, embracing, decades of sisterhood, celebrating my catharsis. Agnes stood on the fringe of the circle, a wide grin on her impish face as a single tear slid down her cheek. It was nearly three in the morning when we arrived at the beach house. After my awakening, we had sat in the moonlight talking to the older women. Emerson had a thousand questions for Agnes about the moon and rituals. Agnes explained the tenets of her spirituality. She called it an earth-based faith that highlights the relationship between people and nature and looks to the Universe as a source of energy and knowledge. For her, the Great Spirit takes the form of the Goddess and God, a dual entity of balance, male and female, light and dark. To all things there is an equal, she said.

Penn didn't say much. I don't know if she was appalled or reflective. She wasn't angry or cold, just quiet. Her sensibilities are a little more delicate and rigid than Em's. After my last few years, I was open to anything that gave me hope.

I fell asleep as soon as I lay down, slept for eight hours and woke a little before noon. I felt really good, maybe great. Someone had taken the chains from me. I felt the world turning under my feet. It was like some great stone that stopped rolling years ago, wedged tight between pity and pain, rotated again beneath me. Slowly at first, with a great groan of effort, the constraints had loosened and pushed forward, propelling me toward the future. My future was Ian. Not because I owed him or couldn't survive without him, but because I wanted him to share my life. I wanted to be the authentic Jade for him and me. I owed that to myself.

I had to know if he still wanted me in his life, his bed, his forever after. I was strong enough now to fight for our marriage, but if I had to accept that it was no longer meant to be, I could go forward alone. I would not break.

"Morning Penn." She was sitting on the porch sipping from a mug I assumed was coffee. That meant she had not been up very long. Of course Emerson was still asleep.

"How do you feel this morning?" she asked. "Quite an emotional night for you."

"I'm doing fantastic. I slept well, no nightmares or lying awake staring at the ceiling fan. I feel hopeful, exhilarated."

"So happy you feel better, this is what this summer has been about, healing you."

Emerson emerged from the house and kissed the top of my head before stretching herself out in the hammock. "Wow, last night was a trip. Agnes is crazy, I love her."

"Her finding me on the beach that morning was the first miracle in a long string of phenomenon that has saved my life. You two were crucial. I can't imagine what would have happened to me without you." I walked around to stand between them. "Some people use this as a figure of speech, but you two truly saved my life. You put your own lives on hold to bring me back to reality."

"So, what are you going to do with this new beginning?" Emerson asked.

"I have a few ideas but first I need to see if I still have a marriage. I love Ian. I need to show him there is a better life ahead for us. It's time for me to go home and show him how much I love him."

CHAPTER FORTY-TWO

Present

James Island

IAN AND I HAD talked only briefly since he left the beach. I called him once, left a message and he returned my call a few days later. He said he needed time to process the news of the abortion. I didn't want to give him too much time. I knew he could bury feelings so deep neither of us would be able to excavate them.

After my experience under the full moon, I wanted to capitalize on my clarity and energy surge, make it work for me to redeem our marriage. Agnes explained that each phase of the moon corresponds to specific magical works. Healing, matters of the home, manifesting desires, love and sexuality were all topics pertaining to the full moon.

"Ian, I love you." That was the first sentence I spoke when he answered the phone. I wanted him to know that it was foremost on my mind. He was quiet. I could hear his brain speak and reject any number of responses. Finally, I felt sorry for him and spoke again.

"I don't want to push you, just wanted you to know how I feel. I've had some extreme revelations lately and it's time we talk. I'm not defending my past, making excuses, or painting myself as the victim. I will answer any questions you have or discuss our unresolved concerns, but my objective is to rebuild a marriage that has tremendous potential. I want our marriage. I want you."

"Come home." His voice was desperate, fragile, and sincere. "I love you too and I want to see what we can do together."

"Are you in town all week? What's your work schedule?"

"I don't travel as much anymore. I can make anything work."

We decided I would come home day after tomorrow. That would give me time to close the house.

Penn and Emerson were making lunch or dinner, some meal for us to eat mid-afternoon, because we were starving and completely off schedule.

"I'm going home." I announced to them. Both froze in mid chop. After a significant pause, they came around the counter for a group hug.

"This calls for wine," Emerson said.

"What doesn't call for wine in your world?" Penn chided

"Bite me."

I listened to their squabble, back and forth, baiting each other, and realized how much I had missed this banter over the years and would miss it again. "Oh my god, I have loved being with y'all this summer, aside from the way it started out, you know."

"We should never lose touch again, sisters for a lifetime. Slainte," Emerson said. We toasted us with wine, promising to get together much more frequently.

"Oh shit, the chicken's burning." Penn ran to the stove to rescue her garlic and butter sautéed chicken. Em was bending forward slapping her knees. I marveled at the ease between us, even now, after we had changed and matured. We had taken very different paths, but those college girls were still inside us. When I closed my eyes listening to their laughter, two decades melted away. They had saved me. They held onto me when I was dying. Be it the universe, the goddess or the great pumpkin, whatever brought us together in the past and in the present, I was grateful. Now, I had a future.

Emerson finished the salad and I poured more wine and set the table.

"When are you leaving?" Penn asked.

"I told Ian the day after tomorrow. I need to close up the house, wash the linens, clean out the fridge, and secure the outside furniture."

Penn sat the food on the table. "Why don't you let me do it? Then you can leave tomorrow. The grandparents are picking up the kids from camp and bringing them home the first of next week. I don't need to rush back for anything."

"I don't have to be back in Charleston until Sunday," Emerson said. "Together we can get everything done."

I chewed the chicken and thought about it. "I hardly have anything to pack. I don't even have a suitcase. There are just the few things I've bought and I can find some beach bag in the linen closet for that, but I can't let you to do that after everything you've done for me."

"Listen," Penn said. "I could use a few days to paint before I go home. I still have a few days to get the house in order before the kids arrive. Besides, Brian has been incredibly understanding about my time here. That's been my surprise of the summer. I thought he would have wanted me home long time ago but he's been so generous and agreeable."

"If you're sure, I'll call Ian and see if that works. The house is probably wrecked. I bet he stopped doing dishes ages ago and is eating out of paper plates and using plastic forks. This chicken is great. Tell me how you made the sauce."

"This is the last night we have at the beach," Emerson said. I was wistful about leaving the safe little nest I had created here, but the excitement of beginning a new life with Ian was greater. I cleaned the dishes and called Ian. He sounded excited about my earlier return. Don't worry about the house, I told him. I wasn't putting any pressure on him. I laid out my best outfit for tomorrow and put the rest of my meager belongings into a frayed beach bag. At least it was sand-free. Then I grabbed another bottle of wine and joined the girls on the porch for one final sunset.

We were quiet for a while watching the colors create another stunning visual reminder that nature was glorious in her manifestation.

"Em, did you see the bones hanging from the trees last night?" Penn asked.

"Bones? The wind chimes? I saw pieces of broken pottery and colored glass and shells."

"No, that's not all it was," Penn said. "Jade saw them. I'm telling you, bones and not rodent bones."

Emerson shifted to stare at Penn. "What are you suggesting?"

"Tell us what you're thinking, Penn," I said.

She was quiet, looking out over the water. The pelicans were flying north to roost for the night. They flew in formation, gliding then flapping their wings, then gliding again, all in unison. I knew that hesitation of Penn's. It meant she thought her idea was strange but was trying to decide if she should tell us. Sometimes, her ideas were genius. Other times, Em was merciless in teasing her for her weirdness and out of the box imagination.

"They could be human." She said it low, a whisper lost on the wind. Did I hear her? Human?

"What have you been smoking?" Emerson exploded. "Human?"

"What would make you think human?" I asked. "How many skeletons have you examined?"

"Y'all have to admit that was some weird shit last night," Penn said. "Praying to the moon and waving a knife around. Oh, don't look at me like that Em. Yes, I'm tolerant of anyone's religious choices. But that was not something I've ever been a part of." Penn grabbed her wine glass and finished the rest of it and poured herself another.

"Well, I thought it was a powerful experience," Emerson said.

"Do y'all remember when we were here in college and that older couple collecting mussels found those human bones? They were from a baby," Penn said. "A human baby." She leaned forward, her eyes wide and paranoid. "What if all that is related?"

"Sweet Jesus! Do you think those two sweet old ladies are killing babies and hanging their bones in the trees?" I asked.

"Holy hell, Penn, you need some new medication," Emerson added.

"Whatever," Penn said. The topic hung in the air just like those bones, but no one mentioned it again.

CHAPTER FORTY-THREE

Present
Charlotte, North Carolina

AFTER A TEARFUL AND prolonged goodbye, I headed west to Charlotte, leaving my beautiful beach behind. I hoped I would be back soon. I realized I needed the wildness of the coast, water crashing against the sand, the wind blowing my hair, and the sun heating my skin like an afternoon sex romp. Untamed and savage, like a feral cat, aloof and independent, I was part of the beautiful symbiosis of nature and the elements.

I turned my attention to home and Ian. I wasn't sure if I could live in the house anymore, but I was going to make every effort. I needed to show him I was devoted to us being a family, regardless of children. A puppy might be a good start. Ian had always wanted a dog but with each pregnancy and miscarriage I found excuses to deter him. I always wanted a kitten but was concerned a cat would scratch a baby.

I was getting into town before the animal shelter closed. I could adopt a puppy through the humane society and we could become a family, doting over this baby and buying a new bed, collar, leash and toys. I could see us walking it together on the beach, throwing a stick in the ocean waves for it to retrieve. It would be a great way for us to spend time together creating a healthy relationship and it would give us something to focus on together.

She was gloriously sweet. A light pale yellow like the inside of a coconut cream pie. The shelter volunteers thought she was a mix of terrier and yellow labrador retriever. She looked like a tiny, yellow lab and was about seven weeks old. I carried the puppy inside the pet store with me to get a collar, leash, bed, and food. The rest, Ian and I would do together. Oh, but she needed toys too, I thought. No, we should do that together. Maybe just one.

I had stopped at the grocery earlier for salad ingredients, wine and French bread. Hitting the fish market on my way off the island this morning, I had shrimp and mussels in the cooler. I also had to say goodbye to Agnes and Maggie. It was harder saying goodbye to Agnes than I anticipated. "I don't know how I will ever thank you," I said. "You've shared your food, your wisdom, even your faith. Thank you for trusting me with your friendship and exhuming me from my watery grave. You gave me the strength to live and I will carry you with me always."

I cried for the next thirty minutes as I drove home. I would miss being there and living the slow, thoughtful life I had found on that barrier island.

This little girl and I were going home to cook Ian a delicious meal. I planned to steam mussels in a wine and herb broth with chopped tomatoes and peppers with toasted bread to dip in the bowl, salad greens, a crisp mix of bitter and buttery and Emerson's vinaigrette with shaved parmesan that I stole from the fridge.

Arriving home, I unloaded the groceries. Entering the house, I heard Ian's voice from the back bedroom. Walking through, I noticed the kitchen was clean, the sink devoid of dishes, everything in its place. As I continued, cradling the squirming ball of fur, I noticed the furniture was dusted, the rugs were vacuumed and tidy, even the sofa pillows were fluffed and placed neatly. Maybe he had a woman living here, I thought. I followed the sound of his voice, hesitating in the hallway, while he finished what I deduced was a business call. Why was he in the guest room on a business call? Weird? He ended the call, and I peeked around the door frame, keeping the wriggling present hidden.

"I'm here."

Startled, Ian jerked his head up from the file folder on the desk separating us, and gave me his best smile, dimples and those sparkling eyes. "Oh my god, Jade, you're early." He pushed his chair back and came around the desk toward me.

"You have a home office."

"Yeah, we'll talk about all that." He tried to hug me, but my twisted position made it awkward. I turned to face him and presented him with his sweet baby girl. He was speechless. He smile faded and he looked at me incredulous. Oh, I had made a presumptuous mistake.

"Jeez Jade, it's perfect." He held her above him to view the underneath. "She's perfect. What made you do this?"

"I want to start a family with you," I said, leaning in to kiss him on his sexy mouth. We kissed, lightly, sweetly. He put the puppy on the office floor, took me in his arms and really welcomed me home, completely and unhurried, with purpose and heat. The sensation electrified me and made me want more of everything. He pulled back, still holding me, and looked into my eyes. Still breathless from the kiss, I continued to caress his chest muscles, exploring, needing.

"Hang on a minute," he said. "Not too long though, because I want you and I can't wait much longer." He left the room and returned holding a box. "Here take the lid off."

Just as I touched the lid, the box moved and I drew my hand back. He laughed. "Go ahead, it won't bite. Actually, I can't be sure."

Then he laughed again. This was more laughter than I had heard from him in two years.

Removing the lid, I peeked in to see a perfect, coal black kitten. Even its tiny, twitching nose was black. "I tried to put a bow on him, but he's not fond of ribbons, eating them, but not wearing them." I took the precious gift into my hands and brought him to my face. He purred like a motorboat and looked into my eyes. I fell in love, swift and deep, with him and Ian.

"I love him. I love you. But why?"

"I want to start a family with you," he said.

We sat on the floor of Ian's office and let the puppy and kitten play together. I looked around at what he had done to create the place.

"This looks great. You must work here more that I realized."

"There have been a lot of changes over the last few months. I was just offered a supervisory position that allows me to work at home. I have staff meetings weekly via the computer and I will go into the office about once a month for a management meeting."

"Oh, Ian that is fantastic. I'm so proud of you. You've worked so hard over the years and really deserve this." I hugged him then nuzzled the kitten that had crawled in my lap.

"I guess I need to think about what I'm going to do. I don't really want to go back to my school job. I'm in a good place right now but it may take me more time to adapt to being here."

"Well, that's the other thing I want to talk about," Ian said. "I've had time to contemplate my life and us." I held my breath, not knowing what he might say. Everything seemed positive, but I was getting a vibe his ideas might bring major change.

"Do you think your parent's would sell us one of the beach houses?"

"They have mentioned they're getting tired of the upkeep. I told them I would help. You know they'll let us stay anytime though. Are you thinking we can vacation more with your new schedule?"

He leaned toward me brushing my hair from my shoulder to graze my neck with his lips. "I don't want to visit the island," he said. "I want us to move there."

The kitten and the puppy were curled together napping in a knot of legs and whiskers, one black, one light. Balance. My new family. I looked at Ian. My one love, my future, hard times, good times, balance.

"I think that's a fabulous idea. As long as I'm in your arms, I'm home."

THE END

Turn of the Silver Wheel

JAMES ISLAND TRILOGY
BOOK TWO

PROLOGUE

1944
James Island, North Carolina
My Dearest Agnes…

My dearest Agnes,

I miss you so very much. How I long to be back on our island, as I have come to think of it, on our strip of sand, in one another's arms. I hope you are well and catching lots of shellfish. I worry about you and wish I was there to take care of you. As I write those words, I hear how they sound, that I would need to take care of you, imagine. Of course you are fiercely independent and quite capable. I just like the idea of you needing me, wanting me. I love you.

We are safe enough here, but I am not allowed to tell you where that is. I can tell you war is a horrible thing. The lands are ravaged, the cities destroyed and the people, all the innocent people, well all I can say about that is this is a tragedy for our world. What these leaders have done for the sake of ideology. I will serve my country with honor, but I have discovered I am not a man for violence. I sink deeper into myself with every passing week.

I must go. We are moving again. I do not know how long it will take for you to receive my letters. I hope you will get them in a timely manner. It would break my heart for you to feel I have abandoned you. I will be back for you, my love.

Your smitten soldier,
Jackson

∽

My darling Agnes,

How I miss you. I need to hold you and feel you with me. This separation is torturous. My grandest hope is that all will be over soon and you and I can begin our new life together. I do not have much time. We are moving or flying missions almost all the time, with only a bit of time to sleep and eat.

War is a devastating display of fear, fear and hatred that rot a man's soul. So much death, so much destruction, and to what end. Conformity. Uniformity. Paranoia. This is a hellacious display of what happens when reprehensible men feel insecure in the world, feeling threatened by others who talk, worship, and behave differently. We will still be different after we finish destroying each other. We were never meant to all be the same.

You know how I feel about all this. I am an honorable man. I will serve but it is beginning to be with a resentful heart. My place is with you, wherever you want to go in this world or if it is just to stay on our island. I will build you a hut and we shall eat shellfish, make love in the sand, and save sea turtles. Dreaming of you and reliving our special times together is what keeps me going.

I am trying to make some arrangements in case, well, you know. I refuse to say it aloud. Our love will triumph over this unholy war and we will rest in each other's arms soon. I will write when I can, hurrying now to post this before my next run. I love you always.

Your winsome warrior,

Jackson

∽

My dearest Agnes,

I hope you are well and that no harm from this war has reached you. I know you are strong and will survive no matter what, but that does not keep me from wishing to be with you, hold you, and protect you. I want us to lose ourselves in our love and shut out the ugliness.

This war is a catastrophic collapse of morality and exposes the devaluation of human life. I find all this repulsive and frightening. I know why we are here and that we have a duty to protect. We must end this ruination, but I have no appetite for this taking of human life and having to do things I abhor in the name of patriotism. Some men are born to be fighters, defenders, and leaders of armies but I think I am meant for a quieter way of life. I would like to teach high school, science or math maybe. We can buy a house, plant a garden, and have some children. That is the favorite part of my fantasy, us making babies. We can practice a lot and then have a houseful. I close my eyes and imagine I am with you on our island, our beach. Moonlight washes over the water and spills onto our naked skin, our bodies wrapped around one another. I can feel your softness as I melt into you, curls framing your beautiful face, your sapphire eyes absorbing my love. Agnes, you take my breath away. Some days I feel I will suffocate if I do not get to inhale your essence. I will starve if I cannot taste your salty skin hot with love, my mouth lingering on yours, always wanting more.

I wonder if some government official reads our letters. Oh well, I am not giving away war secrets. I am just a man in love. Unfortunately duty calls, my sweet.

I have taken care of some arrangements for you, in case, if the worst should happen. Do not dwell on that. I will hold you again. I need you to know that you are my greatest love and everything I could want in life. Your love makes me a better man. I will always love you,

Your passionate pilot,

Jackson

༄

The letters came randomly. I knew he was somewhere in Europe. Days and weeks would pass without a letter and then when I thought I could no longer survive, I would get several at the same time. Wrapping them in oilcloth, I took them in my boat to our island. Sitting on the quilt where we first made love, I read his words to me. Fat, drops of salt water tears dried tacky on my face. Unable to control them, I sat and stared at his letters until they became too blurry to read. Looking east, past the horizon, I imagined Jackson standing on the other side of the Atlantic, waiting for me. I lost a part of myself every day without him. I dreamed his strong hands were gathering me, piece by piece, until I was whole again in his arms.

Made in the USA
Columbia, SC
14 May 2019